THUNDER ON THE PLAINS

BRAVELANDS

THE SHATTERED
HORN

BRAVELANDS

THUNDER ON THE PLAINS

BRAVELANDS

THE SHATTERED HORN

ERIN HUNTER

HARPER

An Imprint of HarperCollinsPublishers

Library of Congress Control Number: 2022952465
ISBN 978-0-06-296696-4

Typography by Ellice M. Lee
23 24 25 26 27 LBC 5 4 3 2 1

First Edition

THUNDER ON THE PLAINS

BRAVELANDS

THE SHATTERED
HORN

Tangled Forest

BRAVELANDS

Cheetah's Hunting Grounds

Grandmother River

'Quaking' Plains

PROLOGUE

The sound of laughter and trumpeting rang out from the watering hole as the three elephant calves splashed and squirted water at each other. Their mothers and aunts waded in the shallows, watchful for movement from the crocodiles who lazed, seemingly disinterested, on the far side of the lake. Young Storm roared with laughter as she flopped over dramatically on her side, sending a huge wave splashing over her little cousins, Sunbeam and Ash. Sunbeam trumpeted and threw his trunk over his head. Droplets of water sprayed all around, sparkling in the clear afternoon sun. A few of them splattered a group of baboons who were drinking at the edge of the water, and they screeched, some in fury, others with laughter. A herd of gazelles were finishing up their visit to the watering hole and preparing to leave, a family of aardvarks snuffled around a nearby anthill, and starlings crowded the bushes along the bank.

Great Mother Starlight gave a long, contented sigh. She felt her bones creak as she adjusted her position on the bank, the better to watch the young calves play. Her eyes weren't as sharp as they had once been, her trunk not quite as strong, not to mention the state of her knees. But she wouldn't have her youth back, not if it meant giving up everything she saw before her. Her calves and grandcalves, and great-grandcalves, her time as Great Mother, the peace that mostly reigned in Bravelands at the end of it—as much as peace could ever be said to reign between predator and prey. There would always be family strife, ruthless competition for food, old resentments between creatures that flared up without warning.

But there would be life, too. Some of it would not have thrived without her guidance, and wasn't that the best thing that could be said for any Great Parent's legacy?

Her ears twitched and flapped as she heard someone in the crowd of animals use her title.

"Well, let's ask the Great Mother!"

A gazelle and a small band of baboons peeled away from the others and headed her way. The first baboon marched up to her with an air of smugness.

"Great Mother," he said, "tell this gazelle that there was never a Great Parent who was nothing but a shadow! That's ridiculous!"

"It's true!" the gazelle snorted. "I heard it from someone who knew someone who was in her herd! Tell him, Great Mother!"

Starlight blinked slowly and flapped her ears to cool the sides of her neck.

"What are your names?"

"I'm Sprint, Great Mother," said the gazelle.

"This is Pebble, Twig, and Trunk Middleleaf," said the baboon. "And I'm Mango Highleaf."

"Not all stories of the Great Parents are true," she said, and saw Mango give Sprint another smug look. "But they are all based on a seed of truth. I believe that Great Mother Prance guided Bravelands from beyond the stars, after she gave her life, when the mountain erupted and the red rivers ran. Whether she was a spirit, a shadow, or something else, who can say?"

Mango's jaw dropped. "You mean the mountain really did explode? I thought that was just a story too!"

"Where did *you* think the black rock valleys came from?" sniffed Sprint.

"Not all the way from the mountain!" Mango snapped back.

"As I said," Starlight reminded them, lowering her trunk to gently rest on each of their heads, "the truth may always lie somewhere we can't quite see. It's certainly an interesting tale, and we know it begins with the Great Mother losing her shadow but failing to die, and becoming Prance Herdless."

She paused, stretching her neck to loosen its stiffness, and also to buy herself a little time while she remembered what happened next. Where did the leopards come into it, in the end? And who was the first to fall to the Sandtongue Curse? She sighed, knowing that even her version of the story was likely to deviate from the truth. Time had passed, and the events of history could never be pinned to the earth forever; they could only travel on the wind, and they would inevitably change as they did so.

"The Great Father before her was Great Father Thorn—a baboon," Starlight began, and the baboons all nodded in gleeful anticipation.

But before she could go on, she felt something strange. Her ears quivered and she raised her head, seeing that a few of the other creatures around the watering hole were doing the same, on edge and alert.

The ground beneath Starlight's feet began to tremble, and a moment later she heard the rattling, groaning noise, and she knew what was coming.

"Is it the mountain again?" Mango gasped, turning and shading his eyes as he squinted in the direction of where he thought the mountain might lie.

"No," said Starlight with a smile. "This is no terrible earthquake. Listen!"

Her ears flapped again, and Mango bit his lip as he concentrated for a moment.

"Oh—it's hooves!" he said.

"It's the buffalo," Starlight said. "The herd are passing by, somewhere close. Every female and calf are on the move, going to meet the males and gather for their great migration."

"Are there a lot of them, then?" asked Twig Middleleaf,

who seemed younger than the others.

"A very, very great many," said Starlight with a knowing smile. "When they are all gathered together, they will *truly* make the earth shake. In fact, the buffalo believe that it's the shaking of the earth, with all their hooves moving as one, that brings the rains down from the sky."

"Wait," said Sprint. "So if the buffalo don't make their journey, the rains won't come? What about the grass? What about the watering hole? If there are no rains . . ."

"Such a thing has never happened, as far as I know," said Starlight, "And I believe it never will. I do not know what would happen if the buffalo failed to migrate. I only know that they believe it. That's why the Great Spirit is so important—it ties us all together, even though we all sometimes have very different ideas."

"Look," said Pebble, pointing over Twig's head. "I can see them now!"

"I can't," said Twig, squinting. "I can just see a big cloud of smoke!"

"That is the dust being thrown up by their hooves," said Starlight. "There are so many of them that when they're all moving at once on a dry day, you'll barely see hide or horn until they're almost upon you."

"Wow," said Twig, his eyes widening.

Starlight looked up to watch the dust cloud rolling across the plain. She thought back with fondness to the many migrations she had witnessed in her time as Great Mother. The herds of buffalo crossing the plains, united in their journey, one great family, with one aim: to go, and to return.

But as she gazed at the passing herd, something seemed to flash across her vision. It was as if the rolling dust was really a dark storm cloud, and lightning burst within its depths.

Something was wrong.

The baboons hadn't seen it—she didn't even have to look at them to know it. This was one of those times when the Great Mother alone could see the truth behind the reality of things.

The thunder roll of the buffalo's hooves echoed in her mind, darker and harsher than it had been, and there was an answering rumble from deep inside her chest.

The Great Spirit was uneasy.

There is something wrong in Bravelands, she thought. *And even the Great Spirit may not know what it is. . . .*

CHAPTER ONE

Stride stretched, his front paws clawing at the dry ground, and rolled over until he was belly up under the striped shadow of the lone tree. Beside him, Pace's rib cage rose and fell as he heaved a sigh. The sun was high in the sky and the day was hot, too hot for sprinting over the plains after prey. The coalition still needed to hunt today, but Stride was perfectly content to sprawl in the shadows with the other cheetahs, waiting for Jinks to decide when it was time. There were some benefits to not being the leader.

"Almost makes you wish that cheetah hadn't stolen the sun in the first place," said Pace, squinting up into the blue.

Stride let his head flop over to look at his best friend, his tail twitching. He recalled the tale well, because his mother had told him as he suckled with his litter-mates. Her voice was still with him, comforting and calm. . . .

"See, once the world was dark, my children. All the time. Everlasting night, forever and ever. But the sun did exist, it was just hidden underground by Death." It sounded fanciful now, of course, but at the time his ears had drunk in her soft words. "Death was jealous of the way the Great Spirit loved the living creatures. Or maybe Death was just hoarding the sun for itself—or something—anyway, it was under the ground in a deep, black ravine where nothing lived. But the Great Spirit knew that life couldn't carry on in Bravelands without the sun, so it picked a cheetah and asked him to steal it back."

Of course the spirit chose a cheetah, he had thought. The best possible animal.

And the cheetah succeeded—obviously—but Death had chased after him, pursuing him over all of Bravelands. The cheetah was faster than Death for a long time; round and round in big circles they ran, until the sun was high in the sky.

"And then?" he had asked.

"Death never gets tired," his mother had said, "so it managed to catch the cheetah in the end, as it catches all creatures."

That hadn't been the happy ending he hoped for, and his mother, sensing his sadness, told him that the Great Spirit had been so impressed with the cheetah's bravery that it made the sun keep going round and round, rising and falling every day "to pay tribute to his sacrifice."

Stride looked up at the blue sky again. The shadows had already moved a little, so that his back paws were sticking out into the light. He sensed movement from near the trunk of the tree. Jinks was stirring, as was his lieutenant, One-Ear. Stride got up, stretched, and then briefly washed the dust from his eyes with his paws.

"You've all lazed around long enough," said Jinks. "Everybody up. Time to hunt."

The coalition leader's words made him swallow a growl. Jinks had been lazing around just as much as the others!

I guess if you're not the one making the decisions, you have to be bossed around all the time instead, he thought, as the four cheetahs stretched their backs and shook out their fur. His mother had told him that life in a coalition would be all about hanging out with your best friends, chasing down the best prey as easily as breathing. She didn't say anything about what to do if your coalition leader was a slick-tailed bully.

"Follow me," said Jinks. "While your parents were telling you nonsense tales about things that never happened, mine were teaching me how to find prey."

Pace looked mutinous, and even One-Ear's muzzle twitched with irritation.

Jinks led them in a zigzag across the sun-drenched plain, from tree to tree, sniffing through long grass and sometimes just standing and staring, as if he was listening to something the others couldn't hear.

But eventually, as the coalition was following Jinks to the top of a small grassy hillock, Stride heard it too: his whiskers twitched at the sound of hooves. Lots of hooves striking the dry earth, and the snorting and heavy breathing of large creatures. Annoyingly, Jinks really *did* have a knack for finding good prey, even if Stride was faster.

Jinks gestured to the others to move carefully, and all four of them crouched low into the grass as they reached the top and looked down at the herd of buffalo crossing the plain below them.

Stride narrowed his eyes as he scanned the herd. All the buffalo seemed to be adult, or near-adult size—much bigger than a single cheetah. Where were the calves? Then he realized, just as Pace whispered aloud:

"It's the males. They're probably heading to join the rest of the herd."

"We could bring one down," said Jinks.

Stride frowned. He couldn't see any elderly or sick buffalo lagging behind. They'd have to target one of the younger males, and what they lacked in size they would make up for in spirit. . . .

"Are you sure?" Pace asked.

Jinks gave him a pitying look. "You don't think you can outrun a buffalo?" he sneered.

"'Course I can," said Pace, hurriedly. "They're slow—but they're so *big*. It'll take all of us to finish it off, and if the others catch us . . ."

"It's not that hard," said Jinks. "I killed an adult buffalo by myself once. You just have to use your brain."

Pace fell silent with a sigh, but he met Stride's eyes behind Jinks's back.

All by himself? Stride thought. *Sure, and I'm Great Father Zag come back from the dead. . . .*

"It's true," said One-Ear. "I saw it."

Stride realized the rangy, thinly spotted cheetah was staring at him, and looked away quickly. But whether it was true or not, did Jinks really think taking on the herd was a smart idea?

"It must have been a great fight," Stride said, trying to sound genuinely complimentary, and not like he didn't believe a word of it. "But wouldn't we be better off focusing our energy for today? Find some smaller prey that we can take down without so much of a fight? If we search over—"

Stride felt the dull blow across his muzzle before he even realized Jinks had moved. The leader's claws were sheathed, but it was still a hard cuff that made Stride yelp and back away.

"*I* am the leader of this coalition," Jinks snarled. "If you want to do your own thing, fine. You can leave and see how you fare hunting all by yourself. My coalition and I are going after the buffalo."

Stride moved his jaw experimentally, feeling it ache as he wiggled it, and then lowered his eyes. "No. Sorry, Jinks. I'm with you."

"Good," said Jinks. "I've already got my eye on the buffalo we're going to take down. There, you see the one with the shiny black horns that haven't formed their boss yet?"

Stride squinted in the direction Jinks was nodding. There was a young buffalo at the edge of the herd, a little separated from the rest. The top of his head was still covered in hair—the boss, the hard covering that happened when the males' horns grew together on top of their head, hadn't come in yet. He didn't seem to be paying much attention to the rest of his herd, instead rooting through the grass.

"He's likely only been with the males for a season. Probably thinks he's a big grown-up buffalo and nothing can touch him. Well, we're going to prove him wrong," said Jinks, and slunk through the grass toward the huge animal.

Stride's heart clenched as he followed. The buffalo was young, and nowhere near as massive as the leaders of the herd that Stride saw farther off. But it was big enough to give the cheetahs a whole lot of trouble. . . .

The herd was moving away from them. The young male was following, but a few steps at a time, getting distracted by tasty grasses or whatever it was that caught a buffalo's eye. The cheetahs kept their movements short and swift, moving when the buffalo looked away, freezing in the long grass whenever his head turned toward them. At last they were almost on him. Despite his doubts, Stride's mouth was watering. Perhaps they *could* do this. If they just let the herd get a little farther away, they could kill the creature and run before the herd could turn, come back for the meat later.

That must be his plan, right? he thought, with a nervous glance at Jinks.

Jinks's eyes scanned the horizon, met Stride's, and then fixed on the young male. His hindquarters tensed as he judged his distance, and then he sprang across the grass, faster than the wind.

Jinks was on the underside of the buffalo's neck before the creature knew what was happening, with Stride, Pace, and One-Ear split seconds behind him.

The young buffalo's eyes rolled in panic as One-Ear leaped onto his back, Pace biting one leg and Stride the other. For a moment, he thought that the creature might topple over and be theirs, as easy as that.

But then it took a huge breath and bellowed at the top of its lungs.

"Help! Help me!"

Stride's heart sank as he saw, between the creature's legs, the rest of the herd turning as one.

The buffalo stumbled, trying to throw Jinks and One-Ear off without falling. One-Ear was half-dislodged, leaving a trail of claw marks across the buffalo's back.

"Quake!" thundered the herd, as if with one voice.

"Jinks, kill it!" Pace growled, through a mouthful of buffalo hair.

Jinks just grunted and lunged again for the buffalo's throat, but the oncoming herd seemed to have given the young male strength, and he tossed his horns, catching Jinks on the side of the neck with the flat of them. Stride winced. A little to the left and Jinks could've been speared on the horn, right through the jaw. Now Jinks was on the ground, the other three hanging on as the buffalo bucked and roared, and the dust was rising as the hooves of the herd drew closer. They would *all* be speared or trampled!

Stride let go and ducked away from the stomping hoof, looking at Jinks.

I'm going, coalition or not, he thought. *So you'd better give the word, or . . .*

"Let's go," Jinks said, and he turned and burst into a run. One-Ear dropped down beside Stride, and Pace wriggled out from beneath the buffalo's shaking back leg, and all three of them made a run for it. Up and over the hillock they flew, leaping rocks, heading for the nearest trees.

The herd was so close behind them as they turned that Stride imagined he could feel their breath on his tail, but they were soon outpacing the slow creatures. Even at a full charge, a buffalo could never catch a cheetah. At last, Stride heard a deep, smug-sounding buffalo give the order to stop, but he didn't risk looking back.

Jinks led them to a halt under a small copse of fever trees on the edge of a swampy, nearly dry watering hole. The buffalo could still be seen in the distance, gathering around their injured herd-mate. They weren't even watching the cheetahs anymore.

For a moment Jinks said nothing while they all caught their breath. One-Ear lay down at the root of the tree and waited, as patiently as a stone. Pace, however, was glaring at Jinks, through one good eye and one that was swelling up. Stride hurried over and sniffed at his friend's injury, but Pace twitched away. "I'm fine," he said. "Just got a bump on the side of the head. It could have been *much worse*."

"It was a foolish idea," Stride said. He met Jinks's eyes as the coalition leader turned.

You could have got us all killed, he thought. *Deny it, I dare you.*

Jinks just stood there, looking at Stride as if he was a piece of muck caught between his claws. Then he shook himself and said, "Come on, there's more prey where that came from," and turned to go.

Stride's claws unsheathed for a moment, scraping in the earth. Jinks was a rash, selfish fool, and he ought to have to acknowledge that he'd made a stupid mistake.

But do you really want to fight about it? Now?

No. I just want something to eat.

With a cautious glance at Pace, Stride followed his coalition leader back out onto the plain.

"We'd better find prey with good meat on it," said Jinks as they were hopping over a thin crevice in the ground that snaked across the dry earth. "I want to take some to Flicker."

Stride hid his sigh and his rolling eyes with a quick pause to clean his whiskers.

Not this again.

Jinks's courtship of the female called Flicker, who lived somewhere on the edge of their territory, was a topic he returned to *a lot.*

Flicker's coat was the glossiest in Bravelands. Her eyes gleamed like the watering hole under the morning sun. She was as strong as an elephant and as fast as lightning and her spots were as black as midnight and she was clever enough to be Great Mother but much too humble, in fact the Great Spirit itself had chosen her to be Jinks's mate and be the perfect mother to his cubs. Or something like that. Stride had stopped listening to Jinks's actual words when it came to Flicker; it all amounted to the same thing.

"I bet she's actually fly-ridden and half-lame," Stride

whispered to Pace. Pace shook his head sadly.

"I've met her," he said.

"Oh, come on," Stride said. "Don't tell me she's really like that? That's the only thing worse than Jinks lying about it!"

Pace chuckled. "Sorry to say," he muttered. "He's exaggerating, but she is pretty impressive."

"Jealous?" asked One-Ear in a snide tone, sidling up to Stride.

Stride didn't bother to hide his rolling eyes for One-Ear's benefit. "I wish Jinks and his mythically excellent mate all the happiness in Bravelands," he said. "I just don't want to keep having to hear about it. I didn't join a coalition to hear about females all the time—I could have stayed in my mother's group for that!"

One-Ear scoffed. "Sure."

"I'll have no trouble finding a mate when I want one," Stride said, vaguely aware that he might be digging deeper into the hole rather than climbing out of it. "I just want to enjoy coalition life by myself for a while. Hunting, independence. Fun."

I was promised fun, he thought bitterly. *Even the failure at the buffalo herd could have been fun, if it hadn't been for Jinks's attitude.*

When I'm leader, things will be different. . . .

A hot breeze stirred the dust around his paws, and all of a sudden, Stride scented something that made his whiskers twitch and his ears prick up. He looked around and glimpsed the long, graceful horns of an impala rising from behind a ridge to their right.

Stride stopped walking.

"What?" said One-Ear.

"Impala," Stride whispered. He hesitated for a moment. In his peripheral vision he could see Jinks stop, turning back and watching him. "I'm going to take one."

"Nah," said One-Ear.

"They're fast," said Pace. "After running from the buffalo . . . if you overdo it now, you know what could happen. . . ."

Stride shook his friend off.

"I'm fine. I can do it," he said. Pace was right, it was dangerous. If he didn't go now, the wind would change again, and the impala could smell them and bolt.

This was his only chance.

He started up the ridge, leaving the others behind him. Jinks could have easily ruined the hunt by calling out to him, but he didn't. Stride wondered if he too was starting to get hungry and thought this might be their best bet. Or maybe he just wanted to see Stride fail. . . .

Slinking on his belly the last few cheetah-lengths, Stride tried to breathe evenly and gather his strength as he came up over the ridge and saw the impala there. Its herd was close by, but they wouldn't charge, they would run.

So let's run.

He sprang. The impala saw the movement and stumbled into a sprint. The herd scattered, and now it was just the two of them, and the long yellow-green slope down the other side of the ridge, the rocks and the trees and the open sky. Stride took an easy pace at first, letting the impala's panic drive it to waste its energy early, and then he really began to push. The strokes of his paws and the beat of his heart seemed to meld together, until the sounds of the world contracted down to just the rhythm: *badabum, badabum, badabum.*

Color leeched from his vision. He was running in a gray world where the black shadows seemed to glow with a strange purple hue that he knew would hurt his eyes if he looked at it for too long.

He was soaring, barely feeling the rocks under his paws, his eyes fixed on the hindquarters of the impala as it tried to swerve and sway to throw him off. He felt momentum dragging on him as he followed it around a clump of trees, but he shook it off, and with a burst of exhilaration he charged after the impala down a long, straight valley. There was no escape for it now, except to outrun him, and no impala could outrun him. . . .

And then, moments from being able to seize the impala's flank in his teeth and bring it down, Stride realized he wasn't the only one hunting.

He was also being hunted.

He didn't know how he knew. Perhaps it was that the painful shadows were growing brighter, violent purple and green swimming in the corners of his vision. Perhaps he just knew.

Something was right on his tail. It made no sound and had no smell, and it would never stop. He could not look back. If he did, he would see what was chasing him, and the idea was unbearable. There was only one way to evade it, but he didn't know if he was brave enough. Panic filled his heart, and the horrible vibrating shadows shifted closer.

He leaped. His claws unsheathed, clamped down around the back of the impala, and together they tumbled to the ground in a crashing heap. He heard a snap of fragile bone, and he dug his claws in deep. Ignoring the shadows and the spinning world around his head, he found the creature's neck and sank his teeth in. It would not get away from him now.

The impala twitched and struggled for a little longer, but as blood flowed over Stride's tongue, the color flowed back into the world. Blue sky, dusty yellow grass, spreading red under his paws.

CHAPTER TWO

Whisper raised her head, chewing on a tasty mouthful of grass, and scanned the horizon.

"Can you see anything?" Murmur asked, for the fourth time that morning.

Whisper squinted into the distance. Was that the telltale puff of dust that meant the males were here? No . . . it was just a meerkat kicking out dirt from its burrow.

"Nothing," she said.

Murmur snorted and shook her head, nudging Whisper with her small horns as she did so. "Where *are* they? Do you think something's happened?"

"What could happen to a herd of buffalo?" Whisper asked. "I'm sure they'll be here soon."

"And when they are," put in a strident voice above Whisper's head, "you will regret that you didn't appreciate the peaceful days while you had them." Thunder, Murmur's mother, smiled as if she was making a joke, and the other buffalo around her all chuckled.

"Don't you want to see the males again?" asked Murmur.

"Of course we do," said her mother, more kindly.

"But they are noisy," said her mother's friend Clatter.

"And they take up so much *space*," said another buffalo.

"And the eating! Everything in sight, all the time," said one more. Whisper looked at Murmur and frowned in confusion. The females and calves ate pretty much everything in sight too; that's why they were always moving around. What were these elders talking about?

"Well, I'm excited!" Murmur said—a little unnecessarily, considering that she was scanning the horizon again and pawing the ground with one hoof. "I can't wait to see Quake again!"

Whisper chuckled at her friend. She thought it was sweet that Murmur was so stuck on Quake. He was a skinny thing whose ribs were clearly visible under his hair, but they had all grown up together in the mothers' herd, and Murmur had always liked him.

"You two acted like you had your horns tangled together half the time," Whisper said. "But he's not exactly Bellow, is he?"

The leader of the herd was growing old now, but the last time Whisper had seen him he'd still been an impressive sight, with huge white horns that curled all the way around his ears twice.

"Even Bellow started out as a calf," Thunder said.

"If only they stayed that way," said Clatter wistfully. "The calves are so sweet."

Not all of them, Whisper thought, looking around for her little brother.

She didn't see him, and panic pulsed in her heart for a moment. Where had he gone?

"Echo?" she called. No answer.

Trying to keep calm, she pushed between Clatter and Thunder and made her way along the edge of the herd, excusing herself as she wriggled between the much larger females and their calves. Oxpeckers chirped and fluttered around her head, then settled back onto their buffalo, ruffling their feathers and plucking out insects with their tiny beaks.

"Echo? Has anyone seen Echo?" Whisper called. The buffalo gave her blank looks, until one small calf looked up and then glanced over her shoulder. Whisper followed her gaze, and she saw him. He was outside the herd—*again*.

This time he was prancing and rearing in a play-fight with a young rhino, the little nubs of their horns pressed together as they shoved back and forth over a line in the dirt.

"I got you!" the rhino giggled, as Echo's hooves slipped and he was pushed back.

"Nuh-uh!" Echo retorted, and put all his weight into a great shove. Whisper could have told him that was a bad idea. She sighed as he lost his balance and toppled over, sprawling on the ground. The rhino tossed his horn in triumph, and both of them roared with laughter.

Whisper marched up to them. Echo looked up at her and

rolled back to his hooves.

"What are you doing?" she demanded. "Come back to the herd! You're going to get eaten and it'll be all your own fault."

"Oh, come on," said Echo. "I was with Rockside, and his mother's just over there. Nothing bad was going to happen!"

Whisper looked past Rockside and saw that a large adult female rhino was grazing on the grass a little way away.

"She's too far away to save you if predators sneak up!" she told Echo. "They could be hiding anywhere! You'll never see them until their teeth are in your throat. Go on, go back to your mother," she added, turning on Rockside. The little rhino looked for a moment like he wanted to argue, but Whisper gave him a hard look and he hung his head and slumped off. "Let's go," she said to Echo, but her brother wasn't listening. She gave a grumpy snort and nudged him with her horn. Echo stumbled and then glared back at her.

"No, look!" he said. "Over there! What's that?"

Whisper's heart lurched as she scanned the plain, searching every bush and hillock for the twitching ears and tails of predators. What if it was hyenas? She hated hyenas. . . .

She was just about to shove Echo behind her so that they could back away from the unseen danger, when she realized his gaze was fixed farther away, on the horizon, where the rolling plain faded into a shadowy swash of forest and far-off mountain. Squinting, she saw what he'd been talking about. A billowing cloud of dust, growing larger and closer with every moment.

"It's them!" Whisper gasped. "It's the males, they're back! Come on, we should tell Murmur!"

They turned and cantered back to the group.

"Murmur! Thunder! We saw them, they're nearly here!" Echo shouted.

A rumble of excited chattering passed through the herd as the buffalo all raised their heads toward the horizon. Thunder pushed her way to the front of the crowd, with Murmur at her side and a few of her friends and their calves in their wake, as the rest of the herd closed in behind them.

"What happens when they get here?" Echo asked, his eyes still wide and fixed on the distant dust cloud. "Will we set off on migration right now?"

"Not yet," said Thunder, looking down at him with a fond smile. "We'll spend some time getting reacquainted first."

They talk about the males being noisy and annoying, Whisper thought, *but they get the same look as Murmur when they're nearly here!* Thunder was staring out to the horizon with a dreamy gaze that seemed like she was already imagining being reunited with her mates and calves, or possibly like she had been hit on the head with a rock.

"I hope that doesn't take too long," Echo muttered to Whisper. "I've never been on migration! I want to see Bravelands, with the rest of the males!"

"We'll be off soon enough," said Whisper. "Enjoy the rest while it lasts. Migration is . . . hard."

She intended to leave it there, but Echo went on. "But we'll get to cross the black rock rivers, right? And we'll see forests and mountains and elephants and lions, and the rains will come, and . . ."

"Yes, elephants and lions," said Whisper. "And dangerous river crossings, and heat, and exhaustion, and other predators. It's a hard march, Echo. It's not a quick stroll to the watering hole and back. There are many dangers on the journey. Not to mention that when it comes, the rain is cold and it's wet and you can get sick and the rivers swell up. . . ."

Echo snorted. "I didn't say it wouldn't be hard," he said. "But we'll have Bellow with us! I heard he gored a lion last time!" He tossed his head, jabbing the air with his stubby horns, and then lost his footing and fell to his knees in the grass. Murmur laughed at him and helped nudge him back up onto his hooves, and Whisper couldn't help blinking at him affectionately too—but her smile felt weak.

He doesn't remember, she thought as she watched her little brother's carefree capering. *He was too little to know what was happening.*

Echo had been born on the last migration. His birth was hard on their mother. Too hard. He didn't seem to remember that awful day, when their mother couldn't keep walking, and the herd couldn't stop, and so Thunder and Roar and the other females had gathered around to say their goodbyes and promised her that they would feed Echo and keep both her calves safe. A kindness that felt more brutal than any lion's bite. And then they had walked away. The herd left Whisper's mother to lie down and wait for death, whether it came from starvation or at the claws of predators.

Whisper remembered trying to get a final glance at her mother, and Thunder ordering the others to block her view.

Telling her, quietly, that she had to be like a mother to her baby brother now, and that meant she had to be strong and not look back.

Without his own mother's milk and attention, Echo hadn't grown as quickly as the others. Whisper secretly worried he might never be strong enough to join the male herd—but worse, so much worse, was the idea that he might not be strong enough for the migration. That she might find herself saying goodbye to him too.

She watched as Thunder gave Murmur an affectionate lick on the ear and tried not to feel envious.

She could make out the shapes of individual buffalo in the distant haze now. They were imposing in the afternoon light, huge horns curling around their ears and across their foreheads. In the middle, she thought she could even pick out one a little larger than the rest. Was that Bellow?

Echo's right, she thought. *With Bellow here, we'll be fine. We will set out on migration, and then the rains will come, and all of Bravelands will be renewed for another year. And Echo will make it back and join the males like he's supposed to. I'll make sure of it.*

CHAPTER THREE

The gazelle was limping now, and Cub could see its sides heaving with each panting breath and gleaming with beads of sweat. But it was still running, as fast as its tough old legs would carry it.

Behind Cub, Skullcracker let out a high, yipping cackle, and the other hyenas echoed it from all around them. Cub joined in too, and she watched with satisfaction as the gazelle twitched and turned its head, seemingly against its own will, to look back at the laughing clan. It cost the herd creature dearly—while it was looking back toward Cub and Skullcracker, the gazelle wasn't watching as Hidetearer and two others put on a burst of speed and managed to circle around their prey, so that when the gazelle looked back, it realized it was surrounded and stumbled to a trembling halt.

"Give up," Skullcracker commanded, grinning as she padded around the gazelle, her yellow eyes fixed on her prey. "Your shadow is gone. Your death has found you. Why keep running?"

The gazelle's legs were shaking, but with a great effort it raised its head into a proud, straight stance.

"I have run my whole life with the Us," it said. "And now I run alone. But telling a gazelle not to run is like telling the grass not to grow. A gazelle outran her death once. Who's to say it can't happen again?"

The hyenas just giggled at her.

"Cub," said Skullcracker, and Cub jumped in surprise. The older hyena licked her lips and looked at her. "It's time. Make the kill. Take your name."

"Unless you want to be called Cub until your teeth fall out," sneered Hidetearer, to another chorus of snickers from the rest of the clan.

Cub gave the gazelle the venomous look she couldn't risk giving either Hidetearer or Skullcracker.

They shouldn't do this. Embarrassment and fury made her ears burn. *They shouldn't need to. I should have caught my name by now, by myself, without needing a kill to be gifted to me like this.*

It was almost tempting to refuse, to say she would remain Cub until she earned her name for real.

But Hidetearer was right. She really couldn't face being Cub much longer.

Even the gazelle seemed to agree. Its head bobbed, staring into her eyes.

"You hesitate," it said. "Do not fear, young Cub. After all, you're only following the Code of Bravelands. You kill to survive."

Skullcraker gave a derisive snort, but Cub steeled herself and approached the prey. The gazelle didn't move, and Cub tensed to spring . . . but as she did, the gazelle leaped away from her.

It tricked me! Cub thought as she scrambled after it, snapping furiously. All around her she could already hear her clan laughing. If she let this stupid old gazelle get away, she would never, ever hear the end of it! She made a great leap and closed her jaw desperately on the only part of the animal she could reach—its tail. The gazelle let out a yelp and bucked and kicked out at her, but Cub dug her teeth into the flesh beneath the fluffy hair and dragged the animal backward until it stumbled and fell.

As soon as the gazelle was down, it was all over. Skullcracker and Hidetearer had their teeth on its throat. The gazelle twitched once, and then its spirit was gone.

The feeding frenzy began, and all the hyenas jostled and shoved to get a good mouthful of the meat—it'd be tough and bitter, on a tired old animal like this one, but still good. Cub was no different, wiggling in between two of her clan-mates to clamp her jaws around the leg.

But then she felt something strike her between the eyes, and she recoiled to see Skullcracker pulling back her paw, ready to swipe at her a second time.

"Weaklings eat last," she sneered. "Wait your turn. *Cub.*"

Cub growled back, but she retreated, spitting out gazelle

hairs, and watched as the rest of the clan scuffled and fought over the best parts of their prey. She glared at the others and tried to sneak in between them to grab a bite—the clan would expect nothing less—but her heart wasn't really in it.

I really am going to be Cub forever, she thought.

At last, the others had eaten their fill, and they backed away, leaving Cub with what was left. It wasn't much. Scraps of flesh and stringy furry hide, and the bones that jarred against her teeth and stabbed into the roof of her mouth when she tried to get a good bite. Flies were already starting to land on the clouded eyes of the gazelle, and a shadow moved overhead— vultures, waiting for their turn.

Cub cracked her way into a leg bone to get at the marrow inside, still warm and tasty but too much effort for the well-fed elders of the clan to bother with. They were already starting to wander off, leaving her alone with her meager meal.

"Congratulations," sniggered Hidetearer. "You should be proud, you've gained your name at last!"

Cub raised her head and frowned at the older hyena. "No, I didn't. I didn't make the kill. . . ."

"I think you did," said Hidetearer, looking at Skullcracker with a sly grin. "Well done, Tailgrabber!"

Cub bristled. *Tailgrabber?* What kind of a name was that for a fearsome hyena? She shot a pleading look at Skullcracker. "That doesn't count! I didn't make the kill!"

"Tough," snapped Hidetearer. "It's not your choice, Tailgrabber."

"Bye, Tailgrabber!" called Backbreaker and Neckbiter, their tails wagging as they walked off, laughing.

"Finish your meal and join the clan as soon as you're done," said Skullcracker. She wasn't laughing, but just stared Cub down as she added, "See you soon, Tailgrabber."

She turned to join the others, and Tailgrabber watched them walk away, her heart in her mouth.

It's just a name, she told herself, slowly lowering her muzzle to her prey once more, if only to keep the vultures from circling any lower. *It doesn't define me. It's not that stupid. I could have killed this thing, I just . . .*

Didn't.

She crunched down on another bone and lapped up the marrow, swallowing the moist, meaty stuff gratefully—it might not be as filling, but the dry season was beating down on them, and it had been a long, hot chase.

Then, suddenly, something sharp jabbed Tailgrabber in the back of the throat. A shard of bone. She tried to swallow, but it scraped across the roof of her mouth and wouldn't move. It was stuck! She threw her head forward and coughed as hard as she could, all her fur rippling with the effort. Panic overwhelmed her, until she couldn't see the prey in front of her or feel the heat on her back; she could feel only the racking coughs shaking her body and the jabbing pain in her throat.

Tailgrabber, a nasty little voice in the back of her head seemed to say. *Choked on the prey she couldn't even kill herself . . .*

Then the shard came flying out of her mouth. She collapsed

onto her belly, still coughing, the plains shifting dizzily around her. If the vultures came now, she wasn't sure she could even get up to chase them off.

She sat there for a little while, until everything stopped spinning, and then looked up at the state of her prey. The vultures had stayed away, but even in the short time she'd left it alone, the head and shoulders of the gazelle were covered in flies.

But there was something strange about the way they were moving. Instead of swarming in all directions looking for food and warm places to lay their eggs, they were crawling over the mostly eaten creature toward her, as if they were one creature with a thousand legs. . . .

Oh, she thought, as all at once the insects lifted from the gazelle into the sky and swirled in front of her, a curtain of vines made from black and shiny bodies that parted and closed again over glimpses of . . . something. *Oh. This again.*

She tried to brace herself, but before she could do more than breathe, the dark vines parted once more, her vision narrowed, and she was drawn into a world that was not the sunlit grassland where she had been before. The sun was setting over an arid, featureless plain. The ground was cracked and dry. It was dead: but with none of the squirming, stinking, thriving decay that came with ordinary death.

Standing on that dead plain, as white and clean as if they'd been bleaching in the sun for a year, and yet upright and whole as if they'd been living only a moment before, were skeletons.

Countless numbers of huge skeletons. Their rib cages were large enough to hold a hyena inside, and their empty skulls bore gigantic curling horns.

Buffalo. A whole herd of skeletal buffalo.

One stood alone, ahead of the herd. It was even larger than the rest, with a single horn curling around its head. The other had been broken off. Tailgrabber couldn't see it. It was lost.

The buffalo was as dead as the others, as dead as the dry earth they stood upon, but somehow Tailgrabber wasn't shocked when it moved its enormous head, turning its empty eye sockets toward her.

"Help us," it said, in a voice like rocks rolling downhill.

Then at last, as if they had all just realized that they were dead and there was no muscle or sinew holding them together, the endless herd of buffalo began to topple and fall into piles of loose bones. The bones themselves crumbled into dust, and the dust flew up and made a black, buzzing curtain across Tailgrabber's vision.

The flies and beetles scattered and were gone, leaving Tailgrabber alone on the sunlit plain with the corpse of the gazelle and the circling vultures.

She tried to take a deep breath and steady herself, but her back paw wouldn't stop drumming against the earth nervously.

Oh, Great Devourer . . . what was that? She scratched behind her ear with her jittery paw, but it didn't stop the creeping feeling underneath her fur.

She had seen things before. The children of the Great Devourer would come to her sometimes and show her things. But she had never seen anything as strange or as frightening as this.

She had to get back to the den.

CHAPTER FOUR

Stride paused in a shallow hole surrounded by grasses, dropped the impala carcass, and raised his head carefully above the vegetation, scenting and listening for predators. It'd be no use making off with his prize, risking Jinks's wrath like this, if it was stolen from him by lions or hyenas before he got where he was going.

Jinks would forgive Stride for eating the impala himself and being too tired from the chase to drag the rest back to the coalition. These things happened. He would understand, even if he used it as an excuse to give Stride a hard time for a while.

Jinks *wouldn't* understand what Stride was actually doing with his prey.

The coalition came first. The coalition always came first.

It was a good thing he could trust Pace. A less loyal friend might have spilled his secret to Jinks in return for a better position within the group, but not Pace. They'd known each other too long, since they were cubs.

The impala smelled delicious, and it was leaving a scent trail that any predator worth their nose would be able to follow, but as long as Stride moved quickly, he would reach the copse with the huge baobab at the center and the ring of marula trees around it, before anyone or anything caught up with him. He paused a little longer to make sure he was alone and then dragged his prey through the long, dry grass toward the distant bulbous shape of the baobab.

As he drew close enough that he had to wriggle underneath a row of bushes, pulling the impala clumsily behind him, he stopped worrying about hyenas, and about Jinks.

What would he find on the other side of the bushes?

A familiar parade of terrible images passed across his mind's eye as he dragged his prey between the marula trees. A limp and lifeless form . . . a flock of vultures . . . or perhaps even worse, nothing at all . . .

"You need to stop coming here," said a voice above his head. Stride jumped, but before he'd looked up, he caught the scent of his brother. He grinned up at Fleet, who was lying draped over a branch in a nearby marula tree.

"Oh, really?" Stride replied. "I'll just take this impala away again and eat it all myself, then. . . ."

"Well, no need to be hasty," chuckled Fleet.

"It was going spare anyway," Stride lied. Fleet shook his head.

"Liar," he said. "Food *never* goes spare."

"It won't now," said Stride, biting into the impala's leg just to emphasize his point.

Fleet laughed again and then climbed down from the tree. Stride tried to pretend he wasn't watching as his brother's trembling paws found purchase on the trunk and he landed in a stagger on the ground below. His chest heaved, fur hanging loose from his rib cage, as he padded over to the impala on three skinny, shaky legs, dragging the fourth uselessly behind him. Close up, Stride saw that Fleet's eyes were dull, covered in a sticky-looking film.

He nudged the impala toward his brother, who fell on it hungrily. Stride joined him, but made sure to take small, careful bites. They ate together in silence for a while, until Fleet's belly bulged against his skinny frame and he lay down for a rest, letting his muzzle fall onto his paws. His back leg twitched as if it had a mind of its own.

"Seriously," Fleet said at last. "You can't keep doing this."

"Dunno what you mean," said Stride.

Fleet just stared at him and said nothing, which was infuriating. At least that hadn't changed. Fleet had been the most annoying brother in the world when they were cubs, always one step ahead, always first to answer any question or chase after any prey. His name had fit him like his own shadow.

Until the warthog, and the hole in the ground, and the horrible sound of his leg cracking.

Now the name Fleet seemed like a horrible joke.

"You can't put your life on hold," Fleet said, at last. "You've got your coalition to think about. They're your future."

Stride stared at him. "You know I can't just stop. What would you eat if I didn't bring you food?"

"I would manage," Fleet said with a sniff.

"Crickets? And lizards?" Stride prodded.

"I caught a snake yesterday," Fleet said.

"Oh yeah? And that filled you up, did it?" Stride didn't mention Fleet's sagging skin and sticking-out ribs. He knew he didn't have to. Fleet looked away. "You'd starve," Stride said. "And you're still my brother. The coalition might be my future, but you—you're my past and my present, so shut up."

Fleet sighed. "Just don't get caught, okay? Don't risk your life for me," he said.

"You can't tell me what to do anymore," Stride retorted. "As it happens, I should get back. But I'm not going because you said so."

"Obviously," Fleet said, with an annoying smile.

"I'll see you soon," Stride said. "I'll bring you a whole buffalo, you'll see." He turned to go, but as he was stepping out of the shadow of the tree, Fleet spoke.

"Thanks, Stride," he said. "Really. Thank you."

Stride just smiled back at him. He wriggled underneath the bushes again, going over the story he'd tell Jinks and the others in his head.

I chased it so far I got lost, and then I was so hungry I ate it all myself.

They'd believe that, right?

Perhaps this time. But Fleet was right—the more he did this, the harder it would be to come up with excuses that the coalition would accept.

He stuck his head and shoulders out of the bushes, the setting sun glaring in his eyes, and then something struck him across the ear and the world went dark for a second.

A voice yowled in shock and fear, and the darkness lifted as the creature who'd sprawled over his face got to her paws. He realized it was another cheetah just as she reared back and smacked him across the face, claws out. He yelped and threw himself out of the bushes, backing away from her.

He was starting to open his mouth to yell at her, when he saw that her eyes were full of panic, widening as she took him in and realized what he was.

"Hey, it's okay," he said, crouching submissively in front of her. "Sorry! I didn't mean to startle you. Don't kill me."

"I'm not going to kill you," the female cheetah gasped. "You scared the spirit out of me! Where did you come from?"

She started to look at the bushes, toward the marula trees and the baobab.

"Nowhere," Stride said quickly. "I mean, I was hunting a warthog and it ran under here, but I lost it."

"Oh. Shame," said the cheetah.

Stride stood up, slowly, not wanting to make any sudden moves and startle this skittish female again. He needn't have worried—she relaxed and then sat down on her haunches and licked her paws. Now that Stride's own heart had stopped racing, he noticed that she was quite beautiful—she had very dark spots and sleek, well-fed fur. In the low sun, the gold in her fur almost glowed. Oddly, she seemed somehow familiar, though he was sure they hadn't met before.

"I don't know you," she said. Her large eyes narrowed in suspicion. "This isn't your territory, is it?"

"Not . . . exactly," Stride admitted. "Is it yours?"

That was going to make things complicated, with Fleet . . .

"No," the female said.

"Well, then we're both just passing through," said Stride, trying not to sound as relieved as he felt. "I'm Stride."

"Flicker," said the cheetah.

Oh.

There *could* be more than one Flicker roaming the plains. Easily.

But more than one Flicker with deep thoughtful eyes and golden fur dotted with spots as black as a starless night? Unlikely.

Shame—I was really hoping she'd be flea-ridden.

"I should get going," Stride said. "Got to get back to the— back to my territory. Bye!"

Before Flicker could reply, he turned and hurried away.

Maybe she just won't mention this to Jinks. He probably doesn't talk about me to her anyway. And even if he does, she'll probably forget my name by then.

He hoped she would. But when he glanced back over his shoulder, Flicker was sitting still where he had left her, watching him go.

CHAPTER FIVE

The herd was a snorting mass of bodies, males and females greeting each other with joy and excitement—and, in a few cases, chilly hostility.

Whisper, Echo, and Murmur kept close to Thunder at first, but then suddenly Murmur looked around and gasped.

"Quake? Quake, is that you?" she cried, and broke into a run. Whisper hurried after her, with Echo on their heels. They wiggled through a gap between two large males, and Whisper stared as Murmur ran up to a young, muscular male, with growing horns but no boss yet, whose hide was stained with blood from two long gashes on his rump. Whisper wondered for a moment who it was, before he turned his head toward them, and she realized Murmur was right. It *was* Quake!

"Hi, Murmur," he said, with a big grin. His voice was deeper than Whisper remembered it too. Murmur stopped a couple of steps from him, staring in amazement.

"You've grown," she said. "You look just like Holler."

That's taking it a bit far, Whisper thought. Quake definitely looked more like an adult than she'd expected, but he still had a long way to go to match his father.

"But what happened?" Murmur added with a gasp. "You're bleeding!"

"Oh, that?" Quake gave a dismissive toss of his head. "It's just a scratch. Some cheetahs tried their luck, but I drove them off."

"By yourself?" Murmur gasped.

"That's right," said Quake.

"Weren't you scared?" asked Echo, looking up at Quake with huge, shining eyes.

"Of a couple of scruffy old cats? Nah," said Quake. "They should've known better than to tangle with me!"

"Wow," breathed Murmur.

"It's just part of life in the male herd," said Quake. "I've learned a lot this last season."

"What about lions?" Echo asked. "They're bigger than cheetahs! Have you ever fought a lion?"

Quake snorted. "Lions are nothing special," he said.

"Yeah," said Murmur, rolling her eyes. "You're just a calf, you wouldn't know. Once you're big enough to fight off a meerkat by yourself, you can join this conversation."

Echo looked hurt, and Whisper sighed. Murmur didn't mean it. She was just trying to look grown-up in front of Quake. Whisper wondered if the obviousness of Murmur's crush might put Quake off, but he still preened and stomped back at her. Even his oxpecker looked smug as it picked a fly from the hair by his wound.

"I've seen a lot since I left," he said. "Once I had to fight off an elephant to get to a watering hole!"

"No! You didn't?" Murmur gasped.

No, Whisper thought, suppressing a giggle. *I bet you didn't . . . but I won't tell Murmur that, she seems like she's enjoying herself too much.*

"Woooow," said Echo, and Quake preened again, but this time Echo was looking at something behind him. Whisper followed his gaze and saw a great black horned shadow that almost blocked out the sun.

"Bellow!" Whisper said. "Look, there he is!"

The herd leader and his brother Holler were coming right toward them, the other buffalo parting to let them through. All four young buffalo held their breath, even Quake, who Whisper noticed was standing up extra straight, as if he could make himself taller by pure effort. He still would have looked small compared to the lumbering forms of his uncle and his father.

Whisper watched in awe as Thunder greeted Bellow with a dignified nod.

Then Thunder and her friends crowded around Bellow and Holler, fussing over them one moment and demanding to know why they were so late the next.

Making sure the other females have a hard time getting close, Whisper thought.

Holler was as large as Bellow, but he was louder, his deep

laughter resounding across the plains even above the noise of the herd.

Now that they were here, at least until the migration began, nothing bad could happen.

Whisper and Murmur stood and watched the males on the riverbank as the sun went down. Quake was with them, tossing his horns in the water and jostling for space with the bigger buffalo. And Echo was there too—Quake hadn't invited him, but another adult male, Shout, had summoned all the male calves of the season to join them. They splashed in the water and stared up at their elders with wide eyes.

The calves were watching the adults, and Murmur was watching Quake.

"I still can't believe he wasn't much bigger than Echo when the males left," she said. "Do you think his boss'll grow in soon?"

But Whisper was watching Echo.

It was both wonderful and achingly difficult to just stand with Murmur and Thunder and watch him splash about in the mud with the other males without sneaking closer, just in case. Nothing could happen to him if they kept an eye on him, and they would. So it didn't matter that he kept vanishing from her sight, or that she didn't know what he was saying to the older buffalo.

She kept telling herself that, over and over again, as Murmur went on about Quake and when they would have calves (*Not till next year, sweetheart,* Thunder told her, as the other grown-up females chuckled to each other).

"He'll be herd leader one day," said Murmur, "and we'll call our second calf Bellow—the first one will be Cry, obviously, after Grandmother."

Whisper noticed that the females were exchanging knowing glances again.

"What?" she asked Thunder.

"Well, darling," Thunder said to Murmur, "don't put *too* much of your heart into one male, or into his prospects, either. His father was supposed to be herd leader, you know. At least, that's what everyone thought when old Rumble was dying. But the Great Spirit chose Bellow, not Holler."

"He was furious," said Stampede in a low voice.

"But the Great Spirit chose wisely," another female said firmly. "Bellow has led the migration successfully ever since. It's not always the most physically powerful who leads."

"And a female's job is not to cling too closely to one future, or one male, but to make sure that no matter what, the herd goes on," added Clatter with a snort.

Murmur snorted right back. "Just because you've never had *romance* in your life, Clatter . . ."

"What does happen when a leader's chosen?" Whisper asked, changing the subject quickly before Clatter and Murmur could really get into the romance versus the practicality of mating. "How come Bellow knows where to go? Did Rumble teach him?"

"Yes, indeed," said Thunder, seeming equally glad to move the discussion on. "The old leader takes the new chosen one away from the herd and passes on the great knowledge of the land. Just the old leader and the new, under the silver light of a full moon—it's a sacred moment."

Her oxpecker punctuated her words with a musical little chirp, and all the oxpeckers, including Whisper's, responded in kind. A thrill passed through Whisper with a shudder. Every time the oxpeckers turned from their constant grooming of the buffalo's fur and did something like that, it felt like the Great Spirit was moving among them.

Whisper looked over at the males again, staring for a moment as Bellow's huge horns dipped and swayed in conversation with the others. One day, he would have to take a younger male for that moonlit talk. . . .

But it wasn't long before Whisper found herself scanning the group for Echo, just to check. She could see a couple of other male calves, but there was no sign of him. Then one of the adult males shifted, and she saw him—he was being jostled back and forth, trying to get into the circle with Bellow, but the others kept shutting him out. As she watched, Quake stepped to the side and his flank sent Echo slipping in the mud. A couple of the other younger males laughed.

Whisper snorted angrily. Whether it was an accident or not—and she wasn't sure it had been—they shouldn't treat Echo like this. He could be really hurt if they actually trampled over him!

She knew she shouldn't go over to him, but right now, Whisper didn't care. She tossed her horns and stomped toward the river. It was time for Echo to come back with her, if the others weren't going to treat him like one of them. . . .

She was so angry, so focused on getting to the river-bank and on the piece of her mind she was going to give the other males—including the really big ones—that her hooves thumped on the dry ground as she walked.

Thump, thump, thump . . .

And then, where a thump should have been, there was nothing. Her stomach turned over and she was down in the mud of the river, sprawled on her side, before she even realized she was slipping. The mud coated her face, and she shook her head and tried to right herself, but she'd walked right into a deep churned-up puddle, and it wasn't that easy. She kicked up water and dirt trying to get back up.

"Whisper!" Echo gasped. Whisper looked up at him and saw that several males were watching her, their eyes widening. She grimaced at them and wriggled even more furiously, splashing water everywhere, angry with herself now as well as with them.

"Whisper, look out!" cried Quake, and it was only then that Whisper saw the fear in their eyes. She twisted to look behind her and saw knobbled hides cutting through the shallow water toward her.

"Crocodiles!" screamed Echo.

Terror froze Whisper where she stood. She couldn't seem to tear her gaze away from the approaching sandtongues. Then Echo's voice called her name again, and she lumbered around, splashing and stomping in the mud, trying to climb the bank. The water farther down the river frothed as the grown-up males realized what was happening and a few of them made for her. She just had to get to them, to get past the adults, and they would close ranks behind her and see off the crocodiles. But no matter how hard she struggled, she was barely gaining ground against the sucking riverbank. It was like a nightmare, pushing and pushing while behind her she heard the splashes of scaly feet splashing up into the mud. Any moment now she would feel teeth close on her hind legs. . . .

Then with a roar the adult males arrived. She looked up and caught the eye of Bellow himself as he charged up to and past her. A split second later she heard a crocodile's screech and felt a splash of water across her flank.

She didn't stop to look. She pushed on, with the help of another adult male who paused to press his side to hers and shove her up and out of the mud pool and onto the bank. Whisper staggered on until she felt her hooves on solid ground once more, and then until she reached Quake and Echo, who were pawing the ground with worry.

"I've got you!" Echo said, and grabbed a mouthful of Whisper's hair to pull her to him—unnecessarily, but it still made Whisper give a panicked little smile.

She looked behind her at last. A wall of stomping wet buffalo seperated the youngsters from the crocodiles now, and the hooting and bellowing was almost deafening. Surely the crocodiles would have turned tail by now, rather than risk having their heads smashed in by the hooves and horns of the buffalo—but the mass of bodies was so confusing, she couldn't even make out one male from another. She caught sight of

Holler, dipping his horns into the water to wash away a gout of blood, and felt a flash of satisfaction. At least one crocodile had met its fate on the end of that horn.

The other females were rushing over too now, keen to make sure their calves and mates were all right, and a few of them splashed into the stream after the crocodiles, howling with fury. Horns thrashed and water shot up in great waves.

"Are you all right?" panted Murmur, making her way over to Whisper and the others.

"I'm fine," Whisper said. "Everything's fine."

"But why did you go into the water in the first place?" Murmur asked.

Whisper looked at Echo. He met her eyes for a second, his eyes widening in recognition, then he looked away. He knew that she'd been coming to defend him. . . .

Then, at last, the churning water calmed and the buffalo began to turn and make their way back to the bank. But as they did, Whisper's neck prickled. Something was wrong. Every buffalo's gaze was pinned on Bellow, emerging from the group alone. He was limping. He staggered up the bank, almost losing his footing in the same mud that had tried to swallow Whisper. The rest of the buffalo gathered behind him, staring and muttering to each other.

Bellow made it to solid ground, and then heaved a great sigh and fell to his knees, right beside Whisper and the other calves. She stared at the wound in his side. Blood was flowing, slowly but steadily, matting his hair to his flank. Bellow was breathing in labored gasps. Thunder and Holler both shouldered through the crowd to his side, and they began to talk in low voices. Whisper couldn't make out his words, but she could hear the pain in Bellow's voice.

"This is my fault," Echo said, in a small voice. "You nearly got killed, and you were only coming over here for me. . . ."

"No," said Quake, and for a moment Whisper thought he was going to comfort Echo. But he gave her and her brother a cold look before going on, in a sneering voice. "*Both* of you are to blame. And not just for nearly feeding Whisper to the crocodiles. You got Bellow injured. You've put the whole migration at risk!"

CHAPTER SIX

The hyena clan was gathered, the males and cubs tearing into the prey that the females had dragged back for them while the females lay in a loose circle, flopped on their sides or sitting up with their legs tucked neatly underneath them. Tailgrabber could tell that they were discussing something intently, even before she came close enough to hear their words.

Perhaps there was something important happening, and she wouldn't have to tell them about the vision. It never went well when she tried to share what she saw, even with her sister Nosebiter.

But the sight of the dead plain haunted her. She shivered even now as she thought of the skeleton buffalo, gazing at her through the swarm of bugs.

Tailgrabber walked up to the circle and quietly took a place next to Backbreaker, but out of swiping distance, just in case.

Spinesnapper was speaking, her tail thumping on the ground with excitement.

"They'll regret the day they moved onto our territory," she panted, a satisfied grin splitting her face. "We picked the strongest cub in the litter—the cream of the pride's next generation," she added, to appreciative cackles from the rest of the circle. "And bit its paw nearly clean off. If it lives, it'll never hunt."

"Good," said Skullcracker. "And there's more where that came from, if those lions don't learn their place."

"They call *us* scavengers!" said Hidetearer haughtily. "They can't even keep their own territory; they have to come to ours and steal our rightful prey."

"Right," said Spinesnapper, licking at the old scar on her flank. Several of the clan bore similar marks. Backbreaker's was still fresh, the puffy pink lines across her muzzle telling the story of the hyena clan's escalating battles with Noblepride.

"This will show them," Hidetearer said. "They'll think twice before bothering us again."

Doubt weighed on Tailgrabber's heart, but she said nothing. Maybe they were right. Maybe it would end here. Maybe *this* time, the lions would see no point in retaliating.

The others seemed like they would go on congratulating themselves about how their final victory over the lions was assured for some time if nobody stopped them, so at last Tailgrabber cleared her throat and spoke.

"I have something to say."

Heads turned toward her. Hidetearer and Backbreaker

nodded knowingly, and Tailgrabber realized they thought she was about to claim her new name. Well, that could wait.

Maybe forever, she thought.

"I had another vision," she said. More than one of the others groaned, but Spinesnapper batted at her neighbor's muzzle and growled.

"Let's hear it," she said.

Tailgrabber steadied herself and began to talk. She focused on talking to Spinesnapper. The older female at least seemed willing to hear her out and made thoughtful, nodding eye contact whenever Tailgrabber looked at her. She told them about the corpse flies, and the dead land, and the buffalo skeleton with the broken horn who begged for her help. When she was finished, the others exchanged skeptical glances, but Spinesnapper shook her head solemnly.

"Wow," she said. "This vision must have come from the Great Devourer itself! We should inform Gutripper at once!"

Tailgrabber's heart soared and then dived like a buzzard that had spotted a mouse moving in the grass.

They were mocking her. Spinesnapper looked sincere, but she'd given herself away. Inform Gutripper? *At once?*

"Ooh yes," said Hidetearer, doing a much worse job of not sounding sarcastic. "The Great Devourer's chosen messenger shouldn't be talking to a bunch of lowly hunters."

"I don't know," said Backbreaker. "Should we consider taking it to the Great Mother herself?"

"And risk angering the Great Devourer?" Hidetearer frowned. "No, no, we mustn't!"

"All right, all right," snarled Tailgrabber. "I understand. No one wants to hear it."

"No, it was a good story," said Skullcracker, cracking into a giggle. "Very imaginative. Maybe you should take it to the males and cubs, I'm sure they'd appreciate it."

Tailgrabber's temper flared. "Shut up, Skullcracker," she said. The older female's laugh died, and she got to her paws.

"What did you say to me, *Tailgrabber*?" she growled.

"Hey," said a new voice. Tailgrabber looked around.

Her sister was here. Nosebiter was approaching the group, her cub trotting behind her on his big, clumsy paws. When she stopped beside Tailgrabber, the cub walked into her and overbalanced, rolling on the floor for a minute.

"Will you lot scram?" she said in a bored tone. "I want to talk to my sister."

Tailgrabber saw Skullcracker thinking about challenging her, but then she sniffed and turned away.

"Come on. I've got better things to do."

The others sloped off after her, casting dark looks back at Tailgrabber.

"Thinks she's important," muttered Backbreaker. "Just 'cause she's Gutripper's daughter. Means nothing if she can't hunt. . . ."

Tailgrabber tried to ignore her. She looked down at the cub instead, who was lying on his back wiggling his tail and making hopeful faces at his mother.

Nosebiter smiled and lay down, letting her cub wriggle into her chest and begin to suckle.

"So," she said. "Tailgrabber? *That's* your name?"

Tailgrabber let out a deep sigh and flopped down beside her sister.

"Apparently."

"Well? Tell me what happened!" Nosebiter insisted.

"There was an impala, and . . . it really doesn't matter." Nosebiter gave Tailgrabber a firm stare, and Tailgrabber continued. "It tricked me. It almost got away, but then I got it by the tail. It's not fair!" she howled. "I didn't even make the kill. I shouldn't get saddled with *Tailgrabber* for a name."

"Better than no name," said Nosebiter. "Now you have to take that name and make it sound fearsome."

"How do I do that?" Tailgrabber asked miserably.

"Do fearsome things," said Nosebiter.

Tailgrabber rested her chin on the dry earth and watched a line of black ants scurrying from one crack to another.

She knew her littermate was right, but it was easier said than done.

"'Fearsome things.' Like, have visions nobody cares about?" she muttered.

Nosebiter partially sat up, dislodging Cub, who let out a squeak of impatience and wriggled around to a teat that he could still reach.

"Insects again?" she asked.

"Yes," said Tailgrabber. "Flies, from the corpse. It was so *clear* this time. They're getting more . . ." She paused, not sure how to describe the power and the horror that seemed to build in her, every time she saw another one of the strange visions.

"More overpowering. What if it's not just a joke—what if they really *are* messages from the Great Devourer?"

Nosebiter frowned. "Come on now, Cu . . . I mean, Tailgrabber. You *know* they're trying to make you sound crazy. Don't do it for them. I suppose you have seen things that are . . . true-ish. But it just sounds like a lot of buffalo are going to die. Why should that concern us? More for us to eat."

Tailgrabber shook her head and examined her paws.

"It didn't feel like that."

But still, her stomach rumbled at the mention of food. Nosebiter smiled at her.

"Focus on the here and now, not things that might or might not ever happen. Focus on hunting," Nosebiter told her. Tailgrabber knew she meant well, but the words stung. What did her sister think she was doing? Did she think she wasn't trying to get better? To not starve?

Despite the irritation, she nodded. "I know."

"What do hyenas say?" Nosebiter said.

"*We survive,*" Tailgrabber sighed.

"That's right," Nosebiter said, and gave her cub an affectionate lick on the top of his little head.

Haven't you ever wondered, though . . . Tailgrabber thought. She knew better to ask out loud. Even her sister would find it hard to understand what she was talking about. *Haven't you ever wondered if there's more to life than just surviving?*

"Come on," Nosebiter said to Cub. "Let's get back to the den, I don't like it out here after what happened to that lion cub. I don't think we've seen the last of Noblepride, do you?"

"Not a chance," Tailgrabber said emphatically, glad that on this at least they were in full agreement.

"Then you should stay," her sister said, getting up and nudging her cub to his feet. He waddled behind her, belly full of milk. "Keep a lookout for them. That's more important than visions of dead buffalo, right? Eyes on the present, sister."

"Right," said Tailgrabber, watching Nosebiter leave.

CHAPTER SEVEN

Stride paused, catching his breath. It was a few days later, and he had returned to Fleet's small territory. This time he'd chosen a much more portable prey, a dik-dik, to bring to his brother—but the wind had kicked up, stronger and stronger, until he'd had to fight to stay upright even with his small prize dangling easily in his jaws.

The bushes didn't provide much shelter, but at least he could put the little creature down without it blowing away.

Jinks and the others hadn't wanted to come hunting. *Storm's coming*, One-Ear had said. Stride had thought he was in luck—this was his opportunity to grab something for Fleet. But maybe One-Ear was right. It seemed to be growing darker, though Stride had been sniffing the air and he didn't think there was likely to be rain. . . .

"Fancy seeing you here again," said a voice. Stride spun

around, stepping defensively over his prey.

It was her. Again. Flicker. She was sitting behind him, giving him a cool and thoughtful look—or trying to; the wind was ruffling her fur and making one of her eyes wink involuntarily.

"This really is a long way from your coalition, you know," she said. "Don't you like hunting with them?"

Stride's heart gave a little skip. *She knows.*

Had she told Jinks about him? About where they'd met?

"I like hunting with them," he said. "They're my coalition. I just . . . like my alone time too."

It was a weak lie, but to Stride's surprise, Flicker laughed.

"I bet you do," she said.

"What does that mean?" Stride demanded.

"Well. Jinks." Flicker tilted her head. "He's not the easiest to get on with."

Stride blinked. Was this a trap? He looked around, half expecting to see Jinks himself watching from the long grasses.

"Don't worry, I didn't tell him you were here," Flicker said. "You can be honest. Jinks is insufferable, isn't he?"

Stride held his breath a moment longer, and then it burst out of him in a laugh.

"Great Spirit, *yes*," he chuckled. He nudged the dik-dik under a bush for safekeeping and sat down, washing his paws. If this was really a coincidence, he'd be able to take it to Fleet in a minute. "Jinks is a pain in my tail, is what he is! I'm sorry, but I have to know, what do you even see in him?"

"Me?" Flicker asked, giggling with him.

"Oh, he's *always* on about you," Stride said. "*Flicker's the greatest hunter, Flicker's got the most beautiful pelt, Flicker's eyes look like deep pools of nighttime* . . . that sort of thing. He's a good hunter, strong, I'll give him that. But *I* wouldn't have his cubs!"

Flicker had broken eye contact as he'd repeated Jinks's compliments, her ears twitching. She'd looked uneasily pleased at the flattery. But when Stride mentioned cubs, she looked up at him, and her ears turned down.

"I haven't told him I'll have his cubs," she said, the hint of a growl entering her voice.

"Oh." Stride pawed the ground, a little embarrassed. "Well . . . he's pretty sure you will. I mean, he thinks you're destined to be mates. He talks as if you already are. . . ."

"I don't believe in destiny," Flicker said flatly.

Stride was saved from having to respond when the wind kicked up around them once more, throwing a wave of dust and sand into their faces. They both turned to shield their eyes and straightened up, spitting out grit.

"I ought to go," said Stride. It would be more sheltered in Fleet's copse. . . .

"Why are you really here?" Flicker snapped. "Other than to get away from my 'mate'? I see you here all the time, every other day."

Stride bristled a little. "I don't see you."

"You're always bringing fresh kills. Half the time you're trying to drag some creature bigger than you are. It makes you easy to hide from," she said. "Are you stashing your prey near here somewhere? Hoarding it from the coalition?"

Stride's mind raced. He couldn't admit to that. That would be unacceptable. It would make him look like a thief and a traitor.

But he couldn't tell her the truth, either. . . .

"I just like hunting," he said weakly.

"I think I know what it is," Flicker said, ignoring him. "I think you *want* to share with the coalition, but you can't. Because you're a better hunter than Jinks is, and his fragile ego couldn't take it. Am I close?"

Stride swallowed. She was pretty far from the truth, but her theory was so flattering it seemed to stick his tongue to the roof of his mouth so that he could only nod.

Also, it was convenient not to have to tell her about Fleet.

"Well, I won't tell him," Flicker said. "But you can't go on like this forever, you . . ." She stopped speaking. Her eyes slowly widened, looking over Stride's shoulder. "Is that what I think it is?" she whispered.

He turned to look, expecting a pride of lions or stamped-ing elephants in the middle distance, or Jinks sneaking up on them. But at first it seemed like there was nothing there. Then he realized that the middle distance wasn't as far away as it ought to be. The far hills and rocks and lone trees that should have been visible behind him were gone, hidden behind a pale curtain that rolled across the plains toward them.

"Sandstorm!" Stride yowled.

His paws kicked up dust from the ground as he spun. Flicker's were already doing the same. Side by side, without speaking, they fled in the opposite direction from the rolling cloud of sand. They pushed through the winds that battered the plain, blowing them from side to side. Stride tried to go faster, but the wind was too strong, his paws not stable enough, to achieve the true speed of the cheetah. Instead they staggered back and forth together, trying to keep their footing. Half a bush sailed over their heads, torn from the ground, and Flicker gave a yell and veered aside as a small tree was bent almost right over, its branches smashing into the earth.

Stride glanced over his shoulder and saw the sand swallow Fleet's copse of trees. Horror seized his heart, for his brother and for himself. The storm was catching up. It would be on them in moments.

"Here!" Flicker yowled, and gave Stride a nip on the ear to get his attention before vanishing behind a large rock that jutted out of the earth. Following her, Stride saw that the ground fell away on the other side, leaving a hollow just large enough for two cheetahs to squeeze in.

They threw themselves against the rock, curling around each other, heedless of any awkwardness that they might have felt if it hadn't been chased out of them by the panic of the oncoming storm. Flicker pressed her chin over Stride's head, covering his eyes, and they both wound their tails up to try to cover her face.

They were barely in time. Sand poured over the top of the rock and crashed down around them, as if they had put themselves in the path of a raging river. In seconds, it was piling up over their heads. Stride pressed his eyes closed, grateful for the soft fur of Flicker's throat, and tried not to breathe.

In a moment, there was nothing but darkness and the roar of the wind, howling across the hollow. Then terrible creaking and tearing sounds, and a thump that rattled Stride's bones. Flicker pressed her chin down hard on the top of his head, and he winced. He could hear her heartbeat, fluttering in her throat like a nervous prey.

And then, as quickly as it had begun, it was all over. The wind moved away, the sounds died, the sand stopped growing heavier on Stride's back.

Stride tried to breathe in, but he inhaled sand. Hot, sharp pain seared his throat. Panic seized him and he burst from the dune that had formed over the top of them, coughing and spluttering, rolling over until he could finally clamber to his paws and retch the grit from his tongue, and shake and shake and shake the sand from his fur.

Flicker emerged more gingerly, her flanks and paws shaking and her breath coming in shallow, hitching gasps. Her back legs were caught, and Stride had to help dig her out.

It was hard work, even climbing out of the shadow of the rock—the ground was coated in drifts of loose, shifting sand. When Stride found his footing, he looked up and saw that the landscape had changed. It looked as if they had been plucked from the familiar plains and transported to some strange desert land, where trees lay uprooted in large brown drifts, and sand covered everything in a bizarre smoothness.

"Fleet," Stride whispered. "Oh, Great Spirit . . . Fleet . . ."

The copse was barely visible beneath the rolling sand, the bushes hidden entirely, just a few trees sticking up beyond the drifts. Their branches were heavy and bending or broken, sand still trickling from the leaves like rain.

Stride scrambled into a run.

"Who's Fleet?" Flicker called, coming after him.

"Fleet!" Stride yowled, skidding to a halt beside the sand dune where the bushes had been. "Can you hear me? Are you okay? Fleet?"

He held his breath and thought he heard a distant mewling noise.

Stride swallowed and then ran headfirst at the dune, half climbing over and half tumbling through it as the bushes beneath gave way. Sand poured over and around him and he almost got stuck again, but then Flicker was there, holding a branch down with her paws and following him through the gap they had made.

Beyond the bushes, the center of the copse was like a dry watering hole, sheltered from the worst of the sand by the bushes and the trees. There was no sign of Fleet.

Desperate, Stride ran to the closest tree, dug around the roots, and stared up into the branches, calling his brother's name. He had to be here. He couldn't have run away. But if he hadn't found shelter . . .

He checked the base of each tree in turn, until he heard the mewling again, and at last he saw something twitch, dislodging a layer of sand.

It was a tail.

"Fleet!" Stride called again, and led Flicker over to the

weakly moving tail. They dug into the sand below, exposing Fleet's back, his broken leg, and finally his head.

Fleet's eyes opened just a crack, but his breath was shallow. Stride and Flicker kept digging, until all of Fleet was exposed, and then Stride gently rolled him onto his side and licked at his face, clearing the sand from his eyes and nose. His brother was breathing, but it seemed to take a long time for him to gather the strength to say anything. Finally, he swallowed and coughed, and his eyes opened a little more.

"Who's this?" Fleet mumbled, turning his gaze on Flicker.

"I'm Flicker," she said. "I'm a friend of Stride's."

Stride felt a warm rush of gratitude at her no-nonsense manner.

"This is my brother, Fleet," Stride said.

"Nice to meet you," Fleet said. He took a slightly deeper breath and managed to wriggle upright a little more. "Sorry about the . . . sandy welcome."

"Hardly your fault," Flicker reassured him. She looked over at the sand dune where the bushes had been. "I'll go and dig it out."

She gave Stride a long look and a small knowing smile, before she turned away. Stride felt more *looked at* in that moment than he thought he ever had before. Flicker had taken it all in in moments: realized what he'd been doing, registered Fleet's injury, introduced herself to him, all with the deceptive smoothness of a sand dune. But her gaze said clearly, *I know your secret now.*

When she was a little way away, beginning to snuffle around the drift searching for the scent of the dik-dik, Stride turned to Fleet.

"Really," he said. "Are you hurt?"

"I'm all right," said Fleet. "Really."

Stride gave his brother a hard stare.

"It is a good thing you were here," Fleet admitted, rolling his eyes. "I would have been fine, but . . . it might have taken a while." He started washing his paws, as if admitting this had made them feel dirty. "Anyway, where did *she* come from?" he said, turning his head to watch Fleet, who'd caught the scent and was busily digging into the side of the sand drift.

"We . . . met," Stride said. "Before."

"*Mm-hmm.* She's not in your coalition," Fleet said.

"No females in the coalition," Stride said automatically. "Mates live outside. You know that."

"Mates?"

"What? No, not *my*—she's . . ." Stride hesitated. Would Flicker thank him for describing her as Jinks's mate? Something told him she wouldn't. "Not," he finished.

"Here you are," said Flicker, trotting over proudly with the dik-dik dangling from her jaws, shedding sand. "It's a little grainy, but it should still taste good."

Fleet thanked her and then stretched, his paws pushing up small dunes in the sand around him. "I need to rest," he said.

"We should go." Stride gave his brother another lick on the top of his head, Flicker blinked at him in a friendly way, and then they made their way back through the bush drift and out onto the sandy plain in silence. At last, Stride cleared his throat. "I should get back to the coalition," he said.

"Jinks doesn't know about Fleet," Flicker said. "He'd never stand for you hunting for a lame, non-coalition cheetah."

"No," Stride said. He bristled a little, searching Flicker's face for a sudden change of heart. She'd said nothing to suggest she would tell Jinks, but . . . "And if he finds out, he'll have me expelled from the coalition, or worse. And if I stop, Fleet will starve. He's brave, but he needs me. Nobody knows I come here apart from Pace. And if you tell . . ."

Flicker looked a little offended. "Why would I do that?" she said. Then she relaxed, and Stride felt his own heart slow to a more comfortable beat in response. "You really are full of surprises, though, aren't you? No, I won't tell Jinks. And listen, my pack is all females, and they don't mind what I do as long as everyone gets fed and . . . well . . . they don't mind where I hunt, anyway. So I can help you."

"What?" Stride asked.

"Hunting. For Fleet. I'll help you, if you want me to."

Stride felt a strange warmth come over him, starting in the pads of his paws.

"I can't ask you to . . ."

"Good thing you didn't, then," Flicker countered. She smirked. "It won't be a hardship—after all, I'm the greatest hunter, with eyes like deep pools of nighttime. Right?"

Stride could only nod.

CHAPTER EIGHT

"I heard he's still bleeding."

Whisper shuddered, trying to pretend she didn't hear Clatter muttering into Thunder's ear. The sun was hot on her back and the ground almost seemed to glow. She was lying on the grass with the other calves, watching the older buffalo mill around, stomping their hooves nervously. Strong winds had whipped up that morning and blown away the clouds, until there was just one thick line of orange-tinted cloud visible on the horizon, and that was moving away. Apart from a few scattered trees and bushes—and the bodies of the other buffalo—there was no escape from the searing gaze of the sun.

"Who told you that?" Thunder snorted. "Bellow is recovering well. He's as strong as ever."

"That's not what I heard. I heard he's sleeping an awful lot, and his leg won't stop bleeding."

Bellow had retreated to the shade of a tree, surrounded by a guard of male buffalo. At first, Whisper had waited anxiously for news, fearing that there would be none for a long time. By the next morning, she thought that no news might have been better than the mixed messages that spread through the herd. Should she believe the gossips who said the herd leader was moments from death, or the ones who claimed he was perfectly fine? Surely the truth was somewhere in the middle—right?

"If he can't stop bleeding," Echo whispered to her, after Clatter had bustled off to spread her news to the rest of the herd, "is that . . . does that mean . . . did I . . ."

"*No*," Whisper snapped. Then she leaned over and gently nosed the side of his face. "You didn't do this."

She knew exactly how he was feeling. After all, she was feeling the same thing—except that his guilt was misplaced, and hers was not. The crocodile attack and Bellow's injury were down to *her* choice to run to the river, *her* clumsy hooves getting stuck in the mud.

Did I kill Bellow?

None of the other buffalo seemed to blame her. But the question still stuck in Whisper's throat, like an unexpected shard of rock in a mouthful of grass.

The sun beat down ever harder. The path to the edge of the river was well-worn, as the buffalo grew thirsty and the wilting grass grew less and less refreshing. Whisper was beginning to think about going to the river herself, despite the shudders that ran through her when she imagined crossing the mud to the edge of the water. The mud was drying into cracked earth, so at least she wouldn't get stuck again. . . .

But before she could make her mind up to go, a commotion of deep buffalo voices sounded from the direction of Bellow's resting tree. She scrambled to her hooves and hurried to the edge of the herd to look. With a rush of relief, she found herself watching as Bellow approached across the dry plain, at the head of the guarding buffalo, with his brother Holler walking close by his side.

He was alive. He was still injured—he walked with a slight, rolling limp. A whole flock of oxpeckers rode along on his back, swaying and flapping with his uneven gait, taking it in turns to fly down and peck at the insects that swarmed from the still-open wound in his flank.

It wasn't bleeding, exactly. But Whisper could see why the gossips had said it was. It was oozing and raw. It did not look good.

"My friends," Bellow called out as the herd gathered close around him. "I hear your concern, and I want to reassure you. My wound is yet to heal completely, but I feel strong. Thank you all for your patience and your kind thoughts."

"Good healing, Bellow," called several buffalo over Whisper's head, and "Thank you, Bellow!" A few voices said things like "I told you so" under their breaths.

Whisper noticed that Holler's eyes were trained on Bellow, barely flickering away for a moment while his brother spoke. And as she followed his gaze, she realized that one of Bellow's legs was trembling. He was doing well at hiding it—if it hadn't been for Holler's concerned stare, she might not have noticed at all. . . .

"Now," said Bellow, in a jolly tone that gave nothing away about how tired or in pain he might be, "please, do not worry about me. Go back to your mates and your calves, and prepare for the great migration!"

With a snorting and snuffling of agreement, the herd began to spread out again, males and females mingling together.

"Thank the Great Spirit," said a voice at Whisper's shoulder as Murmur left her mother's side and came over to her. "It would be terrible if Bellow was badly hurt!"

"Hmm," said Whisper.

"The Spirit must be looking kindly on the herd," Murmur said, her voice full of confidence. "Oh, hello, Quake!" she called, spotting the young buffalo as he crossed in front of them. Quake saw Murmur and headed over. He didn't look concerned about Bellow—far from it, he walked with light hooves and a slight smile.

"Excited for the migration?" he asked Murmur. Whisper suppressed an eye roll as her friend almost shuddered with the thrill of being spoken to—*asked a question*—by Quake.

"Oh yes," Murmur said. "I was a bit worried, you know, for Bellow—but now I can't wait to get started."

"Well, you needn't have worried," said Quake. "Even if Bellow can't lead us, the migration will leave on time."

"What do you mean?" Whisper asked. "Bellow has to lead us—he's the only one who can!"

"My father can," Quake said. "He's ready to take over at a

moment's notice. He's been ready for a long time."

Whisper frowned. "But he can't. He hasn't been chosen. He hasn't learned the Way. . . ."

Quake sighed and flicked his tail dismissively at Whisper, as if these fundamental truths were no more important than flies on his rump. "He's done the migration plenty of times, there can't be much to the Way he doesn't already know. Anyway, there's no time for all that. If the migration doesn't start in the next couple of days, the rains won't come. You know we can't let that happen."

He squinted up at the sky over their heads, and Whisper did too. It was so clear and bright that looking at it made her head spin. Almost as if to prove his point, a dry breath of wind stirred the dust around their hooves.

"Well, Bellow's fine," said Murmur firmly. "He'll lead the migration, just like normal. But it's good that Holler's here as backup."

Quake opened his mouth to respond, then hesitated, sniffing the air. Whisper scented what had stopped him too, and a shiver ran down her hot back.

"Lions!" went the call, several of the buffalo bellowing it out at once. "Form up! Lions!"

"Form the Shell!" Bellow's voice rose above the din.

"Echo!" Whisper called. Thank the Great Spirit, he hadn't wandered far, and they came together as they pressed back into the center of the herd, Murmur right behind them. Chaos reigned for a moment, and then the ranks of the Shell began to form around the calves, the largest and healthiest buffalo on the outside, rings of tossing horns and stomping hooves around the small, the sickly, the old. Whisper found herself and Echo standing in the inner circle beside Roar, who was enormously pregnant, and an ancient male whose name she didn't know, whose skinny knees shook as the Shell closed around him.

Through the shifting legs of the bigger buffalo, Whisper could make out the tawny shapes circling them. Lions, moving fast, keeping far enough from the Shell that no buffalo could strike at them without making a weak spot. And that was just what the lions were looking for, Whisper knew. Somewhere they could dart inside, like thieves, and extract a calf or an elderly buffalo before the rest could stomp them. She pressed close to Echo.

But then she heard Bellow's voice again. "Begone," he cried. "We are at our full strength, and we will crack your skulls if you come close enough. There is nothing for you here!"

An echoing shout went up from the outer ring. Whisper heard Holler's voice, and Thunder's, and many more. The sound was like a hurricane wind, buffeting the lions back. Whisper's heart raced, but she felt safe, even with Echo by her side.

"It's okay," he said to Roar, who was looking a little sick. "They don't stand a chance."

Then, suddenly, there was a different sound. A gasping sound. A sound of dismay that rippled through the herd. Whisper whipped around and peered through the legs of the inner ring again, and she saw a heap of fur where one of the buffalo on the outer ring of the Shell had fallen. Dust was still settling around it.

Was it the lions? Had they decided to try their luck on one of the strongest buffalo?

No—it was Bellow. He had collapsed.

Whisper could see a lion, beyond Bellow, notice him fall. Her eyes glinted with the light of hunger and excitement. There was a horrible moment as Whisper saw all the lions look at the fallen Bellow. They would be making their choice—would they dart in to try to drag the wounded buffalo away, or use the confusion to rush past and make a grab for a calf?

Then Holler's voice rose above the gasps.

"Herd, protect your leader! With me! Move the Shell!"

Energy seemed to crackle through the herd at his command. Whisper's short hairs stood on end. The buffalo began to move all at once. Whisper focused on making sure she and Echo kept pace with the rest, because if they were left behind they could be crushed by their own outer ranks or reached by the lions—but she knew that the outer ranks would be stomping forward, flowing around their fallen leader and closing behind him, until . . .

A few more paces, and Whisper saw the buffalo of the inner rank in front of her shift and open, stepping respectfully but firmly past the fallen body of Bellow.

The herd came to a stop, and Whisper heard furious yowling from the lions. The Shell was complete once more. The vulnerable buffalo had been kept together and absorbed the injured Bellow.

She found herself standing right beside her leader's head. Bellow was breathing hard, a look of terrible pain and effort on his face as he tried to stand. His leg wouldn't hold, though, and his wound was bleeding again now.

"It's all right," she said. Bellow's eyes flicked up to her, and Whisper flushed under her hair as she realized he had recognized her. "It's all right, the Shell is holding, you don't have to get up yet. You should rest."

Bellow blew out a long, frustrated sigh, but he did stop trying to get up.

"They're leaving," said Roar, peering between the ranks. "The lions. They're giving up."

"Thank the Great Spirit," breathed Murmur.

They stayed in the Shell for a little longer. Then Whisper heard hooves on dry earth as a group of the strongest buffalo broke away—they would be sweeping the plain to make sure that the lions weren't simply lurking nearby, waiting for the buffalo to think it was safe. A distant spitting yowl told her that one of them had done just that and was probably regretting its choice now.

The ranks began to dissolve once more. But unlike any other time the Shell was formed, the buffalo didn't relax, didn't turn to chattering to each other or wander away in search of food. Every buffalo in the herd seemed to spin on its heel to face inward, to look at Bellow.

Whisper's breath caught in her throat as she watched the herd leader press his front hooves into the ground. If he couldn't stand . . .

But with a great grunt, Bellow slowly managed to get up. It seemed he couldn't lift his head all the way, his large horns dragging the tilt of his shoulders even more to the side. Echo's eyes were huge and liquid as he looked up at the massive buffalo, and Whisper pressed him close to her. She was partly in awe of their leader being so close, so brave, and in so much pain . . . and partly afraid that if he fell again, he could crush Echo beneath him.

The buffalo parted a little, and Whisper saw they were making way for Holler. He stood, looking down at his brother, who suddenly seemed diminished, not like the legendary force he used to be. It felt like the image was burning itself into Whisper's memory: Holler, backed by the strongest buffalo in the herd, stamping and blowing from their short patrol to chase off the last of the lions. Bellow, standing with the calves, the weak, the sickly.

"My friends," Bellow said, addressing the whole herd, his voice still carrying even though his breath came in pained rasps. "I apologize. I wanted . . . I wanted to be healed, but we must face the truth, together. I am not strong enough to lead the migration."

Another ripple of gasps ran through the herd, and Whisper saw dismay on the faces of the buffalo closest to her, and confusion . . . and a few flickers of anticipation and excitement in the eyes of Holler and some of the other grown-up males, quickly hidden, but definitely there.

"I may get strong again," Bellow went on. "But I may not, and there is no time to waste. My successor must be found at once. I must teach him the Way. The migration *must* begin on time." He looked to the sky, and Whisper saw a tremble around his muzzle, as if the blue sky frightened him. "The rains will not come unless we make our long march," he said, almost to himself.

Then Thunder and his other mates shoved their way to the front and gathered close around him, moving the calves and the elderly out of the way so that they could surround the great fallen leader. With a sigh, Bellow sank back to his knees among his family, dignified but defeated.

CHAPTER NINE

Cub eyed the gazelle with sharp suspicion. It was talking about giving in, but she knew better than to believe it. She relaxed the tension in her muscles to make the creature think that she believed its lies . . . and then she leaped, spinning at the last minute so that her whole body took the gazelle down flat, her paws so strong pushing down on its neck that it couldn't breathe. The other hyenas whooped and cackled as Cub dispatched the gazelle. Gutripper ran to her daughter's side, and Cub stood back respectfully to let her take the first bite, but before she did, Gutripper looked deep into Cub's eyes and said, "Congratulations on your naming kill, Breathstealer. I'm so proud of you." The other hyenas cheered and called out, "Breathstealer! Breathstealer! Breathstealer!"

Tailgrabber batted hard at a pebble. It rolled a disappointingly short distance and got stuck in a patch of grass. With a sigh, she roused herself from her daydream to look around. She was on patrol, checking the edges of the territory for scents of rival predators. It was a job that was somehow both tedious and stressful—there were no lions sneaking through the bushes, waiting to jump out at her, so it was just a long walk in the hot sun across the mostly nondescript plains. But there *could* be lurking interlopers, especially these days, which was why they had to have a patrol at all.

She refocused on the plain in front of her. She would walk as far as the small wood that sprang up a little way ahead and on her left, which marked the border of the territory, and then she would rest in the shade for a moment, maybe see if she could find something to eat in the wood. The others would make fun of her for resting if they knew. But if she pressed on and came back sun-dizzy and famished, they'd make fun of her then, too.

Tailgrabber couldn't win. It was past time for her to accept that.

Breathstealer, on the other hand . . . Breathstealer had the respect of her clan. Her paws probably didn't even sting when she walked on the hot dry mud. Tailgrabber ran the last few hyena-lengths to the shade of the woods and paused to let out a breath of relief as she stepped onto the cooler ground.

The rainy season could be a tough time to live in Brave-lands. Storms and mudslides, and slippery, restless prey. But it would be much worse if they didn't come. The vision flashed across her memory once more, and she frowned. If the others had more respect for her, maybe they would listen when she told them something was wrong. If she'd just taken a less stupid name, then maybe . . .

Breathstealer took the first bite of the gazelle, and as she was finishing
her meal the Great Devourer sent her a terrible vision behind a curtain of
swarming flies . . . but the others were there to see it and they all believed
her, and . . .

And then there was a lion.

It was right in front of her. A young lioness, about the size of
Tailgrabber, weaving around a tree. They were no more than
one hyena-length away from each other. The lion stopped in
her tracks, her mouth half-open in a slightly stupid expression
as she saw Tailgrabber and sniffed the air. For a long moment
they were both frozen, hackles raised, tails swishing.

Tailgrabber's heart was pounding, but she stood her ground
and bared her fangs. The lion began to growl deep in her chest.

"This is our territory," Tailgrabber snapped, a little gar-
bled, realizing that she had to be the first to speak. "Get out."

"Think I'm going to take orders from a filthy scavenger?"
said the lion. She sounded dismissive, but her back arched and
she put out a slow paw to move to the side.

She's testing me, Tailgrabber thought, and she snapped—
catching nothing but air, a good long way from any part of the
lioness, but it still made the big cat pause and hold up her paw.

I'll show her I'm serious. I'll fight her if I have to.

Oh, Devourer, I don't want to fight her.

"Is it just you?" Tailgrabber demanded. "Or are there more
of you prey-thieves lurking back there?"

The lion hesitated before answering. She stared at Tailgrabber and then over her shoulder, as if wondering the same
thing—did either of them have backup coming?

It seemed as if they didn't.

"I'm alone," the lion said at last with a sneer. "But one lion is more than a match for a stinking hyena. You can call me Bold when you're begging for your life."

"And I'm . . . ," Tailgrabber began, but something seized her tongue before her name could escape her mouth. "Breathstealer," she said, instead.

"Heh," said Bold. "Stupid hyena names."

Tailgrabber growled. Breathstealer was *not* a stupid name.

"At least we're named after things we've really done," she said, with only a tiny twinge of shame at the lie she was telling. "You could be a coward for all I know."

"Are you calling me a coward?" Bold rumbled.

"I suppose you'd have to be brave to encroach on our territory alone," said Tailgrabber. "Brave or stupid."

"You keep saying that. This is *our* territory," Bold snarled. "And Noble won't let it fall into your slobbery jaws just because you killed his favorite cub."

Killed? Tailgrabber thought. *They said they just wounded it. . . .*

But so what if the cub had died? The hyenas had to defend their territory, or the lions would take everything, and what the lions didn't take the cheetahs and leopards and wolves would fight over. Tailgrabber drew herself up tall.

"Lions hold no fear for our clan," she said. "Especially not a *male*. Everyone knows males like Noble are lazy and slow. I've never understood why you let them rule your clans. It's pathetic."

"Noble is the fiercest hunter in all of Bravelands!" Bold

snapped. "He is descended from Ruthless, the son of the Spirit Eater, Titan!"

"They're lazy and slow *and* they're liars, then," sniffed Tailgrabber. "The Spirit Eaters are a myth. Hyenas know all there is to know about dead things, we would know if you could eat a *spirit*."

Bold growled louder, and for a second Tailgrabber thought they might fight after all. But then the lion tossed her head and made a dismissive motion with her tail.

"You're lucky, scavenger," she said. "I'm in no mood to fight today. Go back to your clan, Breathstealer."

Tailgrabber forced a laugh to cover her relief. "If we fought, you would be the one who didn't make it home to her pride." She began to back away, just in case Bold took her big words as an invitation to fight after all—but Bold mirrored her backward steps, cautiously keeping the tree trunk close on her right side, until at last she spun around and vanished behind the line of the wood.

Tailgrabber waited for a while, listening for pawsteps and sniffing for fresh lion scent.

Once she was sure that Bold was gone, she let out a deep sigh and headed back to the clan. Her paws pulsed as she walked, and she skipped and chased a leaf for a moment to let out some nervous energy. She rehearsed in her head what she would report to Gutripper. She had important news, after all.

She walked into camp with her head held high.

The hyenas gathered to sleep and share food around the base of a huge, looming baobab tree that stood on the edge of a slight rise in the land, beside a sandy dip that was once probably a watering hole, but certainly hadn't held more than mud in Tailgrabber's lifetime. The thick trunk cast a column of shade that moved around with the shifting sun. Gutripper and the female hunters could usually be found in the shade, especially on hot days, while the males sprawled in the sun or the wind, or prowled the territory in smaller groups hunting and scavenging for themselves—they lived together and were all part of Gutripper's clan, but Tailgrabber didn't really know what the males did with their days, even her brothers and her father. Gutripper was always very clear: it didn't matter what they were up to, as long as they were loyal in battle, and new cubs were born every once in a while.

Sure enough, Gutripper, Nosebiter, Hidetearer, and a few other older females were sitting in the shade of the baobab tree. Cub wasn't with Nosebiter—he must be in the den that had been carved out beneath the roots of the tree, with the other unweaned, unbloodied cubs.

"Mother," she said, approaching Gutripper, who looked up and regarded her with the kind of interest she would pay to a passing flock of birds, or a particularly strong wind. "I've been on patrol, and I have news. I ran into a lion."

Gutripper bristled. Hidetearer began to growl, but a sharp look from Gutripper silenced her.

"Go on," she said.

"It was on the edge of the territory, she was coming out of the woods, but she looked like she was planning to come right onto our land," Tailgrabber said. "I got her to back off." She tried to sound casual, as if she frightened off lions every day.

"You?" sniffed Hidetearer.

"She told me her name," Tailgrabber said, not rising to Hidetearer's bait. "She said it was Bold, and she let slip she came from Noblepride. The cub died," she added. "The one that we injured." She waited for her mother to react to this piece of news, this potentially important twist in the rivalry with Noblepride. But Gutripper said nothing.

"How long were you two chatting?" Hidetearer sneered.

Tailgrabber felt her fur prickle with unease. This wasn't how she'd imagined it at all.

"I made her tell me," she said. "We fought. She was a strong lion, but I got the better of her, and when I had her pinned, I made her spill her secrets."

Gutripper glanced at Nosebiter, and Nosebiter sniffed and then tilted her head at Tailgrabber.

What does that mean?

"Are you sure you fought her off?" her sister asked.

A flash of panic crossed Tailgrabber's mind. "Are you calling me a liar?"

It was the wrong thing to say.

Nosebiter sighed. "You don't have any lion scent on you, Tailgrabber. None. You couldn't have fought her."

All of a sudden, the sound of Tailgrabber's heart seemed to drown out everything else. Nosebiter was saying something... Hidetearer was laughing... but all she heard was her own thumping pulse.

"Did you even meet a lion?" Hidetearer cackled dimly.

"She did," said Gutripper. Her mother's voice was a growl that snapped Tailgrabber out of her embarrassed trance, her eyes fixed over Tailgrabber's shoulder.

Tailgrabber turned and saw the lions stalking through the dry mud of the old watering hole. There were three fully grown lionesses with grim looks on their faces. Bold led them, her eyes fixed on Tailgrabber, glinting with amusement and malice.

She followed me, Tailgrabber thought.

Gutripper put her head back and howled a battle cry that made Tailgrabber's paws dance and her fur stand on end. All around them, hyenas that hadn't been listening in to the conversation scrambled to attention. Males and less favored females came dashing to her side from the other end of the camp.

Bold roared "For Noble!" and the other lions echoed the cry as they charged up the dried-up bank. They were met by a cackling confusion of hyenas' voices, calling out insults or shouts of rage or just giggling nervously.

Nosebiter and Hidetearer leaped at one of the lions, Hidetearer taking a blow to the shoulder that let Nosebiter in to snap at the lion's flank. Tailgrabber was going to join them, but then two other hyenas rushed past her, knocking her over in their wake as they panicked and ran in circles. When she rolled to her paws again, another lion was stalking toward her. He was a male, with one torn ear just visible through his russet-colored mane.

And he wasn't coming for her at all—his eyes were fixed on

Gutripper, who was snapping at the heels of a hyena who'd tried to back away from the battle and hadn't seen him.

"For Noble!" he growled, and pounced.

Tailgrabber threw herself between the lion and her mother. The world turned upside down in a tangle of paws and teeth, and she felt the bones in her shoulder crunch and grind together. The lion was heavy on her rib cage, so she didn't bother trying to stand, just spat out a mouthful of mane and tried to bite down on whatever part of the lion was closest to her jaws. A gratifying roar of pain and anger vibrated through the body above her, and then she saw Gutripper above her head, a whirl of claws and teeth. The lion twitched and recoiled, pulling its leg out of Tailgrabber's mouth, trailing blood. It began to retreat, and Gutripper and Tailgrabber both advanced on it. . . .

And then Tailgrabber heard a sound that made her blood curdle. A desperate, terrible squealing sound from the roots of the baobab tree.

Some of the hyenas didn't seem to hear it, but others stood frozen, eyes wide with horror. Tailgrabber didn't want to move. She wanted to sink into the ground and never, ever find out what that sound was.

But she forced her paws to move, scrambling around with a few of her clan-mates, Nosebiter in the lead. They circled the great tree in what seemed like both a single moment and a lifetime, and were just in time to catch Bold emerging from the cub den.

Her whole tawny muzzle was dripping blood.

Her eyes met Tailgrabber's. Then she sprinted away, as if the Great Devourer itself was on her heels, with a few screaming hyenas following her into the dusk that was falling over the plains.

Tailgrabber let her go. She felt like her paws had turned to stone, standing outside the cub den. She couldn't see inside and couldn't make herself approach, but she didn't need to go any closer to know what had just happened.

The cubs had fallen silent.

CHAPTER TEN

"Before you say anything," *Stride said,* flopping down beside Fleet as his brother tore into the young warthog that he and Flicker had managed to hunt that morning, "I know. You don't have to tell me."

Fleet gave Stride a quizzical look, his mouth full of thick warthog hide.

"There're plenty of things I could tell you," he said. "I'm just not sure which one you're talking about."

Stride rolled his eyes at his brother. Didn't he ever listen?

"Hunting," he said. "With Flicker. Remember? She's been joining me when I go to hunt for you? I was just saying, you don't need to warn me, I know it's a risk."

"Is it?" Fleet asked.

"Of course it is," Stride said. "We've been meeting more

often, staying away longer—all to get food for you, I might add, and you should be grateful, because the prey we can catch with two is far better quality than what I could get on my own."

"Oh, I've noticed," said Fleet, taking another bite of warthog. He hesitated for a moment, chewing, before going on. "She must be a good hunter. Smart."

"Smart? She's a genius." Stride chuckled. "It's funny, Jinks was always going on about how beautiful she is and how fast and graceful, and obviously there's all that, but she's got a real brain for strategy too. The other day, she did this thing where she lay in wait for a passing herd of wildebeest, and she used *their* scent to creep up on an aardvark. . . ."

"You told me," Fleet said.

"Oh. Did I?" Stride scratched behind his ear with his back leg.

"The aardvark was very tasty."

"Oh, yes. Well, it was brilliant. She's always doing things like that. Her cubs will eat well one day, that's for sure, even though you'd think any creature would see her coming, the way her coat gleams, and her eyes . . ."

Stride stopped talking. Something about his brother was bothering him. It wasn't illness—on the contrary, he was looking as healthy as a three-legged cheetah ever could. His pelt was sleek and no longer hung from his bones in a disturbing fashion. His eyes were bright.

No, it was the fact that Fleet was listening intently to him, with a slight smile on his face as he chewed.

"Go on," Fleet said. "Tell me more about how you're in love with Flicker."

Stride growled at him. "Shut up. I just . . . I like that . . . I just think she . . ." He paused. What was he trying to say? *I'm not in love with her—I just think she's the most amazing, smartest, fastest, most beautiful and funny and generous cheetah on the plains and she started helping me care for Fleet just because it's the right thing to do and I'd like to spend the rest of my life hunting with her. That's all.*

He laid his head on his paws and let out a long sigh.

"Okay, I like her. A lot."

"I like her too," Fleet said, blinking happily. "I wish you a hundred fat, happy cubs. And here's hoping Jinks gets trampled by buffalo before he finds out."

"Finds out what?" Flicker said, her nose emerging from the bushes. A startled thrill seized Stride's body, tingling under his fur as she sat down beside the two brothers. "That you've been hunting for Fleet all this time?"

"Yep," said Stride in a slightly strangled voice. He thought he should say something else, but his tongue felt swollen in his mouth. Perhaps it was the confession he'd just made, or the shiver still running down his tail, or just the afternoon light through the leaves, but she looked *particularly* lovely just then, poised and calm with her tail tucked over her paws.

"Stride was just saying," Fleet began, and Stride's heart squeezed as he thought his brother was about to tell Flicker what he'd said. "That he thinks he'll be as fast as I used to be, if he keeps hunting with you."

"Oh, really?" Flicker said.

"Obviously, there's no chance. I was so fast, Death tried to chase me all the time, but I always got away. The Great Spirit probably broke my leg because it wasn't fair to the other cheetahs."

"He was very fast," Stride translated, with a grin.

"Anyway, it's nice to see you," Fleet said. "But did you come for any . . . particular reason?" He said this with a meaningful and deeply embarrassing glance at Stride. He might as well have wiggled his haunches and stuck out his tongue.

"Actually, yes," said Flicker, but she looked solemn. "It's not good news. I've seen that nearby lion pride—Noblepride, I think—coming closer and closer to this spot. I think they're expanding their territory. If they find your den . . ."

Stride shuddered, and this time it was nothing to do with Flicker's presence. Some lions might be merciful and allow a lame cheetah to escape with their lives. Others would see nothing but easy prey. Which was Noblepride? Could their leader live up to his name? And was that a risk they could take?

But Fleet didn't seem worried. He let out a soft *wuff* of amusement. "Even on three legs, I can still outrun a lion," he said. "But I really appreciate the warning."

"Well, just be careful. I'd hate to think I've done all this hunting to feed a bunch of greedy lions," Flicker said with a cheerful flick of her tail. She turned to Stride. "Do you want to go hunting?" she asked. "It couldn't hurt to bring something back to the coalition after all this time you've been gone."

"I'd love to," Stride said. He felt oddly clumsy and shy as he stood up. As he nudged his head against his brother's in farewell, Fleet muttered into his ear.

"Talk to her!"

"All right, see you later," Stride gabbled.

Fleet smirked at him as he turned to follow Flicker.

Stride laughed wheezily as he caught up with Flicker and the young topi. She pulled her fangs from its neck and turned to watch his approach, panting. Adrenaline and triumph vibrated through Stride's paws, and Flicker looked like she felt the same, shaking out her fur before sitting down beside their prey and licking at her tail.

"Good kill!" Stride huffed. "That last burst of speed was . . ." Words failed him, so he simply grinned.

"You're the one who got it to run across my path." Flicker replied. "That was a smart move! And it's paid off. Come on, let's eat, and then you can carry a leg back to the coalition."

Stride bent over the topi's neck, his mouth watering, but something stopped him from taking a bite. The wind had suddenly picked up, and in the breeze that washed over his muzzle he smelled topi, and blood, and Flicker's scent . . . and lions.

His head snapped up, and he saw that Flicker was on the alert too, her gaze fixed on the ridge of rocky ground where Stride had been hiding before he drove the topi toward her. A group of five lions were standing there, watching them, their tails swishing. The largest one gave a signal with a twitch of his ears, and they began to approach. They weren't coming fast, even for a lumbering gang of lions, but they didn't need to. Confidence flowed from them like ripples in a watering hole.

Flicker placed her paws protectively over their prey and growled in the back of her throat.

"No," she snarled under her breath. "This is *our* prey."

Stride glared at the lions, searching for any sign of weakness. Could anything good come of standing their ground? He tried to imagine the fight that would ensue if they decided to stand up to the lions, but even when he imagined himself and Flicker at their absolute best . . . five lions was too many. They were slow, but they were strong. And the topi was too big to carry away with them.

"Come on," he muttered to Flicker. "We have no choice."

Flicker made a loud, furious yowling noise, a shout of rage that made one of the lions at the back of the group briefly pause and blink. But the others kept coming. They would stroll up and take the topi as if it had been their kill all along, and the cheetahs had just been looking after it for them.

Stride's heart missed a beat, thinking Flicker would not back down—but then she spat at the lions once more and delicately, deliberately, stepped away from their prey.

"I won't run," she said to Stride, and turned her back on the lions and began to walk away.

"We won't need to, they'll have the prey to occupy themselves," Stride said. He was certain of this, but he still glanced back over his shoulder more than once to watch the lions gather around the topi and dig in, blood and smugness all over their big hairy faces. Flicker refused. She kept her eyes on the horizon and her chin up, until they had passed beyond a line of thornbushes and the lions were out of sight.

Then they stopped walking and let out matching frustrated sighs, falling into silence for a moment.

"Will I see you tomorrow?" Flicker said at last. "We can hunt on the other side of Fleet's territory, maybe there'll be fewer *pests* over there."

"I think it's full of hyenas," Stride said ruefully, "so no, but we can try. I'll see you there."

"Good." Flicker's expression brightened, and before Stride knew what was happening she had pressed her muzzle to the side of his neck, nuzzling his fur. He took a breath of her scent—did he mention her scent to Fleet? He should—and then nuzzled her back. For a long moment they stood like that, pressed together. He thought he could feel her pulse, a mirror of his own, strong and steady. It felt good. It felt like something fitting perfectly together, like the rains filling up an empty watering hole.

That feeling followed Stride all the way back to the coalition's territory, after he and Flicker had parted. It made his steps light and his breath sing in his chest.

They hadn't even had to speak. Their hearts were aligned, beating in time. They felt the same, wanted the same things. . . .

"Hey, there you are," said a voice, and Stride almost tripped over his paws, before his ears caught up with what they'd heard and he looked up to see Pace draped over a low branch of a tree. Stride grinned up at his friend. Pace's head tilted inquiringly. "You're in a good mood. Where've you been?"

"Oh, you know. I mean, you *do* know. Fleet," said Stride, suddenly feeling awkward.

Pace walked down the trunk of the tree. "I'll come back with you. Listen," he said as the two of them started walking. "I don't know if it's hard finding prey for him or something, but you're gone as often as you're here these days, and Jinks is getting suspicious. Says you're not loyal to the coalition. You didn't even bring anything back with you?"

"I did," Stride said. "I mean, w—I killed a topi. Lions stole it."

Pace hissed under his breath. "*Lions.* Well, that's a good excuse, but it won't work too many more times. I don't suppose you fought them or anything. You could sell it to Jinks easier if . . ." He turned his head and sniffed Stride's shoulder, and then he stopped in his tracks, his nose twitching. "*Stride!*"

"What?" Stride said instinctively, but it was clear by the light in Pace's eyes that he had smelled Flicker's scent on him.

"Who is she? And when were you going to tell me?" Pace reared up and playfully batted his paws in front of Stride's face. "So *that's* where you've been all this time! I mean, Jinks is still going to kill you if you mate before he does, but . . ."

A slightly hysterical laugh bubbled up in Stride's chest, and he made a strangled noise and turned his head away.

"Stride? Stride? What?" Pace bumped his shoulder with his nose.

Stride thought about not telling him, but . . . it was Pace, his best friend, the only other cheetah who knew that he was hunting for Fleet.

Anyway, he clearly needed help.

"It . . . it's Flicker," Stride said. He lay down and put his paws over his muzzle. "That female you smell. It's Flicker."

Pace didn't say anything for a moment, and at last Stride lifted one paw and opened one eye, just to check he was still there. Pace was standing, staring at the horizon, his eyes unfocused.

"But not . . . not *the* Flicker," he said faintly. "Not Jinks's Flicker. Not the Flicker who Jinks is madly in love with, not that Flicker, obviously."

Stride just groaned.

"Because that would make you completely mad," said Pace. "That would be a stupid thing, and you're not stupid, are you? *Are you?* You absolute mud-sucker?"

"I'm not mad or stupid. I love her."

"Oh well, that's fine then!" Pace said, all the fur on his back standing on end and his tail twitching and swishing as if a crocodile was trying to bite it.

"Try not to panic, Pace," Stride said, getting up. "I need you not to panic."

Pace just gave him a wild look.

"I think she feels the same," Stride went on.

"Stride," said Pace. He stood in front of Stride, face-on, his expression as serious as Stride had ever seen it. "Listen to me. Joking aside—and there is part of this that is so bad it's kind of funny—you know that he *will kill you*, don't you? He believes they're destined to be together. To be the most renowned pair of cheetahs this side of the mountain. He believes that to his last whisker. If he thinks you're getting in the way of him and his destined mate . . ."

"Well, he's wrong," Stride growled. "I'll be careful, but I'm not going to stop seeing her because of Jinks. She's certainly not *Jinks's* anything. He says they're destined to be together, but he never asked her what she thinks about it, and she agrees with me—we make our own fate."

He stalked past Pace, feeling a little pang in his chest as he left his best friend standing and stuttering behind him. But he wouldn't give up his time with Flicker just like that. Not for Jinks or Pace. Not for *anyone*.

CHAPTER ELEVEN

"Come on!" Whisper said, nudging Echo in his rump to get him to move. "We're going to miss it!"

"We won't miss it," Echo said, but he did stop sniffing at a patch of tasty-looking grass and hurried along. A few slow, grown-up buffalo were still behind them, so Whisper wasn't too worried about getting picked off by curious predators who had followed the buffalo to Porcupine Hill from the grazing ground, but a new leader hadn't been chosen in many years. Whisper wasn't even sure how many, but more than she had been alive.

Porcupine Hill was hard to miss, even when it wasn't surrounded by the buffalo herd—it was a small hill with steep sides, where a cluster of Elephant Trunk succulents stuck out at all angles. In the growing months they bore tufts of wavering green leaves and bright red flowers, but now they looked brown and their spines were wilting, giving the hill a slightly desolate, and very porcupinish, look.

They reached the crush of the herd, and Whisper tried to squeeze between the bigger buffalo, with Echo holding her tail in his mouth so they weren't separated. It was hard going, until a voice called her name. It was Murmur.

"Whisper, over here! Mother, help them . . . ," her friend said. She must have been able to see Whisper and Echo, but Whisper couldn't find her until she heard Thunder give a loud grunt, and all of a sudden the other buffalo were moving out of their way, some with apologetic murmurs, others grumpy snorts. A path opened to reveal Thunder with Murmur and some of her other calves, right at the front of the herd. Whisper squeezed along it, Echo scurrying behind, and grinned gratefully up at Thunder as the older female made sure they could see the base of the hill, where Bellow stood, waiting patiently for . . . something.

"Thanks," she whispered to Murmur.

"I wasn't going to let you miss it." Murmur grinned back.

"Wow," said Echo, nudging Whisper in the shoulder with his half-formed horn. "Look at all the oxpeckers!"

Whisper had noticed that the oxpecker that usually sat on her back had been missing that morning, but she hadn't given it much thought—though some of the little birds would stay with one buffalo all their life, they came and went as they pleased. But now she realized that there were no oxpeckers on any of the buffalo in the crowd—all of them were perched on Bellow's back, his horns, the spines of the succulents nearby, even one on his nose, right between his eyes. They were almost completely still, their bright orange and yellow beaks pointing up into the sky, as if waiting for something.

Bellow himself was looking a little stronger and healthier than when he had collapsed, but that wasn't saying much. He still held one hoof just barely touching the ground, and there was a redness in his eyes that suggested he was exhausted. But he stood with dignity and as much strength as he could muster, watching the herd and the skies along with his coat of oxpeckers.

"What's going to happen now?" Echo asked. "What's he waiting for?"

"The Great Mother's messenger," said Thunder under her breath. "Starlight will send someone to oversee the choice of the new leader."

"Why can't we do it without her?" Echo said. "It's a buffalo decision, not an elephant one."

"The health of the herd affects all of Bravelands," Whisper said, a slight chiding tone in her voice. "You know that. The migration shakes the rains from the sky, and the leader makes sure the migration goes right. So the Great Spirit needs to know the right buffalo's been chosen. Right?" she added, her eyes flicking to Thunder, just to check.

"That's right," said Thunder kindly. "This is a momentous decision, and not just for us. The wrong leader at the wrong time could prove disastrous for all."

"Wow," said Echo, and fell silent.

At last, Bellow took a deep breath and announced, in a

deep and sonorous grunt, "Candidates! Step forward!"

Whisper held her breath and craned her neck to see along the line of the herd.

Holler stepped out, without hesitation. He didn't have to shoulder past any other buffalo—a path had opened for him as the others looked around expectantly and then shuffled out of the way.

He was the first, but he wasn't the only male to step forward. Several more emerged from the ranks. None of them were as physically impressive as Holler, but Whisper supposed that physical strength wasn't all there was to leading the herd. She didn't know most of them, but she recognized one of her mother's mates, Call, who she knew was a thoughtful kind of buffalo. There was also one young male called Stomp, only a season older than Quake, whose stepping up caused a ripple of derisive laughter from the surrounding males. He held his head high and ignored them. Whisper suspected there wasn't much chance he would be chosen, but she respected his bravery for trying.

"It'll be Holler," said Thunder, surveying the candidates.

"Go on, Holler," said a voice from the crowd, and another joined it, and then several of the males were chanting, "Holler, Holler, Holler!"

Holler dipped his head humbly, but Whisper could see he was pleased.

Thunder laughed a little under her breath, but the other females nearby weren't amused—one turned to her neighbor and began to mutter about tradition and politeness, and soon there was a lively muttered chatter going on as well as the chanting.

"Silence," called Bellow, but Whisper felt like she was the only one who'd noticed. His voice was swallowed by the noise. He took a deep breath, which hitched in his chest as if it caused him pain, but he didn't speak again—instead he looked up suddenly.

Whisper followed his gaze and saw a dark shape circling in the sky.

"There's a vulture!" she said, nudging Murmur.

Thunder had noticed too, and she turned on the herd around her, silencing their chatter with a sharp look where Bellow's shout had failed. "The Great Mother's representative is here," she said.

Whisper watched in fascination as the vulture flew down low, its huge wings splayed and its beady eyes trained on the row of buffalo standing between Bellow and the herd. It circled two more times, low enough that Whisper could feel the breeze as it passed overhead. Then in a blink it had landed on the ground beside Bellow. It looked up at him, and Whisper thought that it was looking at the oxpeckers too. Then it let out a single, loud caw that seemed to ring in the air long after the bird's beak was shut.

The oxpeckers took flight, all at once. Whisper stepped backward at the sight of it, and even a few of the adult buffalo startled. A great flock of tiny birds, almost like an insect swarm, rose over the herd, chittering to each other.

"The oxpeckers are making their choice," Thunder

whispered to the young buffalo. Whisper caught her breath. She didn't know what the vulture had said, but she felt as if she could still hear the dying echoes of its caw in the little voices of the oxpeckers.

True silence fell over the herd now, every pair of eyes turned to the circling oxpeckers. It felt strange and a little bit magical to Whisper, that this choice should belong to the oxpeckers—something so momentous, so important to creatures who were so much bigger than they were.

Every few seconds, one or two oxpeckers would leave the flock and dip down toward one of the buffalo, and the whole herd would hold its breath—but no oxpecker landed. A larger group of them danced around Holler's horns, and Whisper thought that they would land any moment. Holler even raised his head a tiny bit higher, as if he was hoping he could lift his horns enough to force them to set down.

But the oxpeckers flapped away again, to gasps and mutterings of confusion from the other buffalo. Whisper saw Holler's expression freeze for a moment, before his tail began to lash with anger.

"Are they always like this?" Whisper asked Thunder.

"No," said Thunder. "Last time the choice was clear. They landed on Bellow. Nothing like this . . ."

Whisper looked back up at the oxpecker flock, still circling, and thought that it looked a bit different somehow. Was it . . . thinner? Had some of the oxpeckers flown away? Did they get frustrated with their choices and just . . . leave?

Behind her, Echo giggled. Whisper ignored him. Then he

did it again, louder this time, and she turned to tell him to shush.

"Sorry," Echo said when he saw her look around. "It's just that it tickles!"

There was an oxpecker on the nub of his left horn, walking up and down and turning its head this way and that.

"Get off," Echo snickered, his eyes crossing as he tried to watch the little bird and toss his head at the same time. "You've got a job to do!"

The oxpecker was shaken off, but it seemed determined to do whatever it was doing, and it landed on his horn again as soon as his head was still.

Two more joined it, landing on Echo's back. And then another.

"Um . . . Whisper?" Echo said, his voice shaking a little as the flock wheeled around to hover over them, like a heavy rain cloud.

A chill feeling spread through Whisper's body, from her hooves to her horns, an uneasiness that turned to shocking certainty. Slowly at first, and then all in a rush, her little brother almost disappeared beneath a flurry of brown wings and yellow beaks and beady black eyes.

"What's happening?" Echo yelped.

Whisper couldn't answer. She knew what it *looked* like, but it couldn't be that. It *couldn't* be.

The other buffalo were stepping away from Echo, gasping and muttering to each other. Beside Whisper, Murmur gave a nervous laugh.

"Mother, look!" she chuckled, turning to Thunder with wide eyes. Whisper looked up too, half hoping that the older female would say something like *Oh yes, this happens sometimes, it's a practical joke the oxpeckers like to play on us, they've picked another buffalo really.*

But she only saw her own shock reflected in Thunder's eyes.

Murmur's laughter was catching, and a good number of the herd were laughing now, but more of them were muttering urgently to each other, or simply staring at Echo in dismay and confusion.

"Out of the way!" snapped a low voice, and two female buffalo were shoved to the side as Holler pushed his way between them to stare at Echo. There was confusion in his face, but mostly, there was anger. "This is . . . this is ridiculous. This cannot stand. We must begin the ceremony again."

Wait . . . can he do that? Whisper thought. There was an awkward pause while the buffalo all looked at each other, most of them probably wondering the same thing. She looked to Echo, whose face was barely visible beneath the thick coat of oxpeckers. But it was Thunder who spoke. She stepped forward and stood beside Echo, facing Holler.

"Why?" she asked.

Holler's eyes flashed, but his voice was light. "Because this . . . cannot be. The oxpeckers are playing silly games. This is a joke. It must be."

"It is no joke."

Whisper jumped as she heard Bellow's voice right behind her. She scrambled out of the way to stand next to Thunder, as their leader—their old leader?—slowly made his way into the widening circle around Echo.

"The oxpeckers have made their choice," he said.

"What?" Echo said in a small voice that was almost inaudible behind the cries of consternation from Holler and many of the others.

"He's barely weaned!" Holler protested.

As if in answer to this, the vulture let out a hoarse cry. Whisper startled and turned to look at it. She'd almost forgotten it was there.

"Silence!" said Bellow, and his voice seemed to carry a command that went straight to the heart of the buffalo herd. A hush fell.

The vulture called out again. The oxpeckers on Echo's back chittered and chirped in response, and the vulture shook itself and then took off, circling once overhead before vanishing into the deep blue of the sky.

"The vulture returns to the Great Mother," said Thunder. "It's accepted the oxpeckers' decision."

"But a calf can't be leader!" said Quake, shoving past a larger male to stand at his father's side. "It was supposed—it should be someone who's proved himself!"

"His youth does not trouble the Great Spirit, so it does not trouble me," said Bellow. "The choice is made, and we will all understand it in time. For now, the Spirit asks only that we accept it."

A low, rumbling commotion began to build again at these words. Echo was pressing himself against Whisper's side, forcing some of the oxpeckers to circle around their heads or stand on each other's backs.

"Bellow, don't you *dare*," Holler hissed, but Bellow's head snapped around to meet his, almost as if they were going to clash horns, and Holler swallowed the rest of his words. When Bellow spoke, his voice was so low that Whisper had to strain to hear.

"I am your leader," he said. "You will not tell me what I can and cannot dare."

"No, you're not my leader. *That* is." Holler tossed his head at Echo with contempt. "I could trample him without even noticing, and he'd be hardly more than a smear on my hoof!"

Whisper's breath caught, and she stomped a hoof down in front of Echo, almost without knowing she was doing it. The atmosphere in the crowd around them changed too. The females standing nearby stopped muttering in disbelief or watching the clash of brothers with interest, pinning Holler with a stare of uniform shock and distrust.

Whisper found herself being gently pushed back, with Echo and Murmur beside her, as the female herd closed ranks around them, putting their own bodies between Holler and Echo. They lowered their heads, showing their horns to Holler.

Echo is nobody's calf, Whisper realized. *But that means Echo is everyone's calf. There's hardly a female in the herd who hasn't taken care of us both at some point.*

Her heart ached for her mother, wishing she could be here to see this—and to stand up for Echo herself.

"It'll be okay," she murmured to Echo, and peeled herself

away from him to stand next to Thunder, lowering her short horns to match the older females.

Holler was right, in a way. This was mad. Echo couldn't be the leader. But she wasn't going to stand here and listen to him threaten her little brother.

Holler snorted. "No need for the display. I'm not going to hurt the little one."

He sounded as if he thought they were being absurd. But Whisper was still glad of Thunder's bulky form standing at her flank.

"Echo," said Bellow, and Thunder stepped aside to let the leader past. Whisper watched as he approached Echo, who was shivering and still covered in oxpeckers. "Follow me."

Echo looked at Whisper, whose heart skipped a beat. What did he want her to say? What advice could she have for him? He'd been picked, and it was absurd, but he had to go, and that was the end of it.

She took a deep breath and pressed her nose to his cheek.

"The Great Spirit knows what it's doing," she whispered. "We have to trust it."

"I do," Echo whispered back.

"You have much to learn," said Bellow. "We must begin at once."

And with shaking hooves, gradually shedding oxpeckers as he went, Echo trotted after Bellow toward Porcupine Hill and whatever the future held.

CHAPTER TWELVE

There had been five cubs in the den. Now there were five sorry clumps of fur laid on the ground around the roots of the bao-bab tree.

"It's a humiliation," snarled Spinesnapper, pacing to and fro, her tail lashing.

Tailgrabber wished there was room in her mind for thoughts like that. Instead, it was full up with the five dead cubs. With images of Cub nursing at Nosebiter's chest. He had been a living, wriggling, happy little creature, and now he was a tiny heap of flesh and bone and fur. So very, very small.

He didn't know about territory, or humiliation, or any of it.

Did any of them even know what a lion was? The thought seemed to push into Tailgrabber's head without her permission, trailing mental images after it: the dim, soft, safe cubs' den, and then the flashing, almost disembodied fangs, the cries, the smell of blood.

Most of the older hyenas were ignoring the small corpses. Tailgrabber knew why. The cubs were not there. She knew that.

But what if the cubs are lonely? What if it hurts to see us turn away?

She clenched her teeth against a howl of anguish and looked down at her paws.

When she looked up again, Nosebiter was padding toward the bodies. Step by hesitant step, she approached Cub and lowered her nose to his fur. Tailgrabber thought she was whispering something.

"Nosebiter," snapped a voice. It was Gutripper. Their mother didn't hurry over. She barely even turned from the group of hyenas who had gathered around her to talk about the clan's revenge on the lion pride. She just looked over at Nosebiter. "The dead are gone. They belong to the Great Devourer. Turn your back. Now."

Nosebiter stood quivering for a moment, and then she slowly padded around to face away from the dead cubs.

"We survive," she said.

One by one, each of the other hyenas who stood near the cubs turned their backs on them too. "We survive," each one said.

Tailgrabber's paws seemed to move without her say so, turning her around to gaze out over the plain. "We survive," she whispered. The words felt hollow in her throat.

"We survive!" howled Gutripper, in a voice that could be heard all around the baobab tree. "And by the Great Devourer, we will have our revenge!"

With that, she padded off, trailed by Spinesnapper, Hidetearer, and a gaggle of others. Whether they were going to hunt or plot or lie down and rest, Tailgrabber didn't know or much care.

She looked for Nosebiter and found her sitting where she had been, close to the bodies of the cubs but facing away from them, her eyes fixed on the horizon.

Guilt gnawed at Tailgrabber's heart. She forced herself to sit at Nosebiter's side, where she could just see Cub's tiny body out of the corner of her eye.

"I am so sorry," she whispered, her voice coming out hoarse and strained.

"For what?" said Nosebiter.

It's my fault, Tailgrabber thought. *I led the lions here.*

"About . . . about Cub," she said aloud.

"Cub is dead. All things die," said Nosebiter.

Tailgrabber startled. Her sister's mood seemed to have turned around just as she had turned her back on the dead cubs. Was it that simple?

If I have cubs, will I be able to let them go this easily?

"Are you . . . not sad?" Tailgrabber asked hesitantly. "You loved Cub."

"*Love?*" Nosebiter's muzzle was suddenly close to her own, open and snarling, and Tailgrabber almost fell over backward.

"What good is love? Can love bring the dead to life? Can it feed you or fight your enemies? We survive!"

For a moment Tailgrabber thought her sister was going to bite her. She froze. Maybe she could take the punishment, if it would make Nosebiter feel better. She could be like a rock that Nosebiter could thrash and scratch against as much as she needed to. But after a moment, when Nosebiter didn't attack her, Tailgrabber spoke.

"Love is why I hunt," she said quietly, without raising her ears from their flattened position on top of her head. "Love is why I fight my enemies. For you. And Mother. And the clan. And Cub."

Nosebiter slowly, ever so slowly, backed off and sat down. She turned her head, just a little, and Tailgrabber thought she might be sneaking a sideways glance at the sad heap of empty flesh.

"The males do have names, you know," she said quietly. "They choose them for each other just like we do. His father's name was Hearteater. But . . . now he'll never have one."

"We could give him one," Tailgrabber blurted out.

"It's not our place," Nosebiter muttered.

"Great Devourer take our *place*," Tailgrabber said. "I don't care about my *place*. If you want him to have a name, you should give him one."

Nosebiter sighed, and her eyes seemed to properly focus on Tailgrabber's face for the first time.

"You are incorrigible, sister," she said. "Thank you for . . . for speaking with me. For not pretending that nothing has happened. But I'd like to be alone now."

"Of course," said Tailgrabber.

Not really caring about what her mother's plans for revenge were, but with nothing else to take her away from Nosebiter's grief, she headed around the tree to join the gaggle of hyenas. Most of the clan were there, male and female alike. They seemed to be united in their anger—more united than they had been when it had been time to fight. Gutripper was in the middle of it all, her tail lashing.

"We cannot attack Noblepride straight on," said Skull-cracker. "But they've proved that they're not interested in honorable battle anyway."

"Honor is for cubs and gorillas," said Hidetearer. "I want revenge."

"I want *more* than revenge," said Gutripper. "We could kill every cub Noblepride pops out for the next ten years, and it wouldn't be enough."

"No!" howled the hyenas, and "More! More!"

"I want them *crushed*!" cried Gutripper.

"Kill them all!"

"Feed them their own tails!"

"Yes, yes!"

"Make them beg for their lives!"

"Oh, by the Great Devourer!" Tailgrabber barked. The other hyenas stopped their yipping and howling for blood and turned to look at her. Gutripper's gaze seemed to pierce the back of her skull.

Part of Tailgrabber wanted to snap at them and tell them

they were all being fools. But she had their attention now. Was that how she should use it?

"We thought we had beaten them for good when we killed Noblecub," she said, trying to keep her voice calm. "But they just came and killed our cubs in return. If we attack them, won't this just keep happening? If the cycle of bloodshed goes on as it has been, more of us will die than them."

"Then . . . we must kill them all at once," said Spinesnapper thoughtfully.

"*Or*," Tailgrabber added quickly, "we could try something else. I know that she's not *our* leader, but I've heard Great Mother Starlight is very wise. . . ."

The rest of her words were drowned out by a chorus of baffled and derisive giggles from the other hyenas.

"We do not look outside the clan for help with clan problems," sneered Hidetearer. "And even if we did, you think that the Great Spirit would help us, children of the Great Devourer? Your elephant would laugh us out of her clearing."

"And the lions wouldn't listen to her anyway," said Skullcracker. "They only do when it suits them."

"You want us to abandon the Great Devourer, Tailgrabber?" said Gutripper quietly, and the giggles died down, leaving Tailgrabber and her mother locked in an intense silence for a moment. "You, who claim that the flies and beetles whisper His words to you?"

Tailgrabber took a deep breath. "No," she said. "The Great Devourer is the true spirit of these plains. The Great Devourer is all-seeing. I just thought . . ."

"And you would do well to remember it," snapped Gutripper, and with a twitch of her ears, she turned her back on Tailgrabber, as if she were no more important to her than the empty flesh where the cubs had once been.

CHAPTER THIRTEEN

Stride's belly rumbled, and he turned over and wriggled his back against the dry ground, trying to scratch a particularly difficult itch, but not quite managing to get it. Up above him in the tree, Pace was snoring.

Jinks and One-Ear had gone hunting, and they weren't back yet, which was annoying. Stride had hoped to eat before he had to sneak out. That way they'd be less suspicious of his going off exploring without bringing any food back himself. It was a great plan with only one flaw: Jinks and One-Ear didn't know it was a plan, so they had not played along.

Stride lay there debating with himself for a little while, but the sun was getting higher in the sky, and it was nearly the time that Flicker would be waiting for him by the big rock where they'd sheltered from the sandstorm. He could always tell them he'd gotten bored waiting for them to come back and wandered off. They'd believe that.

He rolled to his paws and shook off a fly that had landed on the back of his head.

"Off *exploring*?" said Pace from above, without opening his eyes.

"Do you want to know?" Stride asked.

"Sorry, I can't hear you," Pace said. "I'm fast asleep and have no idea where you are or what you're up to."

"See you later." Stride chuckled. At least Pace had stopped trying to persuade him to stop seeing Flicker. He knew his friend had a point, but his feelings for Flicker were like a storm, or a flood, flattening everything before them.

He wasn't even planning to hunt today. Fleet had enough food to last him a few days. Stride was just going to meet Flicker because he wanted to see her. It was frivolous and unnecessary, but it made him so happy his tail couldn't help twitching as he trotted across the plains. He spooked a herd of oryx, who clearly hadn't expected a cheetah to pass by so close. He carried on without giving them a second hungry look, but even their startled scattering made him smile.

There was a kopje up ahead, like a miniature mountain, one side all jutting rocks and the other a thickly forested slope. He decided to climb it, to get a good look across the plain he would be crossing—after all, he wasn't sure where Jinks and One-Ear had ended up, and it would be terrible if he blundered into them. He wove his way between the trees and came to a large flat rock that stuck out from the top of the kopje. From the top, Bravelands seemed to open out in front of him. Distant clumps of trees looked like sprouting weeds, and ravines and cliffs were faintly visible as dark lines across endless rolling grass. A few shimmering glimpses of water, though many of the watering holes he could see clearly from here were dull brown smudges, almost dried up. A heat haze rose over the open plain, confusing his sight, but the distant blue mountain was unmistakable, dark with trees.

His mother had told him that the black rivers came from the mountain—that once, in a time of great terror and danger for Bravelands, the top of the mountain had opened and fire had spewed down over them. Everything would have burned up, if the Great Spirit hadn't intervened, blocking the fire with her shadows.

Stride sat down and scratched behind his ear with his back paw. To be honest, he didn't completely believe that story—or maybe he was just remembering it wrong. Had the black rivers been made of shadows? Or were they something to do with the fire? What kind of fire could make stone turn as black as night, as smooth as water, as hard as, well, stone?

Some of these old stories are a bit silly, he concluded, and put the whole business out of his mind. The most important thing was that he didn't spy Jinks or One-Ear anywhere in the direction he was planning on going. He could just make out the dim shadow of the ravine where he'd meet Flicker—from here he couldn't see the little spring that ran through it, but he licked his lips thinking about the cool, clear water. Even in the dry season, Flicker said there was always water there.

He set off, springing from rock to rock down the side of

the kopje like a gazelle, or like a little cub chasing a speck of dust around his den. He traveled through the shadows under a cluster of tall baobab trees, and then across a bright, airless plain of dry grass, where the only shadows were the darting shapes of meerkats vanishing into their burrows when they scented him coming.

The ravine was close now, and he imagined he could hear the trickling sound of the stream. He only had to walk around the edge of a small bluff, about as tall as a single elephant with dry grass clinging to the sides of it, and he would be looking down the ravine into the shady space, with its small green pool ringed by reeds. . . .

But as he was approaching the short cliff, a movement above him made him stop. Was it Flicker? Or one of the lions?

But it was Jinks's face that appeared, looking down at him from the top of the bluffs.

Stride's heart felt like it had turned into a heavy, cold stone in his chest. It weighed him down so he couldn't move, or even breathe.

"Hello, Stride," said Jinks, making his way down the slope in a series of short jumps. He stopped a few cheetah-lengths from Stride. His eyes glinted with some emotion Stride couldn't quite read. Humor? Anger? Maybe it was both. . . .

"Jinks," Stride said, trying to sound surprised, but not startled out of his pelt. "Did you catch anything?"

"Not yet," said Jinks. He tilted his head. "I thought you weren't hunting today, Stride. I thought you were staying at the tree. You're a long way from the tree."

"Changed my mind," Stride muttered. "Just didn't catch anything yet. I thought One-Ear was going with you?"

"One-Ear has other things to attend to," said Jinks, and this time Stride was sure that the expression on his face was more like a smirk than a growl.

And somehow that was more frightening.

But perhaps this was all still a coincidence. Perhaps Jinks was here because he knew Flicker came here, and she would spot them and have the sense to stay away, and they could all go home, no real harm done.

"I think I saw some zebras heading this way," Stride lied, with all the casual innocence he could manage. "I was going to head up onto the bluffs and wait there to see if there was one I could pick off. With two of us, we could probably go looking for them now."

"Zebras?" said Jinks, glancing about. "Really?"

He paused. The silence stretched out between them like a long shadow, but just as Stride was about to say *Yes, really*, Jinks's expression changed. It became cold and hateful.

"You're not hunting. You've been doing something unforgivable. After all I've done to welcome you to *my* coalition, to feed you *my* kills and teach you *my* techniques . . . you betray me. You might as well have sunk your teeth into my throat."

It was all over. He obviously knew. But still, over the thumping of his heart, Stride heard himself say, "I think you're mistaken, I haven't done anything. I'll show you the zebras, they're just over that way. It's a shame Pace isn't here,

I bet he could clear this up, maybe we should go back and ask him. . . ."

"Pace," sneered Jinks. "Your dearest friend. Just who do you think told me about this place?"

"No," Stride gasped. "Pace wouldn't . . ."

But who else could have told him? Who else knew?

"Don't worry about it too much," Jinks said. "After all, you'll never see him or Flicker again."

Jinks's leap caught him off guard—despite his words, Stride hadn't quite thought he would really attack. It bowled Stride over on his back. Jinks's jaws snapped at his throat. In a wild blur of panic, Stride yowled and clawed and threw himself from side to side. He heard Jinks's teeth clack together right by his ear and knew how close he'd come to death. But he was faster than Jinks, and his terror gave him an edge at the same time as it left him briefly dizzy and blind. It didn't matter which way was up, he simply writhed until he found a direction without resistance, and then rolled, sprang, tumbled, skidded, and was up on his paws.

His vision cleared as Jinks let out a yowl of fury and pounced again. Stride was standing now with his back to the steep bluff's slope, and he took a wild leap sideways, up onto a rock, and then pushed off to land back on the spot where he had been standing, where Jinks was skidding to a stop.

He raked Jinks's flank with his claws and then sprung away again. Jinks had tried to kill him outright. It hadn't worked for Jinks, and it wouldn't work for Stride.

Keep your distance, and —

Jinks spun to face him, leading with his claws. Stride stepped smartly back, and Jinks's claws cut through the air and buried themselves in the dirt. . . .

Or they should have. Instead, in a flash, Jinks retracted his claws and shifted his weight. He landed securely on a flat paw, charged forward, and raised the other paw, claws out. Stride felt the sting of the trick and of the claws catching in his chest fur at the same moment. He yelped and tried to follow Jinks's momentum and sink his jaws into the back of his neck, but succeeded only in nipping the side of one ear.

Facing off once more, this time Jinks was the one retreating up the steep slope, giving himself the high ground. "I've thought about this for a long time," he snarled. "You've always been a disloyal little pain in my hindquarters."

Stride ignored his words, focusing on his movements. Would he pounce, or was he waiting for Stride to make the first move? A twitch of his tail made Stride leap sideways, just in time to escape another claw to the face. This time, Stride moved faster, feinting to the left and then scampering to the right, kicking up puffs of dusty earth behind him. He heard Jinks splutter and sneeze. Spinning around, he charged back through the cloud of dust to knock Jinks onto his side and managed to close his teeth around Jinks's foreleg. Jinks let out a scream of rage and pain.

Jinks shouldn't have moved. Not until Stride had let go. He shouldn't have risked his mobility, his ability to hunt, everything that made him the coalition leader he clearly thought he was.

But he did move. Stride yelped in surprise as the leg in his jaws was dragged up and away, twisting his neck at an awkward angle. Jinks was stronger and, apparently, crazier than Stride had bargained for. Stride tried to hold on, to give him the disabling wound that he was asking for. His bite could do it, but his neck could not. He had to let go or let Jinks break his spine.

He heard Jinks roar and opened his jaws. He didn't break his neck, but something smacked into the side of his face, and then everything was spinning stars and pulsating black spots across his vision. His jaw ached: not even very much to begin with, but it seemed to worsen with every hitching breath, until he was gasping, and a mewling sound that he couldn't seem to control was coming from his throat.

Paws landed on his side, and Jinks's breath was hot on his ear. "She'll find your body right here," Jinks hissed. "And then she'll know she can't avoid her destiny. Flicker is *mine!*"

A furious growl pierced the air, but it didn't come from Jinks, and Stride was pretty sure it wasn't him, either. The weight on him lifted, a blur of tan fur and black spots passing over his spinning head.

"You are not my destiny, you pathetic bully!"

It was Flicker. She'd saved him. Stride's heart warmed with relief, beneath the dizziness and pain. He heard Jinks yowl, and then Flicker gasp in pain, and he forced himself to roll onto his front and try to get up. He knew he was leaning badly to one side. His legs weren't hurt; it was his jaw. Somehow it felt like one side of his face was numb, and like he had lain down in a bed of thorns, all at the same time.

Flicker was facing Jinks, who sprawled in a crushed patch of dry grass. When he looked up, Stride saw that one of his eyes was a mangled mess, blood dripping down the side of his muzzle.

"You'll pay for this," Jinks hissed at Flicker. "You stupid female, you don't know what you've done. You'll pay for this betrayal."

"You can't betray someone you were never loyal to in the first place," Flicker said, a chill in her voice. "I am not your mate, Jinks, I never was, and I never, ever will be."

"We'll see about that," spat Jinks. "You should think very carefully about your next step, my love. I've negotiated with your family. I've made my claim. Reject that, and you turn against everyone you love. You'll be cast out. Males, females, it doesn't matter. This is your choice. Take me, or be alone for the rest of your miserable life."

Stride's breath caught in his throat. Not because he thought Flicker might relent and take Jinks after all—he knew her better than that, and even if he didn't, he could see her rib cage shaking with rage as she breathed.

No, it was just that he hadn't realized what this was going to cost her. She hadn't said.

He hadn't asked.

"I've made my choice," Flicker said. She turned her back on

Jinks, a move that made Stride tense and the pain in his jaw flare up again. But Jinks didn't pounce on her. He half got up, then wobbled and sat back down. His eye must be even worse than it looked. . . .

Flicker came over to Stride and very gently licked at the side of his muzzle. "I choose you," she said softly. "He's right. My family was clear: if you choose me too, it means we can't rely on other cheetahs from now on."

"Fine by me," Stride said. It was hard to speak, the emotion thick and heavy in his throat. "I choose you, Flicker."

As they ran from the defeated Jinks, his voice carried across the open plain behind them.

"You won't get away with this, Stride! Prepare yourself! A price will be paid!"

CHAPTER FOURTEEN

"Echo, Echo, over here!" called Clatter, and the group of females turned to follow her voice. "This is a good patch."

Whisper was on the outside of the group and could see that Clatter was right. She had found a fairly fresh-looking patch of grass, the vegetation still green all the way to the tips. Whisper's mouth watered at the sight, but she reminded herself that she had eaten plenty of drier, less tasty grass earlier.

It was Echo's right, to be led to the best grazing. Echo was the leader.

Echo himself trotted in the middle of the group, following where he was led, and then fell upon the green grass without hesitation. He didn't even thank Clatter for finding it. Which, of course, he didn't have to. Because he was the leader.

Whisper stifled a sigh.

She didn't know what Bellow had said to Echo, alone on

Porcupine Hill, but her little brother's nervousness about being chosen had melted away like fog on a sunny morning. Now he was frankly *bathing* in the attention of the female herd, in his succulent grass, and in the spotless and shining hide that came from still being the focus of the herd's oxpeckers.

It might be unusual, but Whisper could tell that, after they got used to the idea, many of the females were loving having a young calf for a leader. If Echo had had a dozen mothers before, now he had a hundred, each one keener to make a good impression than the last.

Sure enough, as he was eating his already perfectly nice green grass, Thunder came up with a mouthful of flowers she had found somewhere and started to praise him for how much he was eating—as if Echo had ever had trouble with that.

Whisper failed to stifle her next sigh.

"Are you okay?" said Murmur, following in her mother's wake.

"Oh yes, it's wonderful," said Whisper automatically. Murmur made a low *hmmmmm* in her throat and gently headbutted Whisper in the side of the neck. Whisper snorted. "Well, it's pretty weird," she admitted. "It's just that—I mean—it's *Echo*. He's my little brother—my very troublesome, *very little* brother. How can he be leader? I'm not doubting the Great Spirit, I'm just . . . I've got . . ."

"Questions?" Murmur prompted with a giggle. "Well, so does half the herd, but the Great Spirit knows what it's doing, doesn't it?"

"Of course," said Whisper, because she had to.

* * *

With Echo stuck to the tasty grass like a fly in a spiderweb and surrounded by large buffalo who would give their lives to protect him from harm, after a while Whisper began to feel as if she wasn't needed, or even really wanted, in Echo's entourage. Clatter and some of the others kept giving her sideways looks, especially when she laughed or rolled her eyes when they told Echo how brilliant and special he was.

So she wandered off. Murmur came with her at first, but then said she was thirsty and went to get a drink at the riverbank, and Whisper didn't mind being alone.

It was high time she had some freedom, anyway. Let Thunder chase Echo around trying to get him to stay still and not go playing with rhinos. She'd like to see Quake and the other young males tease and exclude him now, with half the female herd looking down their noses at them from behind Echo's shoulder.

"It's good that he doesn't need me," she muttered to herself as she wandered between groups of buffalo, not really heading in any particular direction. "In fact, it's great. *Great.*"

She made sure not to stray outside the bounds of the herd, but for now that still gave her plenty of room to walk. The buffalo had spread out to occupy the plains as far as Whisper's eye could see—not very far, since they were mostly taller than her and tended to block the view. There were buffalo on the riverbank and buffalo in the dells. These were a few dips in the ground, not sharp or deep enough to be called a ravine but deep and wide enough that you couldn't always see the bottom unless you were standing near the edge. Whisper would normally stay clear of them, especially if she was alone, because predators could be lurking there—but she had seen a few males wander down the slope, so she decided that she would walk along the top of one. Sure enough, in the grassy dip, a group of buffalo were mingling, searching the ground for good grass and talking to each other.

Holler was there, and Quake too. Murmur probably would have called out to him to get his attention, but Whisper was happy not to be noticed by this group. She would just walk along the top of the dell and then head back into the center of the herd. . . .

"I still think it's suspicious!" said Quake's voice, stilling Whisper's hooves. "That little runt is the one who got Bellow hurt in the first place, and now he's leader?"

Whisper turned, anger flaring her nostrils. But the males in the dell still hadn't seen her, and though she wanted to snap at them, she held her tongue. She wanted to see if any of the others agreed with Quake's stupid argument.

"We can't leave the herd's fate in the horns of a calf who's too young to even *have* horns," said one of the males who Whisper didn't know. "But to suggest this calf has done this on purpose . . ." He shook his head.

Whisper relaxed. She could hardly blame them for doubting Echo's suitability to be leader. He *wasn't* suitable by any measure she'd have used before. He wasn't strong or wise or experienced. He certainly wasn't physically imposing.

She turned away, not wanting to get caught up in an

argument with Quake, who she could hear complaining even as she left sight of the dell.

She still didn't understand what was happening.

The Great Spirit had chosen Echo, and Bellow had accepted its decision.

One of those was invisible and all-knowing and not easy to question . . . but the other one was sitting in the shade of a tree not far away, eating grass and watching the clouds.

Could she really go to Bellow and ask him?

There was no other buffalo hanging around him now. He hadn't been abandoned, exactly—it looked like there was a pile of drying grass at his knees that had been picked for him, and there were buffalo casually grazing nearby. But he wasn't surrounded by buffalo either dutifully serving or ambitiously pestering him, as he would have been if another leader hadn't been chosen.

Whisper took a deep breath and then another one, trying to fill herself up with courage at the same time. Then she slowly walked toward Bellow's tree.

He looked up and saw her approaching, just as she was thinking about turning tail and running away instead, and his tail swished in welcome.

"Hello, Whisper," he said. "How are you this morning?"

He remembered my name. Whisper couldn't help feeling a flush of pride as she gingerly walked up to Bellow's side, even though she was sure he probably knew her only because of Echo.

"I'm all right," Whisper said. "How are you?"

"Oh," said Bellow, and then groaned, shifting his good legs a little underneath him. "That is quite a hard question, my young friend. I am all right, for now. I am hopeful, for the future of the herd. And yet, also . . . I am dying."

"No!" Whisper gasped. "It's not that bad, is it?"

Bellow smiled at her. "I cannot join the herd on the migration. I must stay behind. I know what that means . . . and I think you do too."

Whisper's breath caught in her throat. He might have been making a general point about the inevitability of his fate, but the sympathy in his eyes suggested he was referring to her mother's sad end.

"I had a dream," Bellow said, looking up at the sky peeking between the dry leaves of the tree. "Many moons ago. I thought it seemed unusual, significant, but I couldn't say why. I dreamed that my grandmother appeared to me and told me that I would never see the rain again."

"Was it . . . real? Was it really her?" Whisper asked. Could dead buffalo really visit them in dreams? She often dreamed of her mother, but she'd never thought it could be really her. . . .

"I don't know," said Bellow thoughtfully. "But I do believe that I was sent that dream so that when I was hurt, and Echo was chosen as leader, I would not waste time with shock."

"If you weren't shocked, you're the only one," said Whisper in a small voice.

That made Bellow laugh, a deep and sincere laugh. "Well, perhaps a little . . . surprised," he said. "It's true enough that this is not what I expected to happen."

"But it's—you think it's going to be all right? You think Echo can do it?"

"He must," said Bellow. "Look up at the sky."

Frowning, Whisper turned her head upward. She could see leaves, a few distant birds, and whisps of cloud. She was pretty sure that the answers to her questions were not up there.

"Do you see the moon?" Bellow asked.

It took Whisper a moment to find it. A pale daytime moon, not quite full, lingered close to the horizon.

"When the moon is full," Bellow said, "I will pass on the ancient knowledge of the migration to my successor. There are things I cannot explain to any other buffalo, things that will help him lead. I will share these things with Echo. Then he will be more prepared for the role he must play. And after I have passed the wisdom on, there can be no going back. I will no longer be the leader of this herd."

"But . . . ," Whisper said, and then bit her tongue. Then, seeing the patient expression on Bellow's face, she decided to speak her mind. "He's too young! He can barely look after himself, he keeps wandering off, and the others don't respect him, that's why . . . that's why I blundered into the river and you all had to fight the crocodiles in the first place," she finished, in a very quiet voice. It was a relief to have finally said it aloud, and a bigger relief that Bellow just nodded slowly, as if he completely understood. "How is a calf supposed to look after the herd? If something goes wrong, and everyone looks to Echo, he's not going to know what to do! And I think he's being spoiled," she added. "He's off with Thunder and the others right now, I don't even know exactly where he is, and that's . . . he doesn't need me, but he *always* needs me, and it's not . . ."

She stammered to a halt. She suddenly felt like she'd lost control of her own words, like her thoughts were a river, breaking its banks after the long rains. She wasn't sure what she was trying to say, so Great Spirit knew that Bellow wasn't likely to understand.

Bellow made a low *hmmm* noise in his throat, which reminded Whisper oddly of Murmur's skeptical hum.

"Your brother has needed you every day of his life," he said slowly. "And that will not change, believe me. Especially not now. Even the wisest and strongest of us need our families to support us."

Whisper prodded the ground in front of her with her hoof. "That's not why I'm worried," she said.

"I believe that Echo can become a great leader," said Bellow, and before Whisper could speak again, he lowered his voice, and a slight twinkle entered his expression. "But I believe that *this year*, he will be an *adequate* leader, with guidance and patience. And I know that what he needs more than anything to achieve his destiny is his big sister on his side. Your guidance will be far more valuable to him than anybody else's, because you do not love him for his position—you love him because he is your little brother. Do you understand?"

Whisper nodded. She felt as if she had aged several moons in the last few moments. And not just because Bellow had reminded her that Echo needed her after all.

Bellow, the great leader, the wisest of us all . . . he can't help me.

He couldn't tell her why the Great Spirit had chosen Echo, or that it was definitely the best thing. He was just a buffalo, like the rest of them.

And he wouldn't be around to help Echo make the best of the situation he'd been thrust into.

That would be up to her.

CHAPTER FIFTEEN

Tailgrabber deposited the impala's corpse by the roots of the baobab tree, shook herself from head to toe, and then scanned the horizon. She didn't see the others.

They'll be back, she told herself. *Any moment now.*

She had thrown herself into hunting, catching the kind of prey that would once have earned her praise, or at least respect, from her fellow hyenas. Now they barely seemed to notice. Most of the other females, and a few of Gutripper's favored males, had gone to Noblepride's territory.

Again.

It was their third attack since the cubs were killed. Their fifth clash with the lions in less than four days. Tailgrabber herself had been there for only one. She had fought the lions who snuck up in the middle of the night, trying to kill Gutripper in her sleep. They had all fought, driven by fear and fury, and the lions had retreated, seemingly the worse for it.

But Backbreaker lost a paw, and after a few days of bleeding and fever it looked like the whole leg was about to drop off, if it didn't take Backbreaker's life first. And Jawsmasher could no longer hear out of one ear, and nobody was sure if Blood-bather had been killed or simply run away. Not to mention the long list of minor scrapes, breaks, and bruises that were spreading through the clan like a disease.

And for what?

They'd attacked, the lions had counterattacked, and then they had done it *two more times*, and Tailgrabber could see no sign of Noblepride giving up the territory, no matter what Gutripper said.

How long do we do this? Until we're outnumbered? Until we're all dead, or they are?

A movement on the horizon made Tailgrabber's ears perk up. A gaggle of hyenas was approaching. She could see Gutripper and Nosebiter, both still walking on all four paws, and that was enough that she allowed herself to look away and go back to dragging her prey into position.

The warriors headed straight for it, some of them shoving Tailgrabber out of the way to get to the fresh meat. Their hunger suggested the fight had been a long one. She looked to Nosebiter.

"What happened?" she asked, though she knew the answer, if not the details. *We attacked, we were driven off, the lions will retali-ate before dawn.*

Nosebiter glanced at Skullcracker, and Tailgrabber

followed her gaze and winced. Skullcracker's jaw seemed as if it was badly aligned with the rest of her muzzle, off to one side and hanging limply. She met Tailgrabber's eyes and gave a defiant sniff.

"Cosssst me . . . my bite . . . ," she said, thickly. "Buh I blinded that lioness. . . ."

Tailgrabber nodded. She couldn't think of anything to say that wouldn't enrage the others.

"Spinesnapper is gone," said Nosebiter quietly.

"She died for the clan," said Gutripper. "Death comes to everything, but to die for your clan is the best death there is. The Great Devourer will give her pride of place in its kingdom."

The others muttered their agreement, and Nosebiter muttered, "We survive."

"And she took the lion with her," said Hidetearer. "And many of them were mauled, including more of their precious cubs. They must be thinking they shouldn't have started this now."

Really?! Tailgrabber gave Nosebiter a desperate look, still trying to hold her tongue. But Nosebiter was nodding along with the others, even though she looked so tired she could barely hold her head up. Her ears flopped down toward her eyes.

"And when do you think we should expect their retaliation?" Tailgrabber found herself saying. She turned to face Gutripper, determined to show that she was serious—and that she wasn't afraid of their mother. "Dusk? The middle of the night, like last time? Perhaps they'll leave it till noon tomorrow?"

"Tailgrabber," said Nosebiter in a warning tone. Gutripper was simply looking at her, almost as if she was really listening.

"Do we keep on fighting this war until there's just one lion and one hyena left? How many more cubs do we need to kill to make up for the ones we've lost?"

"*All* of them," snarled Hidetearer.

Tailgrabber ignored her and focused on Gutripper. Her mother sat straight and her ears pricked up, but Tailgrabber could see now that she was unsteady on her paws. Was she hurt? Or simply very, very tired?

"And what is the alternative?" she asked.

"A treaty," said Tailgrabber. "We make peace."

"You think they'd make peace with us? They'd just take our whole territory and kill us all!" snapped Jawsmasher.

"We could find a new territory, a better one."

"Hyenas are not cowards!" yowled Hidetearer.

"Then why are we afraid to go to the Great Mother?" Tailgrabber snarled back.

The others groaned—apart from Gutripper, who sighed and tilted her head.

Could she actually be considering it?

"*I'll* go!" Tailgrabber went on, trying to seize the moment. "I'm not afraid of the elephants, and I'm not afraid of the Great Devourer thinking I'm disloyal, either—I don't think He cares! It knows we are His children. Going to the Great Mother to deal with her own lions is not admitting defeat."

She forced herself to stop speaking, before she could talk so much she talked her mother out of the idea. But if Gutripper had been about to give in and say yes, she didn't get the chance, because something was approaching. Tailgrabber's ears twitched, and she spun, sniffing the air. Not the lions already?

No—it was one creature, she could tell that much. But one creature that was louder and heavier and smellier than any lion. The bushes near the baobab tree were rustling, and even the leaves of the tree itself shuddered. For a second, Tailgrabber thought that the Great Mother herself might have come to take them to task for their attacks on the lions. . . .

But the shape that burst from the bushes wasn't an elephant.

"Buffalo!" yelped Hidetearer, and the hyenas startled and backed away, scattering with a chorus of yelps and giggles. Tailgrabber turned and ran, circling the baobab. A charging buffalo would trample any hyena that got in its way, whether they were trying to attack it or not. She ran past the hollow where some of the males were sleeping, past Backbreaker's bed of bloodied moss, and came back around the other side of the tree in time to see the buffalo . . . had stopped. It was pawing the ground and shaking its head, but this was no stampede. It had thundered up to Gutripper, who had held her ground with a wild stubbornness in her face . . . and it had stopped.

It wasn't the biggest buffalo Tailgrabber had ever seen. She realized, now that it was no longer a terrifying blur of sharp horns and crushing hooves and tossing hair, that it must be a young male. Maybe it was lost.

Tailgrabber's eyes narrowed, and she pressed herself against the tree.

Maybe it was prey, after all . . . if enough of them could get behind it . . .

But even one buffalo would be too much for them right now. It wasn't worth the lives they could lose. Not when they had already lost Spinesnapper today.

"We have no quarrel with your kind," said Gutripper as the buffalo snorted in front of her. "We do not hunt you, like the lions do."

"I know," said the buffalo. "I am not here to fight. I've come to talk to you about a quarrel you do have."

Gutripper kept herself looking cool and in control, but behind her Tailgrabber saw Nosebiter's head tilt and heard a surprised *mrum?* sound escape her throat.

"I'm no fan of lions—they try to take our calves and our elderly. I crushed the one that gave me these scars." The buffalo turned his flank so that Gutripper could see. Tailgrabber couldn't make out any scars, but they must have been more obvious from up close. "The buffalo herd have noticed that you have been fighting the lions, without much success. I may have a solution to your problem."

Gutripper's muzzle twitched into a slow smile. "Really?" she said. "Well then, it's only polite for us to listen. Nosebiter, Skullcracker, with me. The rest of you, scram." She snapped at Hidetearer, who gave a nervous giggle and ran off. Tailgrabber watched as her mother and sister and the still-lopsided

Skullcracker began to walk with the young buffalo, talking to him as they went, their voices too low to hear.

Tailgrabber found herself pacing back and forth, her paws twitching, as the buffalo and the hyenas were talking. She didn't know what made her more nervous, the idea that the buffalo could hurt Nosebiter, or that he might actually have the solution to all their problems. The buffalo did follow the Great Spirit, after all, and they were grass-eaters—deadly, but not violent, unless they were provoked. What if he was here to tell them to speak to the Great Mother? Or to tell them that he knew some other way to end the conflict without any more bloodshed?

At last, Gutripper and the others split away from the buffalo, who went into a loping run and headed away at a speed that felt unlikely for a creature that bulky.

Tailgrabber ran to meet Gutripper as she returned, and she wasn't the only one—a whole group of hyenas who had been watching the meeting with the buffalo gathered around, tails swishing in anticipation.

"The buffalo speaks of an alliance," she said. "I am inclined to trust him. I know what he wants, and it is something I know we can provide. In return, we will be rid of Noblepride. For good."

The hyenas whooped and cheered. Even Tailgrabber, though her heart sank to hear that there would be more fighting. At least if the buffalo drove Noblepride out, then perhaps it would finally be over. . . .

* * *

Perhaps the lions had had spies watching and they'd seen the buffalo, or perhaps they were more injured than Tailgrabber had assumed, but either way the hyenas passed a lion-free night for the first time since this conflict began. Tailgrabber woke up in the morning with an equal sense of relief and foreboding. The relief ebbed away as the day went on, but the foreboding only seemed to grow. As the heat rose and the sun became too sweltering to stay in, she lay down in the shade of a tree, a little way from the main hyena baobab. She longed to nap here, but every small noise had her startling and sniffing for lions, or for buffalo.

What did the buffalo and Gutripper have planned? What did Gutripper mean by *something we can provide*?

She tried to lie down and save her energy. Either the lions would be back, or she would need to hunt later, and she wasn't looking forward to either.

But now there was a new sound that wormed its way into her ears. A buzzing sound. She opened one eye, and something flew past, too fast to see properly. Then another, and another.

Not flies, this time—wasps, with shiny black-and-yellow bodies and pointed stings. They were intent on something nearby. Not Tailgrabber herself, but a hole in the ground where she guessed that there must be ants, or whatever it was that wasps hunted.

They must be hunters. Otherwise why would they be so good at stinging?

Tailgrabber tried to be calm and still, knowing the wasps wouldn't bother her if she didn't startle them, but watching them was making her strangely dizzy.

Oh, she thought as her vision seemed to contract down to just the sliver of air around the hole where the wasps were swarming.

She fought the urge to tense up, which never helped, but this time instead of a parting curtain, it seemed as if her sight was focusing and focusing on a single wasp, almost as if she was riding on its back, seeing what it saw as it wheeled and danced in the air, and then down, straight for the hole, and darkness . . .

. . . and then Tailgrabber was walking out of darkness, onto a dim, gray plain.

There were hyenas in front of her. Gutripper in the lead, walking with purpose. The others were following her, as they always did, without question. Tailgrabber wanted to call Nosebiter's name and ask where they were going, but she couldn't make a sound. She could only follow.

The plain was featureless, not like the cracked earth of the buffalo vision, but more unreal. The ground was wreathed in mist, so Tailgrabber couldn't see her paws. Outlines of trees and rocks came and went, passing by the hyenas just slightly too fast.

Up ahead, though, was a different strange sight. The horizon was coming closer. It was a cliff edge. Tailgrabber walked faster, trying to catch up to her mother as she in turn drew near the cliff. Tailgrabber wanted to look down and see what was below. Were the others leading her to something, something she needed to see? But when she did get to the edge, there was nothing there but more mist, far below.

She turned to look at Gutripper, hoping that she would speak, like the skeletal buffalo had spoken . . . but Gutripper didn't look up, didn't so much as take a deep breath, as she walked off the cliff.

Tailgrabber tried to cry out, but still she could make no noise, and now she couldn't move either. She could only watch as one by one, their eyes fixed on the horizon as if they had total faith that there was solid ground ahead, her sister, her cousins, bullies, comrades, all the hyenas walked off the cliff and fell into nothing.

Tailgrabber was left alone, with a harsh buzzing sound reverberating in her ears.

She closed her eyes, and the buzzing faded to the ordinary zooming sound of the wasps. When she opened them again she was lying in the shade, surrounded by dry wild grass and a soft breeze.

She sat up with a start, making the wasps buzz angrily, but not attack. Tailgrabber got to her paws and backed away, her mind racing. What was the Great Devourer trying to tell her? What cliff were the hyenas moving toward?

She stepped out into the sunlight and blinked against the bright, hot glare for a moment. She felt like a fool. She hadn't even thought, when the buffalo had come to speak to Gutripper, that it could be connected to her previous vision. The big, hairy, puffing creature hadn't reminded her of the strange skeletons she had seen, but she remembered now.

The buffalo in her vision needed help. Perhaps this buffalo who had come to them was her opportunity to help, after all?

As she was standing there debating with herself, something else buzzed past her ear, and she jumped. But it wasn't a wasp—this time, it was a little brown bird. Tailgrabber narrowed her eyes. Was that an oxpecker? She turned around, half expecting to see the buffalo approaching. Oxpeckers usually didn't go too far from their buffalo, and if they did, it would usually be a little flock of them following a herd.

This one, though, appeared to be entirely on its own, and heading toward the baobab tree. Tailgrabber watched it until she could barely see it anymore, until it was just a speck in the air, bobbing and fluttering down to land . . . on Gutripper's resting paw.

Tailgrabber blinked. Was that really what had just happened? Perhaps she'd imagined it. . . .

Then the little brown fluttering thing lifted from Gutripper and went to Skullcracker, and then to Nosebiter and Bonesplitter. They jolted awake from their afternoon naps, stood up, and shook themselves, but not one of them tried to bite the bird, and the bird didn't seem afraid of the hyenas.

Unease prickled at the back of Tailgrabber's neck. What was happening? None of the hyenas seemed *surprised* that an oxpecker was landing on them one by one. It was almost as if they *expected* it.

She started to hurry over, trying to follow the movement of

the bird at the same time. It didn't wake every hyena. It left
most of the males alone, and many of the females—the ones
who were badly injured were avoided by the bird, as well as a
few young females and all the elderly ones.

By the time Tailgrabber arrived at the baobab, the group
of hyenas who'd been visited by the oxpecker was starting to
look very much like a clan who were ready for a fight. The
toughest, strongest, and healthiest were all there.

So why not me? Tailgrabber thought.

She suspected she didn't want to go where the others were
going, and yet . . .

The others were setting off now, following the oxpecker
across the plain. Tailgrabber put on a burst of speed and managed to catch up with Nosebiter.

"Hey," she said. "What's going on?"

Her sister turned to her with a frown.

"Nothing," she said. "Just stay here."

"But why? Where's the buffalo taking you?"

"Keep your muzzle out of it, will you?" Nosebiter snapped.
She huffed an annoyed sigh through her nose and briefly
touched her cheek to Tailgrabber's. "We'll be back soon. Just
don't do anything stupid until we return."

She turned away and began to follow the rest. Tailgrabber's
eyes stung as she watched them walking away from her, slowly
passing over the plain. The sight was so immediately familiar
that it felt as if she was being gripped by the scruff and shaken.
The plain was blurred with brightness rather than dim mist,

but all the same, the hyenas were setting out, and she did not know if they would return.

And they expected her to just stay behind, to stay out of trouble.

Keeping well back, slinking to shadows whenever she could, Tailgrabber followed them.

CHAPTER SIXTEEN

Flicker's paws kicked out more little clouds of dust and dry grass as she stomped across the plain. Stride was happy to be swept along in her wake, it was better than anywhere else he could think of to be, but he was struggling to keep up with her furious pace. The tooth that had cracked under Jinks's blow had finally fallen out, and his jaw felt much better for it, but still, the ground under him tilted and swayed more than it used to.

"I won't just lie down and be exiled from my own life," Flicker was muttering. "Who does he think he is? He doesn't get to tell my family whether to speak to me or not. I won't just accept this. And you won't either. You're my family now, I'm not going to let them bully you."

For a moment, Stride's real vision was overtaken by a flash of an imagined future: Flicker defending their cubs against anything that could threaten them in Bravelands.

He felt a little guilty for the thought. It was a nice thing to imagine, but it wasn't real. They had to face what was real first.

He sighed and cleared his throat. "I still can't believe Pace betrayed me like that."

Flicker stopped pacing, and her tail drooped between her legs. "I . . . don't think you have anything to worry about. I don't think it was Pace, whatever Jinks claimed. I told my litter-mate, Softpaw, and she . . . well, she wasn't supportive."

"Neither was Pace," admitted Stride. "He said if I didn't stop seeing you, it was all going to go horribly wrong and we'd get hurt. And he was right," he muttered.

"It sounds like he was just worried about you," Flicker said. Her expression darkened. "Trust me. This is something Softpaw would do. Pace is probably innocent."

Stride nodded. He was relieved, but the feeling was muted, when Flicker's family hung over their heads like a dark cloud. He realized that he knew they hadn't treated her well, in an abstract way: encouraging Jinks even when she said she didn't want him. But he hadn't quite realized that her own litter-sister would turn on her. He hoped never to meet this badly named *Softpaw*.

"Even if Pace didn't do it, I can't go back to the coalition," he said. "That'd be putting him in danger as much as me. We're on our own." He paused. "I want to go back for Fleet. Without our help, he'll die."

"Stride . . . ," Flicker said. Stride felt a prickle of unease. "What?"

"It's just that . . . I like Fleet, and I want him to live, but . . . if we have to run, go far away, how are we going to bring him with us? We can't carry him. You know we can't."

Stride shook his head. "I—I don't know. We'll think of something. We always have before. *I'll* think of something."

Flicker nodded, but Stride could see that there was something more she wanted to say.

He didn't want to hear it. It was a new feeling where Flicker was concerned, and he didn't like it. But she didn't know Fleet like he did.

They walked on together, slower this time.

"What? What is it?" he finally said.

"I don't know how to say this," said Flicker slowly. "It's just that I don't know what Fleet wants. Fleet's the one who has to live his life. Is he happy?"

"What? What do you mean, *is he happy*? He's alive! That's all that matters!"

Even as Stride was saying it, he felt a sliver of doubt enter his mind, like a splinter in his paw. *Is that all that matters? Is he happy?*

"It must be hard for him," Flicker said. "He's hidden away behind those bushes. He can't even see the plains properly. It's better than death, of course it is. I just wonder if there's something else for him, something we haven't thought of yet."

Stride looked down at his paws. Was she right? Was Fleet

secretly miserable? A flash of suspicion came over him. Had Fleet told Flicker something, things he wouldn't tell Stride?

"I can't leave him behind," he said. "That's all I know."

Flicker didn't argue. Instead they turned for the copse where Fleet lived.

As they passed the rock where they'd sheltered from the sandstorm, with sand still piled in drifts between the cracks, Stride put on a burst of speed. He wanted to get to Fleet. They could think about what to do when they were all together. He just wanted to get there. . . .

He wriggled through the bushes with Flicker on his heels, but as he emerged on the other side, he immediately knew something was wrong.

There was no sign of Fleet, but there was a smell. Blood, and fear. He took in the scene in flashes, standing still, his heart racing. There was blood on the ground. There was loose fur clinging to the trunks of the trees.

"Lions?" Flicker whispered, a slight tremor in her voice. "Maybe he was ready for them. . . . Maybe he got away. . . ."

Stride's gaze drifted over the copse and alighted on something sticking out from behind a tree. A long, tan, and black-spotted tail. Unmoving.

The dread felt almost like a strong wind pushing against him, but Stride forced himself to walk through it, to circle the tree until he could see what lay beyond.

There was a dead cheetah in the clearing. Stride felt the world sway underneath him. The cheetah's head was tipped back to expose a throat that had once been pale, now red and dark, torn muscle and sinew hanging out. Its legs were splayed, unmoving.

Wait . . .

Four legs, all the same length and shape.

"It's not him," Stride gasped, and rushed to the cheetah's head. "It's *One-Ear*!"

Jinks's words came back to him in a flash: *One-Ear has other things to attend to.*

"Fleet!" Stride called again. *Jinks sent One-Ear here to kill him. They knew he was here. They came for him because of me. . . .* "Fleet, please be alive! Fleet!"

"Stride, hush," said Flicker urgently. "Listen."

Stride held his breath, the effort of it instantly making his heart pulsate in his ears. But over his heartbeat, he managed to catch what Flicker had heard—a snuffling, wheezing sound.

They found Fleet up against one of the trees. He was sprawled, almost as motionless as One-Ear, and almost as bloody. A wide gash had been clawed across his stomach, and he struggled to lift his head as he heard Stride and Flicker approach.

But to Stride's shock, he didn't seem distressed.

"Oh! You're here," he wheezed. "Good, good. Wouldn't want . . . find me gone. Good to say goodbye."

"Don't," Stride gasped instinctively. He felt Flicker's tail rest on his shoulder, steadying him.

"You really held your own," she said to Fleet.

"Heh! You should have seen me," Fleet said. He bared his

fangs. They were bloody. Stride didn't think all of it belonged to One-Ear—blood was bubbling up in the corners of Fleet's mouth even as he spoke. "It was like old times, Stride. It was . . . good. I'm . . . dying, I think, but . . . it was good."

His bad leg suddenly began to twitch. He groaned in pain as it kicked. Stride jumped back, horror and shame filling his heart, knowing he could do nothing to help. After a few moments, the leg stopped, and Fleet lay back, exhausted.

Guilt gnawed at Stride, until it almost consumed him. *How long have they known about Fleet?*

"This is my fault," Stride whispered. "It's because of me and Flicker. I'm so sorry, Fleet. . . ."

"Shush," hissed Fleet. "Don't . . . don't put guilt . . . I don't need it. You be happy. That's . . . an order. Don't look back."

Fleet winced, and with a great effort, he stretched out one paw toward Stride. Stride dipped his nose and nuzzled against the paw, closing his eyes. For a moment he was back in their mother's den, squished up against his littermates, feeling every twitch and wriggle. They had been one thing, then, not Stride and Fleet and Zip and Leap, but only *the litter.*

He missed those days.

When he lifted his head again, Fleet was gone. His eyes were blank, his wheezing breath stopped.

Flicker lay down beside him, and Stride pressed his flank to hers. For a little while, they didn't move or speak, just lay beside Fleet's body and breathed together, taking solace from each other's warm pelts and softly moving chests.

Then Flicker turned her head and gently licked Stride's ear.

"We should go," she whispered. "Jinks will come here looking for you. We have to go."

Stride leaned forward and gave Fleet a final farewell lick across the top of his head.

"We won't look back," he whispered.

CHAPTER SEVENTEEN

Well, we got this far, Whisper thought as she climbed the high bluff alongside Echo.

The herd was watching the sun set over Bravelands as the full moon rose to meet it. It was time for the passing of the Way. After tonight, Echo would have the knowledge he needed to lead the migration.

They had come to this high place to see Echo off on his journey into wisdom, as Thunder called it. She wasn't sure where he would go to meet Bellow, only that the herd could go no farther than the bluffs. Echo and Bellow would spend the night alone, with a guard of strong buffalo stationed nearby to make sure they weren't disturbed.

The wind was strong up here, and it whipped Whisper's hair up into her eyes and made her blink and squint into the sunset. Down below, Grandmother snaked her way through the landscape, gleaming golden in the setting sun. The river that looked like an endless golden snake. Whisper couldn't remember why they called it Grandmother, but it seemed an appropriate name. It was a friendly sight, warm and welcoming. There was always some water, even at the height of the dry season, though it was thick with mud and silt.

"Whisper," Echo muttered. He didn't say anything else, but he sidled up to her until his small body was sheltered from the wind by hers.

Whisper smiled at him. She didn't feel all that confident herself, and she wondered if it would help him to hear that. But in the end, she just nudged him with her nose. "You'll be fine. It's exciting! You're going to get to know something no one else knows, for the rest of your life."

Echo nodded silently.

"Mother would be very proud of you," Whisper added, and Echo looked up at her with big, wet eyes. "I wish she was here to say so, but I know she would."

"Me too," said Echo.

"It is time," said a low voice. It was Grind. He was walking up toward them.

"What happens now? Where's Bellow?" Echo asked. His voice hardly shook at all as he looked up and met the gaze of the much larger buffalo, and Whisper felt a burst of pride.

"First, we will escort the new leader down to the river," said Grind. "We will take the twisting path, and you will be cleansed of your lifetime's ignorance, so that wisdom can take its place."

I guess that won't take long, Whisper thought to herself. *He hasn't had much life to fill with ignorance.*

Echo stepped forward and was immediately surrounded by an escort of five large males. Whisper shifted her hooves, wishing she'd had a last chance to tell him good luck—but he would be fine. She would see him afterward. He'd probably be better than fine. Echo with the wisdom of the ancient buffalo might well be insufferable.

The large buffalo led the way to a dip in the bluffs, and they started to descend toward the river. Many parts of the bluff ended in sheer cliffs, but here Whisper knew they could take one of a few steep paths that had been trodden into the earth over all the ages of Bravelands by animals heading for the river. After waiting for a few moments to give them space, she went up to the edge of the bluff and looked over.

There were crocodiles in the river, farther down. She could see them lazing on the surface. But they didn't frighten her— they wouldn't do anything to Echo with this mighty escort on his heels.

The rest of the herd began to mill about, not quite dispersing entirely, but spreading out to munch on the grass of the bluffs. Whisper looked around and saw Murmur coming to her side, ignoring Thunder's calls to be careful near the edge.

"Isn't it magical?" Murmur said. "The sunset on the river, the moon in the sky . . . Can't you feel it?"

Whisper paused, trying to feel the magic. Perhaps there was something there. The sun and the moon, the gleaming river, the ceremonial trudging of the escort down the steep hill . . . but it was hard to feel it over the background hum of her nerves.

"I wonder where Bellow is," she muttered.

"Well, we can't expect him to climb down that path and back up," Murmur pointed out reasonably. "They'll probably escort Echo to him after he's been washed."

"Of course," said Whisper. Murmur was right, but Whisper still didn't like it. It was a part of the process she didn't understand, and she wanted to understand all of it.

She went back to scanning the path ahead of Echo and his muscle-bound escort as they drew closer to the river. She wasn't sure what she was looking for. Big rocks he could trip over, maybe, or crocodiles that looked like they might try something despite being outnumbered. But she felt as if the moment she stopped looking, he would vanish from her sight, and she wasn't ready for that yet.

Then she startled and almost lost her footing, as if she'd tripped over a rock without even moving.

"Can you see that?" she hissed to Murmur. "There! Eyes, in the bushes!"

Between two rocks, in a patch of long grass, close to the winding path, she had seen something. Two somethings, glinting golden in the sunset.

"Lions?" Murmur gasped.

"Lions?!" said Thunder loudly. The word spread through the herd like a fire across a dry plain. Suddenly Whisper was surrounded by buffalo, stamping and snorting and trying to see what she'd seen.

And then the dry grass parted . . . and a single hyena poked its head out, looked up at them, and streaked away with its fur standing on end.

A breath of relief passed through the herd. "One hyena wouldn't do much harm to Echo," Thunder told Whisper. "Even without the escort, it would almost be a fair fight!"

Whisper didn't respond. Thunder was right, of course. A random hyena passing by had been no reason to panic. But she couldn't seem to move, as if the panic that had gripped her was struggling to let go.

"Don't worry too much," Thunder added, blowing air into Whisper's mane with a kindly chuckle. "You can stay to watch if you need to, but you should join us and eat something. Echo will be fine."

"Yeah," said Whisper. "I know."

Still, after Thunder and Murmur had both turned away from the edge and wandered off to find food, Whisper stood where she was. She watched Echo, then she looked around for the hyena, then she looked up at the moon. It seemed to be watching her back, like a great eye that could see everything in all of Bravelands at once.

Then she heard Echo scream.

She looked down. She couldn't see him or the escort.

This time, she didn't freeze. She didn't even cry out to the others; she couldn't hesitate even to do that. Her hooves carried her over the edge and down the path. She stumbled and slipped at first, instinctively trying to control her descent, aware somewhere deep down that a broken leg would be the end of her. But she could not go fast and careful at the same time, and as she was trying to, Echo screamed again.

Whisper tossed away her caution and hurtled down the path, half running, half flying—a one-buffalo stampede. Her vision contracted down to the point where the path vanished behind the rocks. Echo was there. Echo *had to* be there. And whatever was making him scream like that, Whisper would crush them.

Her hooves juddered against loose stones, and long grasses whipped at her face and tangled in her hide. She didn't slow down until the slope of the ground evened out, and she realized that if she didn't turn *now*, she would end up stampeding right into the muddy river. With great effort and a frightening moment of skidding, she managed to turn around the corner where Echo had disappeared.

She saw them immediately. The five big buffalo, panting and snorting. One hyena lay motionless on the ground. She heard others cackling somewhere.

No Echo.

"Where is he?" she gasped.

"Ran off," said the escort leader, looking worriedly in the direction of the cliffs. "The rot-eaters startled him. . . ."

Whisper didn't stop. She thundered past them, cursing them in her head. Weren't they supposed to protect him? One hyena wasn't a problem, but a pack of the things . . .

The path went on, parallel to the river now, until it made a last turn down to the water. Echo wasn't there, either, but it was clear where he had gone—strings of buffalo hide were caught on a half-trampled bush with spiky leaves, off the path in a straight line from the hyenas' ambush. She heard more hyena noises and raised voices calling to each other, from somewhere up ahead, and shouldered through the bush after them.

The land sloped sharply upward, and no well-trodden buffalo-way had evolved here, so it was hard to clamber over the rocks and the wild bushes, but she could see and smell that Echo was just ahead of her. And sure enough, she crashed through another bush and stumbled out onto a jagged rock shelf, halfway up the cliff, and saw Echo surrounded by hyenas. She almost came nose-to-tail with one of them. They were snapping and sneering at him, calling out insults and laughing in their creepy, hysterical way.

Echo was bleeding. There was red, matted hair around his nose and mouth. He swayed dizzily.

She bellowed out, "Echo, I'm here!" and then reared up and stomped on the closest hyena. It managed to avoid getting its spine broken, but her hoof landed on one of its paws, and it shrieked and rolled away. She lowered her head and thrust her horns at the next, sideswiping it in the ribs with a grunt.

The rest of the hyenas turned, in a confusion of fur and snapping teeth.

"She's not supposed to be here!" one of them yelled.

"Just another calf, take care of her!" snarled another.

Three of them leaped, all at once. Whisper just managed to brace before they were on her, claws tangled in her hide. One overshot, tumbling down behind her, and she kicked out with one hoof and felt a satisfying *thump*, hearing the hyena whine in pain. The one on her back weighed her down and tried to bite her neck, and she yelled and threw her head forward, sending the hyena overbalancing onto the ground in front of her. The one on her flank, though, hung on with claws and teeth, still trying to get a good bite in despite her thrashing from side to side, until Whisper let out a grunt, squeezed her eyes shut, and flopped down hard on her side, on top of the hyena. There was a nasty crunch, and it let go, whimpering.

Wincing with pain and with horror, Whisper managed to get back onto her hooves.

Most of the hyenas had run. One reared up right in front of her and scratched at her eyes, but Whisper tossed her head away and got only a rake of claws across her chin and throat, just catching the skin. But then that hyena scampered away too.

There was just one left. It was standing by Echo, facing him, panting.

"Get away from him!" Whisper rasped, stumbling forward.

But the hyena wasn't attacking. It wasn't even growling. It was *saying* something, in a low voice. She couldn't quite hear it all; wind was whistling past them now and the thudding of her own blood in her ears was too loud.

She caught just a few words.

". . . step away," it seemed to say, "I won't hurt you. . . ."

What's this trickery?

Echo was staring at the hyena with wide, confused eyes. He backed away from it, his hoof meeting the edge of the rock. His back leg slipped over. The hyena leaped at him, and Whisper scrambled forward—but she was too slow. They were both too slow, even though it seemed to happen in a strange, dreamlike way. Echo startled and slipped farther back, and then tumbled, pawing uselessly at the ground and then the air with his hoofs, off the edge of the rock. He let out a high-pitched cry that echoed off the cliffs around them, and then he was gone.

"No!" Whisper screamed. She ran for the edge. The hyena had been looking down but glanced up at Whisper and then dodged out of her way. It pounced up onto a higher rock.

Echo had fallen into the river. The shelf jutted right out over it, the drop taller than the tallest tree she knew. She could see him, small and brown, turning and bobbing gently in the current. For a moment she held her breath.

Is he moving? Is he alive?

But it was just his hide, drifting in the water. Whisper glanced briefly at the hyena, who seemed to be watching too. It met her eyes with what might even have been a glance of sympathy, then skulked off. Where to, Whisper didn't know or care. She looked down again at the water below.

Her little brother's corpse spun for a moment longer, and then the river current caught it, like a mother nudging a hesitant calf, and gently carried it away.

CHAPTER EIGHTEEN

Tailgrabber caught her breath halfway up the cliff, pressing herself against the rocks. If she looked down, she could still just about make out the buffalo calf—the living one—still standing and staring down at the now-empty river.

It was so scared. . . . If it had just listened to me . . .

She folded her legs underneath her and huddled on her perch for a moment, her mind spinning.

Why had she even tried to save the calf? Any other day of her life, the clan would be right to chase down a buffalo calf and kill it, and she would be crazy to try to stop them. That was the normal way of things.

But not like this. Something was wrong, something was . . . *stupid*.

She couldn't see the other hyenas anymore, even the ones who had been badly hurt by the buffalo, but she knew that at least one of them had died. Maybe more. They had attacked *five large buffalo* to get to that one calf, and . . . they had succeeded? Tailgrabber still didn't understand what she'd seen. How, and more importantly, *why*?

Gutripper and Nosebiter at least had gotten away, along with most of the rest. The answers she was looking for would be found back at the baobab, but considering they hadn't even wanted to share the plan with her, she was sure she wouldn't get them.

She had barely come within sight of the baobab when she found out how wrong she was.

"Tailgrabber! She's back!"

Tailgrabber jumped and braced herself as she saw a hyena running across the grass toward her. But it wasn't Hidetearer or one of the others; it was Nosebiter. And she wasn't angry. Her tongue lolled from her mouth in happiness, and when she reached Tailgrabber, she gave her a big lick on the side of the face.

Tailgrabber stared at her, nonplussed.

"You did it!" Nosebiter said. "You pushed that buffalo right off that cliff!"

Tailgrabber opened her mouth to say no, she'd been trying to save it, but she realized just in time that would have been a very foolish thing to say. She swallowed her objections and continued her walk back to the tree, with Nosebiter trotting alongside her proudly. As they drew closer, more and more hyenas looked up and grinned at her. Hidetearer was there, giving Tailgrabber a startlingly genuine-seeming friendly tail-wag. Other hyenas who'd mocked her or just ignored her suddenly seemed to think that she was important.

I've had dreams like this . . . she thought, walking in a sort of daze up to Gutripper, who gave her a quiet, proud smile. *Am I asleep? Am I about to wake up?*

"You should not have been there," her mother said, but she didn't seem remotely angry. "But if you hadn't been, that female buffalo could have ruined everything. You stayed, even after Legsnatcher was killed, even when the rest of us ran, even me, and you finished the job. I am so proud of you, Tailgrabber. You have just won the war with Noblepride!"

A chorus of howls and cheers went up from the other hyenas.

Tailgrabber thought she was going to faint. Could it be true? How? Should she admit that she didn't understand? If she did, would they realize she hadn't done it on purpose . . . whatever *it* was?

Despite her confusion, though, she felt her tail begin to sway. She couldn't help it. Her mother had just said the words she had daydreamed about for so long. . . .

"You must be wondering, why that calf?" Nosebiter said.

"Yes!" Tailgrabber said gratefully.

Gutripper laughed. "I should have allowed you to know the plan from the beginning. Nosebiter, gather the clan. I want everyone to hear this."

It didn't take long—most of the hyenas who were anywhere near the baobab had either joined them already or were loitering just in earshot, waiting to find out what all the fuss was about. But it was still impressive, and intimidating, to see every living hyena gathered in front of them, females and males, young and old, watching Gutripper and Tailgrabber with expectation.

"This is a great day," Gutripper announced. "Noblepride will trouble us no more. Very soon, Noblepride will be driven from their territory, and it will be ours for the taking!"

Hoots and howls greeted this news, and Tailgrabber waited impatiently for them to shut up and let her mother keep talking.

"The buffalo that came to us a few days ago brought us a proposition. We made a deal: we kill one particular calf from their herd, and in return, the buffalo herd will run their migration right through Noblepride's territory, trampling the lions as they go. They will be eradicated. No lion who still follows Noble will be safe."

The other hyenas cackled.

"The buffalo made sure we had the opportunity—the ones who were with the youngster knew to expect us, and we were allowed to hunt the calf with impunity. Still, we might have lost it, thanks to a buffalo being where she wasn't supposed to be. But my daughter, Tailgrabber, saved the day. Without even knowing why the calf was our target, she crept up after us, ignored the threat from the female buffalo, and drove the calf to its death!"

Cheers, whoops, cries of *Tailgrabber!* and *That'll show them!*

"I'll admit, I once had some doubts about Tailgrabber," said

Gutripper. "But I am pleased to say that they were unfounded. Let this be a lesson to all of us. Some take longer to earn their names, but do not count them out!"

"Tailgrabber!" Nosebiter cried. "Let's hear it for Tailgrabber!"

Tailgrabber felt as if she had to physically brace herself as the wave of adulation passed over her. It was like that sandstorm that had passed by, luckily missing the baobab tree, but leaving other territories sand-worn and half-buried. If she was careful, the feeling of all her dreams coming true wouldn't take her head off.

"Mother," she said, as the cheers died down and the clan turned to chattering and congratulating themselves and each other and planning what they would do when they took over Noblepride's territory. "Why that calf?"

She held her breath, hoping against hope for an answer that would stop her guts from twisting whenever she thought of the terror in the calf's eye. *Was he . . . bad, somehow? Was he not just . . . a cub, like Cub?*

But Gutripper snorted. "The buffalo didn't say much, only that it was a threat to the herd. I didn't ask how. It was too good a deal to risk it by asking stupid questions. Who knows what kind of thing buffalo care about?"

With that, she turned away from Tailgrabber to talk to Nosebiter, and Tailgrabber suddenly felt more alone than she ever had before, despite the friendly tails and the admiring glances of the rest of her clan.

She thought of the grief and fury of the female buffalo.

She thought of her visions, the skeleton buffalo on the dead plain asking for her help, and the clan walking thoughtlessly to their deaths right in front of her. The memory sat across Tailgrabber's shoulders like a heap of heavy stones.

I have a horrible feeling this victory's going to have consequences we can't imagine....

After a while, the celebration came to a natural end as most of the hyenas got bored and wandered off to look for food or sleep. Tailgrabber longed to do the same, so it was a relief when Gutripper barked out, "Nosebiter, Hidetearer, Skull-cracker, to me."

Tailgrabber turned to go, partly wondering what was going to happen now, but mostly just glad to get away.

"You too, Tailgrabber," said Gutripper. "I made a mistake not including you before. You've proved yourself now. I want you here."

Feeling like her heart was tearing in two, but trying to show nothing on her face, Tailgrabber joined the others in their huddle with her mother.

"I don't want this to drag on any longer than it has to," Gutripper said firmly. "We've fulfilled our part of the bargain, the calf is dead. You four will go to the herd at daybreak and find the one called Holler. It's time to make sure the buffalo hold up their side of things. By sunset tomorrow, Noblepride will be no more!"

CHAPTER NINETEEN

Living on the run really isn't so bad, Stride thought. *I've got Flicker, and my freedom—as long as we don't go too close to any other cheetahs, or their territory. But we don't need them. We'll find our own place.*

He felt the warmth of her pelt against his as they sat on a rock in the sunset, looking out over the land. It was quite a sight to see. Red earth and pale green-brown grass, black rock, dark green forest, and fiery pink-and-orange sky. Herds of animals moving across the land farther away, flocks of birds swirling, and a single star glinting somewhere beyond the fiery clouds. At midday Bravelands was stifling, but if the clouds stayed thin and far off it would be cold tonight, and they might be glad of the warmth radiating from the stone beneath them.

His mind wandered to Pace, and to the coalition. Could it even be a coalition now, with Stride gone and One-Ear dead?

It was just Jinks and Pace, and even if Jinks didn't attack Pace for not giving up Stride's secrets, it would be miserable, being the non-leader in a coalition of two.

He hoped Pace had the sense to leave before that happened.

"What would your perfect territory look like?" Flicker asked. "Since we're looking for somewhere to make our own. What would say to you, *This is it, we've found our home?*"

"Well, *perfect* would be . . . long grass, deep watering holes . . . crystal clear, like that stream, the one that comes right out of the rock. Plenty of good trees to sleep in, and all around the watering hole it'd have those reeds that look like waving tails, to confuse the prey. Oh, and it'd be on a major migration route," he added, licking his lips. "Because of the perfect watering hole, obviously."

"Obviously," Flicker said, nodding vehemently.

"So every day there'd be a different herd of grass-eaters passing through. And they'd all be deaf and have no sense of smell."

Flicker laughed. "That would be perfect," she agreed.

"What about you? Anything to add?"

"Well . . . I'd like a cave, as well as a tree," she said. "I like caves. And *no lions.*"

"Ooh, that's a good one. Absolutely no lions allowed." Stride looked around the landscape in front of him, wondering what else would fit on his perfect territory. It didn't matter which birds there were, really. Some smaller mammals, like the one he could see snuffling through the underbush over there, would be welcome too. The cheetahs probably wouldn't even need to hunt them, not with vast herds of big, juicy, and stupid grass-eaters passing through all the time. . . .

Stride squinted and tilted his head. The little creature he could see making its way through the shade of the bushes growing along the edge of a dried-up watering hole . . . what *was* it? He didn't often meet creatures he didn't know, but this thing was oddly unfamiliar. It had a gray-white back and a black underbelly, head, and legs, so it almost looked like a smaller white creature was floating a little way off the ground as the thing moved through the shadows.

"Hey, Flicker," he said. "Do you see that . . . that thing there? Looks a bit like a big mongoose . . ."

"Oh, the honey badger?" Flicker said.

"I don't think I've ever seen one before," Stride said. "It's weird-looking. Are you hungry?" He threw her a meaningful look but didn't wait for her response before getting up and slipping off the rock.

"Um," Flicker said behind him. "Stride . . ."

Stride flicked his tail at her urgently. The honey badger was close enough that it might be able to hear them. If she kept talking, it could ruin his hunting!

"Stride, I wouldn't," she said.

Stride did pause at that. But he'd killed mongooses before. They were a bit bitey, but once he had it in his jaws, he'd make quick work of it.

He heard Flicker mutter, "Well, okay then . . ." as he stalked closer to the small creature. It was ambling through the bushes as if it didn't have a care in the world. This wouldn't be hard at all. He lowered his belly to the earth and slowed his breath, his haunches shifting slowly side to side, alert for any sign that the creature had scented him there, and he prepared to pounce. . . .

"Don't bother," said the honey badger in a gruff voice.

Stride froze. His eyes flicked back and forth. There must be another of the creatures nearby.

But there wasn't.

The honey badger began to dig at the ground. "Yes, you. Cat. I know you're there."

Stride still didn't move for a moment. This had never happened before. The prey creature knew he was there, but he didn't stop digging, except to pull out a chewy-looking root.

Stride stood up awkwardly. The honey badger still ignored him.

"Aren't you going to run?" he growled, trying to claw back a little dignity.

The honey badger made a noise through his mouthful of root that sounded like *no*.

"Eating," he eventually said. "Can't eat and run at the same time, can I?"

He turned, at last, and fixed a beady eye on Stride. Then, against all the unspoken rules of the hunter and the hunted, he turned his back on him again and returned to eating his root.

"You look like you could do with a good meal," he said. "Very skinny for a leopard."

Stride's hackles rose. *Is he mocking me?*

This had never, ever happened before. Prey animals sometimes begged for their lives or spat insults at him. Mostly they were too out of breath to say anything.

"I am a cheetah," he snarled, and stepped closer. He'd teach this fuzzy thing not to be so . . . *weird*. "I'm the fastest thing in Bravelands."

"Well, there'd obviously be no point in running, then," chuckled the honey badger. "Would there?"

Stride came even closer. Where was the best place to bite this creature? The neck was strangely long, the fur very coarse. . . .

Then in a smooth whipping motion, the honey badger turned on him, hissing like an angry snake and opening its seemingly small mouth to reveal rows of small, sharp teeth.

Stride recoiled quickly.

Those are not the jaws of a grass-eater. . . .

The honey badger held up one paw. It had five long, jagged, lethal-looking claws. "I'll slit you, neck to navel, before you can blink."

Stride hesitated. His head was spinning. Was this really happening?

"Bigger and nastier flesh-eaters than you have pushed me, Cat, and regretted it," the honey badger said, and all the casual jokiness had gone from his voice, leaving just the gruffness and the absolute confidence behind.

Stride backed away. "You look like you'd taste of dung anyway," he muttered and then danced a few steps away in case that was enough to provoke this strange, angry little creature.

"Goodbye, then," said the honey badger, and settled in to chewing on its root, as if nothing had happened.

When he got back to the rock, Flicker was doing a really good job of pretending not to find anything funny.

"How'd it go?" she asked.

". . . not hungry," Stride said.

Flicker's muzzle twitched. "If only there was some way you could have known . . . ," she sniggered.

"Yes, all right," Stride said, and tried to laugh along with her. "Are they really *all* like that?"

"That's what I heard. I've never faced one myself, but I've heard stories that would persuade me not to. . . . *Oh!*"

Her face had suddenly turned serious, her ears pricking up, her nose twitching. Stride knew that expression. He turned to face the same way, and sure enough, a dusk breeze was passing through, carrying a scent he knew.

"Springbok," he whispered.

"Come on." Flicker slinked down from the rock into the grass, and Stride joined her. Side by side, moving through the plain like crocodiles barely disturbing the surface of the water, they crept toward the source of the scent. Around a pile of rocks and thick spiky plants, they saw it. A herd of springbok, partially camouflaged against the dry grass and sandy rocks— though they couldn't hide their delicious, meaty scent. Stride scanned the herd, looking for weakness, for any springbok that was moving slower than the rest, or better yet, already injured. . . .

"That one," Flicker whispered, and a moment later, Stride

saw what she'd seen. One of the deer was standing on the edge of the herd, a piece of grass dangling from its mouth, staring out with a vague, distant look in its eyes. Its hide looked a little rough, and it had gray hairs around its muzzle. But meat was meat.

Stride's muscles quivered as they crept closer and closer, tensed and ready for the moment—

One of the springbok raised its head, and the others followed. That was their signal. Stride and Flicker both soared into a run, right at the elderly springbok, while the rest of the herd scattered.

The old deer wasn't completely doomed yet, either—it reacted slower, but once the herd's collective panic took over it too turned and broke into a run that would have left other predators standing. Before Stride got within five paces, it took a leap over a high rock, pushing off with its hooves and turning in midair, making the two cheetahs skid and scramble in the dirt to keep up with its sudden change of direction.

But then they were on flatter ground, and the harder the springbok tried to lose them, the farther it strayed from the rest of its herd. Stride felt the shadows around him lengthening and shimmering as he flew across the ground, and when Flicker snapped at the springbok's heels and steered it toward him, he took his chance, pushing his paws to go *faster*, until the final leap that bowled the deer over onto the ground with Stride's teeth buried in its side.

He knew better than to let go yet, and sure enough, even though it was old and wild-eyed with exhaustion, the springbok tried to get up. Stride clawed his way to its neck, bit down as hard as he could, and shook his whole body. The springbok was yanked up and down, its neck snapped, and it lay still.

"Whew!" Stride gasped. He licked his lips, tasting the blood of the springbok on his tongue, and looked around for Flicker.

She wasn't there.

"Flicker?" he called out. For a moment, there was no answer. Then he heard a weak gasping from a little way back, and with that to guide him he could see the shape of a spotted cheetah lying sprawled in the grass, maybe twenty strides back the way they had come.

His heart in his mouth, Stride shouted, "Flicker! Hold on, I'm coming!" And he sank his teeth into the springbok once more and dragged it over to her, gripped by the throat.

Flicker was alive and conscious, but she was panting desperately, as if in a panic. Stride realized she was crouched on the ground, not sprawled—her claws were digging into the earth as if she was afraid she would fall off.

"What's wrong?" Stride gasped. "What happened?"

"I'm all right," Flicker said. "It happened again . . . it . . ." She tried to stand up and managed to pull herself to her haunches, her legs shaking. "It's just something that happens sometimes. Everything goes gray, and the shadows . . ."

"The shadows hurt when you look at them," said Stride.

"Yes," whispered Flicker. "And then if I don't slow down in time, everything goes black and I pass out."

Stride's heart thumped, and he nudged the springbok in front of Flicker. "You should eat something. That's what makes me feel better, when I've been . . . when that happens to me."

"You too?" Flicker said, looking up at him for a moment with large, glistening eyes, before falling on the springbok hungrily. "I didn't know it happened to anyone else."

"I've never passed out," Stride admitted. "But the rest, yes. Does it . . . does it feel like something is . . . chasing you?"

"Yes!" Flicker said.

Stride nodded. An eerie chill passed over his neck, and his fur stood on end.

"That's the story I heard," he said. "That when a cheetah runs too fast . . ."

Suddenly he didn't want to say what he'd heard. It felt too real, in this moment. As if anyone—anything—could be right here with them, listening in.

"Eat up," he said. "There's plenty for both of us, but you have to get your strength back."

Flicker gave him a grateful blink, and Stride tried to focus on the delicious scent of their prey and the fact that she was fine. Apparently, she had escaped the hunter even though she had collapsed before she caught anything.

Apparently today, a cheetah had raced Death, and the cheetah won. . . .

CHAPTER TWENTY

The oxpeckers were singing, but it wasn't the usual soft chatter of a flock greeting a new day. The little birds of the herd had begun to make their frenzied racket as soon as Whisper had returned alone, and it had only slightly died down overnight. Now they were cheeping at each other in tones that sounded like anger and distress, and hopping from buffalo to buffalo in flocks of four or five, barely settling enough to eat.

Whisper watched them, wretchedly, as they landed on Quake, walked up and down his head, making him snort and complain, and then flew off again. She didn't blame them. She didn't know what to do with herself either.

The day seemed dark to Whisper, even with the glare of the sun rising over the distant treetops. When she had finally returned from the cliffs, she had told Thunder what happened to Echo, and then she had simply lain down in the shade of a tree and hadn't moved since. It seemed right.

Someone had brought her a mouthful of grass while she was asleep. She had woken, seen it, thought, *Like they would have done for Echo*, and been so blinded by the wave of grief that she'd had to squeeze her eyes shut and lay her head on the ground for a long time.

At some point, she had become aware that buffalo had been tramping up and down the cliff, searching for Echo— or perhaps just going to the place where he died, for reasons Whisper couldn't understand. He wasn't there. His empty body was in the river, but Echo was gone.

Murmur came to sit beside her. She said a lot of things that Whisper didn't really hear, but there was one thing she said several times, as the sun crawled up into the sky. Something that broke through the invisible fog that had settled over Whisper, like flashes of distant lightning.

"It's not your fault, Whisper, you couldn't have stopped this. It was just a terrible accident."

Just a terrible accident. An accident.

Whisper let Murmur settle down beside her and rested her head against her friend's shoulder. She didn't say anything aloud, but she was glad of Murmur's presence as her mind spun and wheeled like a seed on the wind.

Something isn't right about what happened. It's not my fault. It's someone else's.

Her thoughts kept on returning to the escort.

Five big buffalo, protecting one small calf. They had failed. Sure, they killed one hyena, but after that they'd just . . . *stood there*. They didn't follow Echo and the rest of the hyena clan. They told Whisper he'd run off, as if anything that happened to him now was fate, a forgone conclusion, his own fault.

Either the escort had happened to be five of the stupidest, laziest buffalo ever, or, or . . .

. . . They let him go.

So Whisper had to ask herself, did someone want her little brother dead? The answer came back horribly fast: yes, of course they did. He'd been chosen to lead the herd. Half the males had been passed over when the oxpeckers picked him.

And there was one male who had the backing of most of the others, who had *assumed* that leadership would fall to him, who had even seemed to threaten Echo before. She had heard Quake and the others discussing it, in the hollow.

If Holler had my brother killed, I . . .

She couldn't finish that thought. She didn't know what she would do.

A shadow fell over her and Murmur, and she looked up. Quake was standing, watching. She felt her nostrils flare and fixed him with a stare that she felt ought to have set his hair on fire, or at least made him turn around and walk away. Instead, Quake tossed his head and let out a derisive-sounding snort.

"I'm sorry about your brother," he said. "But we all have something to learn from this. The Great Spirit made things right, in the end."

"*Right?*" Whisper rasped.

"We were too quick to believe the oxpeckers, even though it was clear they were wrong. Echo couldn't even defend himself against a couple of hyenas—he could never have led the migration."

"Quake!" said Murmur, looking shocked.

"I'm just saying what everyone's thinking."

"Well, don't!" Murmur snapped. "For the Spirit's sake, Quake, she's just lost her little brother. Do you think she cares what people are saying? Go away!"

"A proper successor," Quake said under his breath, but not so quietly that Whisper couldn't hear him clear as day. "A successful migration. That's what's important."

Murmur's eyes flashed, and Quake turned and walked away before she could leap up. Murmur blew out a snort and hung her head.

"Ignore him," she said.

Part of Whisper warmed at the sight of Murmur, steaming over Quake's insulting lack of tact. A few days ago, if things were less awful, Murmur might have taken his side.

But a bigger, angrier part of Whisper was stirring. Quake hadn't just been tactless. Quake knew what he was saying. Even if he wasn't personally involved, Quake had come to tell Whisper that he knew what she knew, and he didn't care.

"I have to see Bellow," Whisper said, getting to her hooves. "Thank you, Murmur. I have to see him."

"All right," Murmur said, a little surprised. "I don't know where he is right now, but Mother usually does, she's still over by the cliff."

Whisper nodded and trotted away, before Murmur could volunteer to come with her. She wanted to have this conversation with Bellow alone.

She looked for him first, in case she could avoid the females and the cliff altogether, but the old leader—the current leader, again, now—was nowhere to be seen. A thrill of alarm passed through Whisper. Had he even returned from wherever he'd been waiting for Echo? Had anyone told him?

Had something happened to him?

Thunder, Clatter, and some others were loitering near the cliff, not quite close enough to look down over the edge, but close enough that they couldn't stop glancing toward it. They were shifting their hooves and talking in low voices.

"Thunder," Whisper said, "I need to speak to Bellow. Where is he?"

"I'm not sure," said Thunder. "I haven't seen him since we went to tell him Echo . . . wasn't coming."

So he does know.

"I need to speak with him," Whisper said again.

"Whisper," said Clatter, in an exaggeratedly kindly voice that grated in Whisper's head, "I know that you've suffered an awful loss, but Bellow must be very busy. . . ."

"Thunder," Whisper said, ignoring the other grown-up female, "I really mean it. It's important. It's about what happened."

"He knows all about what happened," said Thunder, in a much more sincerely kind tone.

"But it's . . . I've got . . ." Whisper hesitated. She wanted to keep her suspicions to herself. It would only make things more complicated if her worries spread before she could speak to Bellow himself. But then, Bellow wasn't here, and if she didn't say something, she was afraid that time would roll on without her being able to say anything at all. "I think someone wanted Echo gone," she said in a rush.

"Oh, Whisper," said Clatter.

Whisper took a deep breath and plunged in. "Don't you think it's strange? That half a clan of hyenas could slip by five of our toughest males? Don't you think if Echo was going to be killed by predators, it would've been any time in his life other than *now*, right before the ceremony, when he was supposed to be being guarded, when he was about to take the role that a lot of other males wanted? Doesn't it bother you that Holler basically threatened him right after he was chosen . . . ?"

"Enough," Thunder snapped.

"But Thunder . . ."

"*Enough, Whisper*," said Thunder, putting her head to Whisper's. The gesture was comforting, but intimidating too. Thunder was so very much larger than she was. "You've been through a lot, and I don't blame you for searching for answers, especially since *there are none*. But I beg you to hold your tongue before you offend someone."

For a moment, Thunder held still, her horns encompassing Whisper's entirely. Then Whisper nodded.

Thunder was right—whether she was protecting Whisper, or Holler, Whisper wasn't sure, but she was still right. Whisper should have trusted her instincts. She *had* to talk to Bellow.

The herd leader couldn't have gone very far with his injury. Whisper was about to set out to find him, determined that nothing else would stop her until she did, but then she was stopped in her tracks by a loud voice calling over the herd.

"Buffalo, to me!"

It was Holler. Whisper bristled at once. She didn't like the commanding tone of voice, and she liked it even less when most of the buffalo turned to gather around him without hesitation. She went too, pushing her way through the crowd so that she'd be able to see him when he said whatever he was about to say. As she wiggled through a small gap, she looked around for Echo. Where was he? She had to make sure he was with her, or . . .

Oh.

Whisper's breath caught in her throat, and for a moment she was frozen to the spot, overwhelmed with the absence of her brother.

The other buffalo jostled her and then looked down and muttered, "Sorry."

"My friends," Holler said loudly. His voice cut through Whisper's grief. She sniffed and pushed herself forward. "A grim morning dawns. We have lost one of our own. A calf. And not just any calf—our chosen leader, beloved of the Great Spirit." He closed his eyes and dipped his head solemnly. "But our mourning must not keep us from our duty. The migration must take place. A new leader must be chosen, and quickly, or all will be lost."

Whisper found herself nodding, not because she agreed, but because everything he was saying was exactly what she would expect him to say.

I, Holler, will shoulder this terrible burden. . . .

"I know I was not chosen," Holler said, which was a little humbler than Whisper had expected. "But what the herd
needs now is a strong leader to get us through the migration,
perhaps not as the Great Spirit's chosen, but as my poor ail-
ing brother's representative. I hereby volunteer to take on this
difficult task."

There it is.

Whisper stared into Holler's face, searching for some clue.
Had he killed Echo for this? Or was he just taking advantage
of a terrible accident?

He didn't meet her eyes, but looked around at the rest of
the herd, who were all starting to murmur their agreement—
some reluctantly, some a lot more cheerfully.

Except for one voice that spoke out in a low, firm tone.

"No."

Whisper looked around to see Bellow, at last, limping
slowly through the crowd. Her eyes narrowed as she glanced
back at Holler. Had he made sure his brother was far away
before he proposed his plan to the others? She had no evi-
dence for that guess, other than . . . well, who would begin a
herd meeting without their leader?

"Bellow," said Holler softly. "I know it's irregular, but what
choice do we have? We must leave, and soon! If you would
teach me the secrets of the migration, then when we get
back . . ."

"No," said Bellow again. "Dear brother, I know that you

want only the best for the herd, and for all of Bravelands. But Echo's death was a tragedy, and I am deeply troubled by it."

He looked at Whisper, who startled.

"I am so very sorry," Bellow said to her.

Whisper couldn't speak, but she nodded.

"But more, I am troubled by the death of the Great Spirit's chosen. I do not believe the herd can simply leave now, without seeking the Great Mother's guidance."

"There's no time," Holler said. "If we delay, and the rains come late, or not at all . . ."

"I am still your leader," said Bellow calmly. "And I say, we are not there yet. There is time to seek the Great Mother's advice. She is a reasonable elephant, is she not? If she chooses a new leader to take over, just for the migration, as you suggest, then that is what we will do."

Holler took a deep breath and bowed. "I understand," he said. "But we must go at once." He lowered his voice, so that Whisper couldn't quite tell if he meant the herd to hear him or not. "If the rains do not come, creatures will die. How many deaths are an acceptable price, to satisfy our *curiosity*?"

Bellow regarded his brother steadily, lowering his voice to match his. "This is Bravelands," he said. "Death lurks behind every rock and tree. I am a buffalo who cannot follow the migration, Holler. Do not speak to me of the inevitability of death."

Whisper shivered.

"The Great Mother will know what to do," said Thunder

in a loud and firm voice, breaking the tension between the brothers. "But Bellow, you are too weak to leave the safety of the herd."

Certainty welled up in Whisper's heart like a watering hole flooding after a long rain.

"I'll go!" she said. "He was my brother. I would like to go," she added, belatedly offering a respectful bow in Bellow's direction.

"Another calf?" Holler muttered.

"This calf is wise beyond her years," said Bellow. His eyes glinted as he met Whisper's. "And she's right. Echo was her brother, and it is right that she should seek answers on his behalf. But Holler is right, too, young Whisper—you cannot go alone. You will need companions on your journey."

"Can I go?" said Murmur, looking up at Thunder. "I want to go with Whisper."

"I don't know," said Thunder, suddenly nervous. "Perhaps a grown buffalo . . ."

"A grown buffalo can come with us too, right?" Murmur said. She stepped up to stand beside Whisper, and Whisper leaned against her for a moment, grateful for her friend.

There was a snort over beside Holler, and then Quake stepped forward. Whisper caught a movement from his father, as if Holler had given him a nudge.

"I will take them to the Great Mother," he said. "I will be their protector."

Whisper's breath caught. She didn't want Quake with them, not after what he'd said about Echo. But Murmur's expression had gone all longing again, even though she'd told him off before, and Thunder and Bellow were both nodding approvingly.

Well, whatever he thinks, she told herself, *the Great Mother will know what to do. And I guess it'll be satisfying to see her tell Quake his father can't be leader, right to his face. . . .*

"This is such a waste of time."

Traveling with Quake was somehow even worse than Whisper had imagined. She thought he was going to be dismissive about Echo and throw his weight around about "protecting" her and Murmur, even though he was only a year older than them. She hadn't realized he would complain the whole way too.

"What is she going to do? Send another vulture to not do anything?" Quake rumbled on. "It just sat there and let the oxpeckers choose last time. I don't see why we couldn't have picked a new leader by ourselves."

"You didn't have to come," Whisper said through gritted teeth, for the fourth time since they had left the herd.

They were mostly sticking to well-worn migration paths—Thunder had told them that the risk that they would be watched by predators was balanced by how much faster they'd be able to travel. They had passed by herds of impala and dik-dik, who had dodged respectfully out of their way. At one point they scented lions nearby, and Whisper briefly felt her heart leap into her throat and regretted that she hadn't insisted on a half-herd of adults to escort them on their journey—but the lions kept their distance.

"Somebody with some sense had to come on this fool's errand," Quake retorted as they trudged across a very wide, but shallow and muddy, riverbed. "You two are clearly much too trusting of this Great Mother character. Why do we bother listening to what she says at all? We're buffalo! Nobody tells us what to do."

Whisper and Murmur exchanged wide-eyed glances. Had he really said that?

"B-because . . ." Murmur cleared her throat. "Because the Great Parent maintains the harmony in Bravelands. She's the one who knows what to do when things go wrong."

"Harmony, really?" Quake rolled his eyes, and Whisper briefly fantasized about headbutting him into the mud. "Solving squabbles between monkeys and meerkats, while we're running from our lives from lions and hyenas all the time. Why doesn't she just drive them all out? Things would be a lot more harmonious then."

Murmur looked at Whisper, a pleading look that said, *Please, can you answer this time?* Whisper blew out a sigh through her nostrils.

"The Great Mother is guided by the Great Spirit," she said. "The Great Parent can . . . *do things* that other creatures can't. The Great Spirit has been in Bravelands since the first animals came here, and it has always helped us when we needed it! I suppose you don't believe the stories," she added, anticipating Quake's scorn.

"What? Great Father Thorn and his battle against the

heart-eater? The Great Mother who turned into a shadow and flew away? You really are still a calf," Quake said.

Whisper stared down at her hooves for a few steps, trying to focus on the squishing sound as they pulled up out of the mud and then splatted back down.

"You're so grown-up," she muttered. "Did any of the males in Echo's escort tell you what happened?"

Quake hesitated. "Didn't speak to them," he sniffed at last. "Why?"

"Because five big strong adult males couldn't protect one little calf. And they must have included you if they talked about it, what with you being a *real* adult who doesn't believe in *calf* stories."

"It's not their fault Echo bolted at the first sign of hyenas instead of staying where he was told," Quake grumbled.

"I think we're nearly there," said Murmur in a fake-bright voice, before Whisper could say anything to Quake. She broke into a trot and approached something on the bank of the shallow river that had looked to Whisper like a heap of mud, until it opened one eye and lifted its bulbous head.

"Hmm?" said the hippo. "What's this? Who's here?"

"Hello," said Murmur. "We're on our way to see the Great Mother. Are we going the right way?"

"Oh yes," said the hippo, with a yawn that showed off his enormous teeth. Whisper took a respectful step backward. The hippo had no reason to trap them between those massive tusklike fangs, and she intended to keep it that way. They were unpredictable animals, prone to fits of temper. "She'll be at the dead tree clearing near the edge of the forest. Just over this rise, past the black river ravine. Look for the stumps. If you find yourself deep in the forest and being shrieked at by baboons, you've gone too far."

"Um . . . thanks," Whisper said.

They climbed the bank and found themselves looking at the ridge the hippo had mentioned: a long, shallow rise in the ground, beyond which they could already just about see the faint dark smudge of treetops. It was a long trudge to the top, but when they got there, Whisper found her breath catching in her throat. The land sloped gently away again, except for one part, close on their right, where it ended suddenly in jagged rocks and strange, leafless trees. Whisper wasn't sure what kind of trees they were, until the three buffalo passed closer to them and discovered that they were the dead, skeletal, burned remains of trees.

She risked a glance over the jagged edge of the cliff. The ravine floor below was glossy, pitch-black. Even with plants growing through cracks in the strange rock, and dirt and sand gathering around the edges, it was one of the biggest black rock rivers she had ever seen, snaking away along the bottom of the ravine to vanish into the rock wall somewhere beyond sight.

"Wow," said Murmur.

"It's just rocks," Quake said. "Come on, if you're so keen to talk to this elephant. We're almost there."

Murmur made a sad sound in the back of her throat and trotted after him. Whisper followed more slowly.

"Anyway," Quake said, as if he was carrying on a previous conversation, "don't you think it's weird that the Great Parent is an elephant so often? What's so special about them, with their giant ears and weird noses? You *hear* about other ones, like Thorn, but how often does any other creature get to be Great Parent?"

"Elephants live a long time," Whisper pointed out. "Is it lots of elephants, or is just a few elephants for a long time each?"

"And when was the Great Parent last a buffalo, eh? Tell me that!" Quake said. "You can't, can you? A buffalo Great Parent would come with hundreds of loyal followers, *and* they'd be able to make sure the rains came all by themselves. It would make *much* more sense to have a buffalo Great Father."

"Or a Great Mother," Murmur said.

Quake just made an obnoxious snorting noise.

Whisper sighed with relief when they approached the trees and she spotted the broken tree stumps. Some of the tree trunks were lying on the ground nearby, half-disguised by brush and weeds. Others were simply gone.

It felt like an ominous way to enter the presence of the Great Mother, until Whisper stepped through the gap between the trunks and found herself in a long, dim tunnel of trees. It was still green here, even at the end of the dry season, and Whisper realized that it didn't feel scary at all, just . . . impressive. Many trees on both sides had broken-off branches, raising the height of the passage, and some of them seemed to have gotten the idea and stopped growing branches there at all. Some tree trunks had what Whisper briefly thought were claw-marks across their middles, but the big cat that made them would have to be . . . well, the size of an elephant.

Tusks, she thought, slightly awed. *Their tusks scrape across the trunks of the trees. . . .*

She had seen elephants before, plenty of times. Sometimes even up close. She knew how big they were. But it was different out on the plains, where there was plenty of space for everyone. Suddenly, standing in this tunnel they had carved out for themselves, Whisper felt extremely small.

"Come on," she whispered, steeling herself to walk down the long passage into the forest. At the end of the tunnel, she could just make out a bright space, maybe a clearing, where the forest was open to the sky.

But they hadn't gone more than halfway down the path before the ground beneath Whisper's hooves began to shake. The three buffalo all stopped and drew closer together—even Quake, who tossed his horns and muttered something about not being frightened. The rumbling earth was not the same as the passing of the buffalo herd, or a stampede—it was fewer, heavier hoofsteps than that.

The elephant ducked under a branch and stood, staring, yellow tusks swinging around to face them—and also to block their way. Whisper gasped as one, two, *three* more full-grown elephants stepped into the tunnel, their massive bodies completely obscuring the light from the clearing.

No, it was five elephants, altogether—one of them had a calf, a little bigger than Whisper, hiding behind one of her huge front legs.

"Greetings, friends," said the first elephant, her eyes glinting. "What is your business with the Great Mother?"

Despite the calf, and the elephant's cool and polite greeting, it took a moment for any of the buffalo to speak. Quake stepped forward, and Whisper could see his sides rising and falling, as if he was gasping for breath, or trying to make himself look bigger than he was.

"We . . . w-we . . . ," he began, and then cleared his throat and fell silent.

Whisper stepped in front of him, even though that put her in easy swinging reach of the elephant's tusks.

"We come from the buffalo herd," she said. "We were sent by our leader, Bellow, to seek Great Mother Starlight's help."

CHAPTER TWENTY-ONE

"That's a lot of buffalo," said Skullcracker. Her jaw was still swollen from the lion battle, but her voice was back to normal.

The four hyenas were peering through the dry leaves of a bush, just out of scent-range of the buffalo herd: Tailgrabber, Skullcracker, Hidetearer, and Nosebiter. It was, indeed, a lot of buffalo. Their big hairy bodies covered the plain almost as far as Tailgrabber could see.

"How in the name of the Devourer are we supposed to tell which one of those is the one called Holler?" Skullcracker went on.

"The other buffalo said he was the biggest," said Nosebiter. "And he had a twisted horn."

"Nosebiter, they've *all* got twisted horns," Skullcracker complained.

She did have a point, Tailgrabber thought. From here she

could see several that could plausibly be the biggest and have the curliest horns. The range wasn't exactly huge; they were all roughly buffalo-sized.

But something told her that going up to any old buffalo and talking about the dead calf and the deal they'd made would be a very bad plan.

"He's expecting us," Nosebiter said. "He'll be here. We just have to wait until we think we see him, and . . . hope we're right."

Hidetearer let out a nervous cackle, and all four of them settled in to wait and watch. Tailgrabber tried to keep track every time she saw a new largest buffalo, but she kept finding her mind wandering, her eyes drawn to the smaller ones. The calves and the barely adults. Would the female she'd seen before be there? The one who had called out Echo's name as he'd fallen?

"Hey, I think that's him," hissed Nosebiter.

Tailgrabber followed her pointing nose, and she immediately saw the buffalo her sister meant. He *was* bigger than the rest, if only a little, and his horn didn't just curl around his head, it had a kink in it that turned the end back on itself.

Taking a deep breath, her ears swiveling back cautiously, Nosebiter padded silently out of the shadow of the bush. She didn't go far, simply sat there, exposed, watching.

Sure enough, the big buffalo eventually looked around and saw her, but it didn't cry out to alert its herd—instead he tossed his head and began to walk away from the others. The hyenas watched intently, until the buffalo reached a copse of umbrella thorns and vanished from sight.

"Come on," whispered Nosebiter, and the four of them slunk across the plain toward the copse, casting glances over at the rest of the herd as they tried to keep to shadows and long grasses.

At last, the umbrella thorns were between them and the herd, and the hyenas were alone in a shaded space with Holler. He was facing away from them, but there was no way he couldn't hear or smell them, and he didn't turn when they approached.

The buffalo who'd come to the clan had seemed large to Tailgrabber, but up close this one was something else. His horns were long and sharp, the twist in them probably only making them more deadly, and his long, matted hair hid a body that could crush bones without breaking his stride.

"Gutripper sent us," said Skullcracker. There was a nervous growl in her voice, which Tailgrabber wasn't sure was wise. "You are Holler, I presume."

The buffalo grunted but still didn't turn around.

"We're here to talk about our deal," said Hidetearer. "We did our part. Now it's up to you. Crush Noblepride, and we'll be even."

"Yes, the deal," said the buffalo, almost under his breath. "I think you should turn around and go back where you came from."

Tailgrabber and Nosebiter looked at each other.

What was he saying? That he would handle it? Or that he would *not*?

It's a grass-eater, Tailgrabber told herself. *A big one, but still a grass-eater. They follow the Great Spirit. They don't even kill to survive. He can't be saying what I think he's saying. . . .*

Skullcracker cleared her throat. "What do you mean?" she said. "We . . . need confirmation. For Gutripper. We fulfilled our side of the deal—we killed the calf. . . ."

"No," said Holler. "You did not."

"We *did*," gasped Hidetearer. "He's dead! And we lost one of our own doing it."

"The *river* killed him," Holler said. "*You* were supposed to do it. I was very specific. *That* was the deal."

"Well, what's the difference?" Hidetearer snapped, her voice rising in annoyance.

"I thought you wouldn't understand," sighed Holler. "I could have pushed the little brat off a cliff myself, without all this trouble."

All of a sudden, the buffalo swung around, making the hyenas jump back in alarm. Tailgrabber swallowed a yelp, her throat constricting painfully. His eyes were fixed on hers, and her paws were rooted to the spot.

"Interesting that *you* would come here, asking for my help," he rumbled.

"What?" whispered Nosebiter.

Tailgrabber couldn't move. She was pinned by the buffalo's dark gaze, and no more than a toss of the head from being impaled on its terrible horns.

What does he know? she thought desperately. *And how does he know it?*

She couldn't speak. She could barely hold down her last meal. But she didn't need to make a sound, because the others were staring between her and the huge buffalo with suspicion written clearly on their faces.

"What do you mean?" said Hidetearer.

"*This one* is the reason you were interrupted before you could kill the calf," said Holler. "She alerted the sister. The sister saw her, she was on edge, so she got to you before you could finish the job. She betrayed you all."

"No," Tailgrabber gasped, desperate and grateful all at once. *Thank the Devourer. He doesn't know!* "That was a mistake!" She risked looking away from the buffalo's hypnotic eyes to look first at Nosebiter, then the other two. "You left me behind, and I wanted to know where you were going, so I followed, and—yes, one of the buffalo spotted me, and she raised the alarm, but it was just me, so they didn't do anything. It's not my fault."

"That's right," said Nosebiter, though her voice sounded less certain than Tailgrabber would like. "Tailgrabber's not a traitor, she's a hero. She finished the calf off when the sister drove the rest of us away."

"Is *that* what she did?" said Holler, and Tailgrabber's heart sank into the bottom of her pawpads. "Because I heard she tried to *save* the calf. He was about to go over all by himself, and this one tried to stop it."

Nosebiter stared at Tailgrabber in confusion, but Skullcracker and Hidetearer began to growl, turning on her. Tailgrabber opened her mouth to deny it, but she choked.

Bright, awful lights came into the other hyenas' eyes. Even Nosebiter's expression turned cold.

"That is a matter for your own herd," said Holler, before the hyenas could turn to violence. "But the fact remains, you *did not* kill the calf. One of you almost ruined my plans completely. So our deal is off. You can deal with your lion problem yourselves. I wish you luck with that."

"*What?*" snarled Skullcracker, wheeling around to face the enormous buffalo. "You can't do that!"

Holler swung his head and snorted hot air into her face. She yelped and backed off, but she didn't stop growling.

"You haven't heard the end of this. Nobody betrays Gutripper. *Nobody*," she added, her lip curling toward Tailgrabber.

"Leave!" shouted the buffalo, and stomped forward. Tailgrabber scrambled away, tumbling in her haste, as if a great paw had grabbed her by the scruff and thrown her. The others were falling over their paws to get away too, yelping and giggling in panic. "I fear a hyena like I fear an ant!" Holler roared. "I can crush either one just as easily!"

"Go!" Nosebiter said, and all four hyenas broke into a run, shooting out of the shade of the thorns and into the tall grass. Tailgrabber ran with them, guilt pounding in her ears along with her racing heart.

This is my fault, she thought. *Just like the lion attack. This is all my fault.*

The hyenas skidded to a halt when they reached the relative safety of the trees where they'd watched the herd before, Nosebiter and Hidetearer colliding in a pile of fur. Hidetearer nipped at Nosebiter's ear out of pure adrenaline and then collapsed with a gasp.

"Tailgrabber," Skullcracker snarled.

"I know," Tailgrabber panted. "I'm sorry—I didn't mean—I was thinking about the cubs and saw the calf and I thought . . ." She hung her head. "I wasn't thinking."

Skullcracker sighed. "I should have known. Tailgrabber, hero of the clan? What a joke." But when Tailgrabber risked a glance up, the murderous light was gone from her eyes. Against all odds, Holler's betrayal might have saved Tailgrabber's life.

"Let's go back," said Nosebiter. "We need to tell Mother what happened. Everything that happened."

Tailgrabber tried to give Nosebiter a grateful look, but her sister wouldn't meet her gaze.

"Oh yes," said Skullcracker. "Gutripper's going to hear all about this. There will be a reckoning."

CHAPTER TWENTY-TWO

It's not perfect, Stride thought, looking out over his territory, *but it will do.*

The grass was long enough, with enough trees, casting enough shade. There was a rock heap, not as big or green as a kopje, but a place he could sit and see for some distance. The river that trickled across the plain was sluggish and muddy, but it was drinkable, and when the rains came it would flow as well as any other. There were some crocodiles living in it, but not so many that the prey avoided it. They had seen zebras, antelope, and kudu, but no other cheetahs and, most importantly, *no* lions.

Flicker had scented hyenas, but you couldn't have everything.

He hopped down from the rocks and wound around Flicker, his tail swishing. Flicker pressed the top of her head under his chin for a moment, and joy welled up in Stride, despite missing Fleet and running from Jinks, despite everything.

They set off to hunt together, their first official hunt on their new territory. They were heading for the riverbank, hoping that the kudu they'd seen yesterday were still lingering by the water, but as they were passing by a clump of bushes and thorns, something suddenly popped up into sight above the grass. It looked like the head of a bird, with a beak and beady eyes, but the neck was bizarrely long, and he just saw the shape of a bulbous-looking, black-feathered body. The bird-thing looked around, then the head vanished into the grass again.

"What on earth is *that*?" Stride mewed quietly. "It looks like a bird, but what's going on with that neck?"

"Oh, Stride. First honey badgers, now ostriches? You really didn't stray far from your first territory, did you?" chuckled Flicker. "It's a bird, all right. But they don't fly."

"Ostriches," Stride said, the unfamiliar name feeling strange in his mouth. "And they don't fly? I suppose it would be too heavy," said Stride. "But it's got wings! Are you sure?"

Flicker tilted her head. "Well, I've never seen one fly, only run," she said. "And not that fast—well, fast for a bird that can't fly, but not compared to us. My mother said they're so greedy, they'll even eat rocks. But you have to watch out for the claws, they kick like an angry zebra."

"So . . . it's huntable?"

"Oh yes. Tasty, too."

Stride gave Flicker a grin, already starting to drool. "Then let's go!"

Sneaking up on birds was always hard. They were jumpy, and what they seemed to lack in sense of smell, they usually made up for in eyesight and hearing. But together, watching the bobbing head and alert for each other's tiny signals—the twitch of an ear, a hesitation before placing a paw down—they got within a few cheetah-lengths of the ostrich without it spooking. Stride's mouth watered. Nothing but the wind could outrun a cheetah from this distance.

Finally the ostrich looked up, its black eyes widening in panic, and turned to flee, the cheetahs springing into pursuit. It was faster than Stride had expected, and now that he could see it running, he could understand what Flicker had said about its kicks. Instead of the short or spindly legs most birds had, its legs were long and muscular, and it had cleared several cheetah-lengths before Stride had found his rhythm.

Stride caught up to it quickly, but then he lost ground again, ducking to the side to avoid a desperate stomping from the ostrich, which flapped its useless wings as it hopped, jumped, and kicked out at Stride. Flicker came streaking up from the other side of it, growled, and leaped at the bird's throat, claws out, in a pounce that would have taken down a creature twice its size—except that the ostrich's neck turned boneless and flopped to one side. Flicker couldn't get a good grip, overshot, and ended up sprawled on the ground in front of Stride. He couldn't stop in time, so he leaped over her, trying to keep pace with the big stupid bird.

But Flicker's attack had made the ostrich dizzy, and it stumbled and lost speed. In a few more leaps Stride was on it, claws sinking deep into the thick feathers. It kicked and pecked at him, but it went down, and Stride finally got his teeth into its neck, biting down hard until it finally stopped writhing.

Flicker hurried up behind him, panting.

"Whoo," she breathed. "That was fun!"

"Mff!" said Stride, looking up with his jaws full of black feathers. Flicker laughed as he spat them out. "This thing's tough!"

"Tough but tasty," said Flicker, nosing in around the ostrich's legs and tearing off a strip of feathery skin.

They began to feast, laughing and joking over the feathers that kept sticking to Stride's nose. The scent of ostrich meat and the joy of Flicker's company filled Stride's world.

Until suddenly, there was another scent. An unwelcome stench of hot breath and fur and dried blood. Stride sat bolt upright and saw them at once, coming over the muddy stream.

Lions.

"Flicker," he warned, and Flicker looked around and saw them too. She yowled in anger and disappointment as they approached.

Stride wasn't sure if it was the same pride they'd encountered before, but if so, something had gone wrong for them in the time between. Most of them carried recent wounds or scars, and patchy or missing hair on sagging skin. They looked hungry and angry.

For a moment, once again, Flicker looked like she might try to fight them. Stride almost wondered if they could—but even in this state, there were too many.

"Come on," he sighed. Flicker backed away, reluctantly, growling, and they made their way back into the long grass they had chased the ostrich through.

But when Stride glanced over his shoulder, the lions hadn't fallen upon their prey. One lion was standing protectively over it, but the others—four of them—were still advancing on the cheetahs.

He nudged Flicker, and she looked around too, then let out an aggrieved huff and spun to face the lions.

"We're going," she spat. "You have our kill. What else do you want?"

"We want you off this territory," said one of the lions, a female with one mangled ear. "There's no room for cheetahs here."

"That's not true," Stride called back. "We didn't even scent you here before."

But his heart was already racing, and the tips of his paw pads tingling, even as Flicker said, "Right, this is our territory, not yours!"

The lions roared and charged.

"Run!" Stride gasped. There was something in their eyes that made him think that had been the wrong thing for Flicker to say. They seemed furious, beyond the natural anger of predators who thought they owned the whole world.

The two cheetahs turned and went into another sprint, through the long grass, over rocks, alongside the slowly flowing muddy river. Stride's muscles already ached a little from the chase with the ostrich, but he was sure they could still out-run the lions. The bigger cats would get tired, or bored, any moment now. . . .

Except then he pulled up short, the shock of the sudden stop vibrating up through his bones, as another lion lurched out of the undergrowth to his left. He cried out to Flicker, and a second later heard her do the same. Two lions were coming out from behind a big rock on her right.

It was an ambush.

Why?! Stride thought, but he saved his breath for putting on an extra burst of speed. *This isn't even their territory, all I could smell before was hyena. . . .*

The lion to his left swiped at him as he passed it, missing by a cheetah-length. In fact, it never had a hope of catching him with its claws, it was too far away . . . but perhaps it hadn't needed to. As Stride threw himself to the right, and Flicker went to the left, he saw even more lions ahead, closing in. The lions they had left behind were still coming.

If they make us stop, there's no hope for us. We have to keep going!

"There!" Flicker gasped out. "The rock!"

Stride saw it. The lions had parted around a jutting rock. There wasn't room for the two cheetahs to jump it side by side, but if they went one at a time, they might make it. . . .

"Go!" Flicker said. Stride wanted her to go first, to be safe—but he knew if he so much as paused to think about dis-agreeing, the lions could be on them. So instead he nodded and sped up, aiming for the rock. The lions were too close. He felt one of them catch the fur of his tail with their teeth, but apart from a prickling sensation as a clump of hair came free, he sailed over the jutting rock and landed back on flat, brown earth.

He didn't stop. He couldn't stop. Their only hope was to keep running. But he couldn't help looking back over his shoulder, even though it cost him balance and made him stub one paw on a rock and stumble. His heart gave a painful judder, remembering Fleet, knowing if he tripped now, it would be the end of his life. . . .

And there was no sign of Flicker.

A lion roared, and Stride's paws faltered.

Then a dark shape flew up and over the rock. Her eyes wide, pupils so huge her eyes looked black, Flicker soared through the air. She landed on paws that were already moving, barely seeming to touch the ground, and was past Stride in a flash of spots. Stride took a deep, relieved breath and followed her, though he could barely keep up even when he was almost flying across the plain. She was just a blur, running faster than Stride had ever seen.

The lions still gave chase, for a while. He could hear the scrambling and furious roars behind him. But now that they had escaped the ambush, the cheetahs finally outpaced them. At last, Stride was sure that they could stop, and he began to slow. His breath was rasping in his throat, his head pounding.

Ahead of him, Flicker was still soaring over the grass. He wanted to call out to her, but he couldn't gather the breath.

Then she looked back at him over her shoulder. Her ears

pinned back, her mouth open in terror and something like grief.

A trickle of dark blood spilled out of the corner of her eye.

Then she fell, hitting the ground, sliding, and rolling over in a spray of dust and grass.

"Flicker!" Stride screamed, pushing himself into a dash. He stumbled to a halt at her side.

She was breathing, but her eyes were filmed over with blood. It was coming out of her ears, too, and a pink foam collected at the corner of her mouth.

"Stride . . . ," she gasped. Her voice bubbled in her throat. "I saw it . . . I saw . . ."

"Get up," Stride said. "It's okay, Flicker. We got away. We . . ."

Stride nosed desperately at Flicker's side. If she could get up, if she could keep walking, maybe it wouldn't have caught her. She could get better. She could . . .

Flicker tried to lick her lips. She blinked and for a moment seemed to focus on him.

"My life . . . has run out," she whispered. "My future was with you. My future . . . was you." Then her eyes went wide and glassy again, and she seemed to be looking at something over Stride's shoulder. He saw, one last time, the look of defiance he had fallen in love with cross her face.

Then all the light left her bloodied eyes, her tongue lolled from her mouth, and Flicker died.

CHAPTER TWENTY-THREE

The sun had set, and the light in the clearing turned from the green of the afternoon to a soft pinkish glow, and finally to a silvery moonlight. Fireflies danced between the trees, in and out of the roots of tree stumps that had seemingly been torn from the earth and rolled aside to make more space. It was as if the stars themselves had come down to earth to be with the Great Mother. One of them landed on Whisper's nose and sat there, blinking softly, for a few moments, before Whisper's oxpecker grew a little too interested and it flew away.

Great Mother Starlight herself stood in the center of the clearing, her enormous trunk swaying gently before the three buffalo. Whisper looked up into her deep brown eyes and felt something stir in her heart. Starlight's presence was like a warm sunbeam on a chilly day.

"It is rare for a buffalo to seek my help," said Starlight. Her voice was low and rumbly, but gentle. "But I have some sense of why you have come. I sent a vulture to your herd not long ago, and when she returned she told me that the choice of leader was . . . controversial. Do you come to me to question the oxpeckers' choice?"

Whisper swallowed, her throat suddenly closing with grief. She tried to speak but could not seem to form words.

Murmur came to her rescue. "No, Great Mother," she said. "I'm afraid that Echo, the calf who was chosen, he . . . he died."

A look of alarm crossed Starlight's face, her large ears flapping. Whisper felt a chill under her hide: the smallest hint of anger or agitation from such a huge creature was terrifying, no matter how gently she spoke.

"The vultures did not tell me of this," the Great Mother said, her low voice louder in the quiet clearing. She looked up to a tree branch, where a vulture sat. It leaned down but made no noise.

"He . . ." Whisper cleared her throat. "They wouldn't have found . . . he was washed away in the Grandmother river. The hyenas pushed him in. His . . . his body might be lost for good."

Starlight turned her gaze on Whisper, and her ears sagged a little.

"I am so sorry," she said. She reached out her trunk and touched Whisper gently on the top of the head, just for a moment. "He was dear to you."

"He was my little brother," Whisper managed to say.

"Oh, my poor calf. It must have been hard on all of you," she added, looking at Murmur and Quake.

Whisper glanced at Quake too. His head was lowered, humbly, and Whisper wondered if coming into the presence of the Great Mother had changed his mind.

"I had a brother," Starlight said, and Whisper looked up at her again in surprise. "He was killed when we were young. Bravelands can be a cruel place. We walk in the presence of death every day, but that doesn't make it easier when we lose someone we love—or when the Code is broken."

Whisper took a deep breath. This was her chance. "We didn't come just because we need a new leader," she said. She could feel the others staring at her, but she hurried on before she could second-guess herself. "I heard that the vultures can taste when a death was natural, and when it went against the Code. I . . . I want to know if Echo died because the hyenas were hungry, or . . . or for another reason."

Quake made a noise in the back of his throat, like a snigger quickly masked with a cough. Whisper glared at him. Apparently he wasn't cowed by the presence of the Great Mother at all; he was just stifling his derision. Whisper wanted to stomp on his tail.

"It is true," said Starlight, seemingly ignoring Quake. "As I said, the vultures have not brought me any news yet, but I will send more birds, at once. They will find him, and if there was anything improper about his death, the whole herd will know it."

"Thank you," Whisper breathed.

"In the meantime, we did *actually* come about the leader," Quake said. "We need a strong leader to take us on migration.

The one the oxpeckers picked was a bad choice, and now he's gone. So now we need you to tell us who should lead, or tell us we should choose someone, or something."

The Great Mother's trunk swished impatiently for a moment, before she stilled it.

"It is not my place to choose a leader for the buffalo," she said. "But nor is it yours, young calf."

Quake visibly bristled at being called a calf, and Whisper tried to hide her smile.

"It is for the Great Spirit to decide. I am merely a vessel. The Spirit has told me nothing of your plight, so I cannot appoint a new leader for you."

"Well, this was a waste of time," said Quake. Whisper and Murmur both gasped at his open dismissal of the Great Mother. Starlight herself remained calm but looked down her trunk at him as he went on. "You're no leader. You probably can't even punish the hyenas who killed Echo, can you?"

"I guide," said Starlight, a chill in her voice. "I do not punish. And in any case, as I suspect you know, most hyenas do not follow the Great Spirit. They have their own ways. The Great Devourer is a spirit of the earth, not the stars."

"So I was right," said Quake. "There's nothing you can do, and we shouldn't have come here."

"What should we tell Bellow and the others?" Whisper put in, willing Quake to shut up before the Great Mother really did lose her temper. "What should we do about the migration?"

The Great Mother took a deep breath. She looked to the

vulture in the tree again and then turned her face to the sky, letting the moonlight wash over her.

"I suggest the herd stay put, for now," she said. "The migration cannot wait, but it *must not* fail, and that is what will happen if it takes place under a leader who does not know how to lead it."

"But couldn't Bellow teach Hol— teach another buffalo the secrets, just for this year?" Murmur asked in a small voice. "We have to go. That's what my mother always taught me. Staying put means . . . death."

"He could teach another," said Starlight slowly. "And perhaps he will have to. But I do not know what would happen if the secrets were bestowed upon the *wrong* buffalo. No, tell Bellow not to do this, not yet. I do not like the news that the Great Spirit's chosen one—a young calf, with his whole life ahead of him—has been killed like this. I suggest you wait while I learn more of Echo's fate and what it means. I will send word as soon as I know anything. Be patient, my dear calves, and the Great Spirit will answer all questions in time."

With that, the other elephants appeared again, out of the darkness, and ushered the three buffalo away.

"*Be patient*," Quake sneered. "What a load of nonsense."

"Quake, by the Great Spirit, if you don't shut up . . . ," Whisper hissed back.

They had decided to travel straight home to the herd, even though that meant crossing the plains by night, with exhaustion creeping up on them. Whisper's knees ached, and she longed to lie down and sleep, but that would be madness now.

Their ears were pricked and their noses always sniffing for any sign of predators, as they tried to hurry without making too much noise in the dry grass. The nighttime sounds of Bravelands were loud in Whisper's ears, the hooting of owls and chittering of insects, and she was certain she had heard scrabbling in the undergrowth a little way back that sounded like something roughly lion-sized. But it hadn't attacked them.

They had been walking in tense silence, until Quake started to complain, yet again.

"Well, it is nonsense. What if it takes her too long to figure out that the hyenas were just trying to eat Echo, and all of Bravelands dies of thirst because the rains don't come? It's insane to risk that just because you're sad about your brother. You shouldn't have said anything."

Whisper's throat burned with anger, and she couldn't reply. How could he make this her fault?

"Hey, leave Whisper alone," Murmur muttered. "You heard the Great Mother—the wrong leader on a migration might be worse than no leader! We'll wait, like she told us."

"She didn't tell us anything," Quake said. "She was just covering for herself, because she doesn't know what to do either. We're buffalo! We can make our own destiny."

"That is ridiculous," said Whisper.

"We can't make rash decisions right now," Murmur said.

"Hmm," said Quake. But he didn't argue, and the three buffalo fell back into silence.

They trudged on through the night, under the stars, listening for danger and trying to ignore each other. Whisper began to shiver as the last of the searing heat of the day finally seeped out of the ground, and a cold mist began to rise up around them. The noises of birds and small mammals seemed to quiet, even as the stars began to fade and the sky took on a strange blank, gray hue.

It had to be almost dawn.

"This way," Quake said suddenly. "Over here. I know a shorter way back."

"Really?" asked Murmur. Her tone was bright and eager. Whisper followed the dim shape of her as she followed Quake.

"Yes, we came this way when I was with the male herd," he said. "Just over this ridge, there should be . . . yes, here it is."

Whisper hurried up to his side and looked down. In the predawn light, the land beyond looked strange, like pooled silver—but when her eyes adjusted, she realized it was a shallow dip in the ground. The earth here was barren, not a blade of grass or a reed in sight. It must have been a watering hole once, she thought.

"We met a rhino here," Quake said, stepping aside to let Murmur go first. She and Whisper made their way carefully down the slope, Whisper expecting to find either hard, cracking dirt at the bottom or maybe slick and slippery mud. "It had gone crazy, maybe from the heat, and it was convinced that it was a flamingo, and we were its flock!"

"What?" Murmur laughed.

"It's true, swear on my horns! It wanted us to stay forever.

In the end we tripped him up and he fell in the mud, and we ran away while he couldn't see us!"

"I don't believe you," Whisper chuckled. It was true, she didn't, but it was such a stupid story that she still felt it lighten her spirits a little. Maybe this was Quake trying to make peace.

She had walked onto the strange grayish earth now, and sure enough, her second guess was right, it was mud—it slipped a little under her hooves.

"Tell us another one," Murmur said. Whisper heard a challenge and a smile in her friend's voice.

"Well, there was this antelope . . . ," Quake began.

"Wait," Whisper said, at the same time that Murmur made a startled noise and she saw her friend's shape in the darkness start to shift backward and forward.

The ground under her hooves had sunk, in a way that mud would not. It was unsteady, and as she tried to pull her front hoof back out, her back hooves sank deeper. She dipped her head to it and blew out a frightened breath, and could just make out the grains of the earth skittering away from her.

This isn't mud. It's sand.

And not just any sand.

She looked over her shoulder and saw the shadow of Quake against the gray sky, standing behind them on the firm, grassy ground.

"Quake," Murmur gasped. "Help! I can't pick up my hooves!"

She was stomping and thrashing, churning the sand around her. It was already up to her stomach.

"Don't move so much!" Whisper gasped. "It's quicksand! Quake, please . . ." She looked back at Quake, but he was already backing away. "Quake, help!"

"How?" he said. He took a hesitant step forward again but came no closer. "I can't do anything—if I get in there, I'll get sucked down too! I'll get . . . I'll get help." He began to move away.

"Don't you leave us, Quake!" shouted Whisper. "Don't you dare."

She couldn't make out his expression in the shadows. "I can't do anything," he said breathily. "There's . . . there's nothing to be done."

And then he had turned. With another glance back, he hurried away.

Fury lit up Whisper's heart, but she forced herself to stay as still as she could. The sand was over her hooves, even though she'd barely moved.

"Quake, no!" howled Murmur. "Come back here! Come back!"

"Murmur," Whisper called out. The sand had reached Murmur's chin. "You've got to stop moving, please!"

Murmur stopped thrashing, but she was panting hard.

"He . . . ," she gasped.

"I know," said Whisper. "You have to stay calm. I'm going to get us out of here."

But how? said a treacherous voice from inside Whisper's heart. *I can't move. How can I pull Murmur out without dooming us both?*

She would find a way. She *would*.

She couldn't lose Murmur too.

"Whisper," said Murmur. "I'm scared."

"Me too," said Whisper, desperately looking around. There were no plants in reach she could somehow throw to Murmur, no trees she could try to knock down if she got herself out, no rocks, even. The whole bank of the quicksand pit was barren and bare. It struck her, even in her terror, that Quake had *chosen* this route. He knew this place from his time with the males. Did that mean . . .

"I can't believe he left us to die," Murmur whispered. There was a cold horror in her voice. Whisper shivered and sank a tiny bit lower in the sand. Quake was annoying, and mean, but was he capable of something as terrible as leading them deliberately to their deaths? And why?

"I'm going to get out and get help," Whisper said. It was the only way. "Don't move, okay? I'm going to get an elephant or something big, and they'll save you. Please, *please* don't move!"

She leaned her weight, experimentally, on one hoof. It immediately slid lower in the sand. She let out an involuntary scream and heard a rush of sand as Murmur jumped and struggled.

"No!" Whisper yelped. "Don't move, Murmur!"

Murmur let out a whimper but stopped moving.

I have to try something. I won't just lie down and die. . . .

Perhaps that was it. If she lay down, she might be able to roll herself over and scramble to the bank, without having to put her hard hooves down on the soft, sucking ground.

If it didn't work, she'd die in moments.

But she had to try.

She bent her knees and flopped down onto the sand on her side, her heart in her mouth. Immediately, she felt the ground almost crawling around her, trying to drag her down. She rolled and rolled again, until she could feel solid earth beneath her. Clambering gingerly up onto her knees, then her hooves, testing the muddy ground, she let out a small whimper of relief. Then she shook the sand out of her hide and spun around, desperately seeking something she could use to help Murmur. If she could throw enough rocks or branches, maybe she could fill up the sand and make a way for her to climb out . . . or maybe she would just disturb it and make it swallow her faster.

"I can't believe that worked," said Murmur, a slightly hysterical laugh in her voice.

"I'm going for help," Whisper said, but when she looked back, she realized that Murmur had sunk even deeper. She was panting for breath, her eyes wide.

There was no time. By the time she returned, Murmur would be gone. Horror made Whisper's hide prickle all down her back.

"I can't just . . . I don't want to die here," Murmur croaked. She shifted again and then let out a yelp as she listed to one side, the sand rising so much she had to raise her head to the sky. Her breathing was ragged and panicky now. "I can't . . ."

"Murmur, please," Whisper begged, pacing the bank. "Just hold on. . . ."

"I can't, I can't die like this, please, help me. . . ."

Whisper cantered up and down the bank, desperate to find some way to help. But she knew there was nothing she could do. Sand was flowing over Murmur's back.

"Whisper, find . . . find my mother, tell her . . ." Murmur gasped and coughed as sand went up her nose and she sank deeper with every convulsing cough. "Oh, Spirit, I don't want to die!"

Now she didn't even need to move to be swallowed by the sand. It seemed to rise around her ears of its own accord.

"No . . . ," Murmur sobbed. "No, pl . . ."

And then, all in a terrible rush, the sand filled Murmur's mouth, covered her eyes, and then all that was left were a pair of small horns, and then there was nothing but swirling sand.

CHAPTER TWENTY-FOUR

Tailgrabber sat with her back to the baobab tree, trying to pretend she was a rock, or a kind of brown-spotted bush. Around her, the males stalked back and forth, pretending not to stare— well, some of them pretended, others simply stared and turned to each other to exchange gossipy whispers that Tailgrabber was glad she couldn't hear.

A little group of them approached her, four males in a formation like a flock of geese, with one at the head and the others following behind, sniggering. The one in front giggled at her but didn't address her at first. He just looked at her and laughed. As if she was inherently funny. Tailgrabber's hackles rose, despite herself.

"You're in trouble," he finally sneered.

Tailgrabber didn't reply.

"Mother's little hero not so heroic after all?" said one of the smaller hyenas behind him.

"Yeah," said the one in front, taking a step closer. "Little Tailgrabber messed up, like she always does?"

He went for a nip at Tailgrabber's jaw, and Tailgrabber reared back and brought her front paw around, as hard as she could. She struck him hard on the side of the head, and the male went down in a cloud of loose fur. His companions all cackled with laughter.

"Go away, Cub," Tailgrabber spat.

"My name is Pawbiter," snarled the male, picking himself up, furious spittle flying from his mouth.

"Go away," Tailgrabber said again, squaring up to him. "*Cub.*"

She looked up at the others, fixing them with a stare that she hoped carried every last drop of the hatred she had been saving up in her heart for herself. The males yelped and scampered away, and their supposed leader followed them.

"Tailgrabber," said a voice, and Tailgrabber startled and turned on the hyena who'd crept up on her, before she realized it was Nosebiter. She sat back down, ears back and head drooping.

"What's happening? What did she say?" she asked.

"You should follow me," Nosebiter said.

Part of Tailgrabber wanted to run. But this was her family. Her clan.

Meekly, she got up and followed her sister around the baobab and across to the bank of the dry riverbed.

"Nosebiter," she said as they walked. Nosebiter didn't reply.

"I'm sorry," she said. "I was just . . . confused . . . I was just thinking about Cub. . . ."

She thought she saw Nosebiter's fur ruffle, as if she had shuddered a little. But that was all the reaction her sister gave.

As they approached the bank, and Tailgrabber looked down into the dip in the ground where the water once was, her heart gave a sharp lurch. Arrayed along the streambed were all the other female hyenas, Gutripper in the center, her favorites beside her. They all faced Tailgrabber, looking up with grim and angry expressions.

"Sit," said Nosebiter, tapping the ground at the top of the bank with her paw.

Tailgrabber sat down. She felt so strange up here alone, with the rest of her clan staring up at her in judgment. Almost every hyena she had known, loved, fought with—and against—was down there.

Gutripper stepped forward. She regarded Tailgrabber with a cool, assessing gaze. But she didn't say a word to her. Instead she turned to address the rest of the hyenas.

"We all know that in the attack on the buffalo calf, we lost one of our own. Legsnatcher was tough. She was faithful and loyal, and when the Great Devourer came for her, she died with honor. Which makes it all the more unacceptable that her sacrifice was for nothing."

Now Gutripper turned on Tailgrabber, who fought not to recoil under the white-hot glare of her mother's stare.

Legsnatcher's death had nothing to do with me, Tailgrabber thought desperately. *But that's not going to matter now.*

"You, Tailgrabber, stand accused of treason. You interfered with the mission, and your actions have put the survival of the clan at risk," Gutripper said. "Do you have anything to say for yourself? Why did you do what you did at the river?"

For a moment, Tailgrabber didn't know what to say. There was probably nothing she could say that would change her fate now.

And in realizing that, Tailgrabber felt herself stand a little taller, taking a deep breath. She felt some of her jangling nerves relax, just a little.

In that case, she thought. *I will tell the truth, and that will have to be enough.*

"I had a vision," she said.

Immediately, several hyenas below her grumbled. She saw Hidetearer and Skullcracker both rolling their eyes. Skullcracker sat down and began to clean between the pads of her paws with her teeth.

"I see things," Tailgrabber said. She took a deep breath and tried to speak clearly. Saying it aloud, in front of everyone, felt freeing and terrifying at the same time. "Insects and dead things show me strange visions, and sometimes they come true. They showed me Gutripper's victory over Eyescratcher when I was just a little cub."

A lot of the other hyenas still scoffed at this, but a few of them made gratifyingly thoughtful faces. Gutripper herself kept her expression blank.

It was true. Tailgrabber had seen her mother's bloody battle with the previous matriarch, old Eyescratcher. It had been terrifying, and she had told nobody but Nosebiter. . . .

"This time, I saw a vision of the clan walking into fog," Tailgrabber went on quickly. "I saw all of you sleepwalking across the plains and off the edge of a cliff. So when I saw hyenas walking off, and I hadn't been told what was happening, I followed them."

"Because you wanted to stop us walking off a cliff?" Nosebiter asked softly, a confused look on her face.

"Because you were jealous that you hadn't been included, more like," snarled Skullcracker. "You wanted to sabotage our mission so that you could step in and be the hero!"

"No! I—I don't know," Tailgrabber said, her confidence shaken. "I thought it might be dangerous, I was curious, and confused, and I thought . . ."

She looked down at her mother. How could she explain that she suspected Gutripper hadn't told her about the plan because it was a bad plan? Questioning her mother's decisions had never gotten her anywhere.

"I want what's best for the clan," she said quietly. "And I want what's best for Bravelands. That's all I've ever wanted."

Gutripper stared at her a moment longer and then turned to the others. "We will vote," she said. "Decide her fate. Now."

Skullcracker was the first to move. She turned her back on Tailgrabber, sitting down and facing the other way.

A long shiver ran up and down Tailgrabber's spine as one by one, in silence, the hyenas turned their backs on her.

Just like Cub. It's as if they've decided I'm already dead.

Gutripper kept her back turned. It stung, but it was not a

surprise. Nor was the fact that every other hyena followed her cue.

In the end, the only surprise was that Nosebiter did not turn. She looked up at Tailgrabber with her ears drooping, and a whine left her throat.

"Tailgrabber," she said.

Tailgrabber's heart swelled. It didn't matter—her fate was decided already. But her sister was on her side, and maybe that mattered more than the rest ever could.

"I . . . I wanted to believe so badly," Nosebiter said. "I thought you could stop this nonsense with the visions and just be a good clan-mate. But that didn't happen."

Tailgrabber's swelling heart felt as if it had turned to a sliver of ice and stabbed into her chest.

"Something is wrong, Tailgrabber. With you," Nosebiter went on. Tailgrabber frowned at her paws. She'd gotten the idea, her sister had made her point—why was she still going? "All this talk of visions, the Great Spirit, wanting the best for Bravelands . . . having sympathy for that buffalo cub. None of that matters, don't you see? The only thing that matters is survival. And if you don't understand that, you have no place here."

Tailgrabber didn't look up. She refused to give Nosebiter the satisfaction.

In the silence, she heard her sister's paws on the earth as she turned around.

"We survive," said Gutripper, and every other hyena echoed her.

"We survive."

Tailgrabber looked up and saw that Gutripper had turned to face her.

"This hyena is no longer one of us," she said. "She must leave the clan and the territory. She must never be seen here again, on pain of death. And to all hyenas, she will forever more have no name. She will be addressed as Cub."

Tailgrabber—Cub—didn't move for a moment. She felt as if she had been winded, thrown down in a bone-breaking slam—and then stung by a wasp, on top of it all. Banishment would change her life. It could *end* her life. But taking her *name* . . .

"Please," she said, trying to keep her voice even. "Let me stay. Let me try to earn a name, and your respect, back again. I will stop the visions. . . ." She didn't know *how* she would do this—she had never managed it so far. "I'll live with the males and *never* take a name, if that is what I need to do. Don't send me away."

But Gutripper's gaze was implacable.

"Hidetearer. Skullcracker," she said. "Take this cub to the edge of our territory and make sure she doesn't return."

Tailgrabber didn't move. She couldn't. That first step away from her family seemed impossible.

But Hidetearer was happy to help. She barged into Tailgrabber with her shoulder, forcing her to take a step to avoid falling on her face.

"Go on," she snapped. "Walk."

In a daze, Tailgrabber found herself putting one paw in

front of the other, flanked by the two hyenas. She had left the baobab and the dried river behind, almost before she knew it. Eventually her spinning mind slowed enough that she thought of turning back to Gutripper, to Nosebiter, and saying something defiant—but it was too late. She could never, ever go back.

The two escorts were walking on either side of her and a little behind.

"Better for all of us if she was never born," said Hidetearer. "Such an embarrassment to her mother."

"To *all* hyenas," Skullcracker agreed. Tailgrabber sighed. However thickly they laid it on, they couldn't hurt her now. No more than Nosebiter already had.

"We'll be rid of her soon," said Hidetearer.

"Yeah," Skullcracker said, and Tailgrabber felt her crash into her, almost tripping her up. She turned, snarling, but pulled up as both hyenas snarled back at her, hackles raised.

Don't. Don't fight them. There's no point.

Tailgrabber tried to listen to the sensible voice within her heart. She sniffed and tried to look dignified while turning her back on Hidetearer and Skullcracker and setting off at a faster pace for the line of trees that marked the edge of the territory.

She knew she hadn't succeeded in being dignified, even before the other two burst into cackling laughter.

"Still thinks she's a hyena," Skullcracker giggled.

"Still thinks she's *anything*," agreed Hidetearer, and Tailgrabber jumped and swallowed a yelp as she felt a nip on the back of her ankle. "Go on, *Cub*. Run. Make us chase you."

Tailgrabber tried to moderate her speed so that she neither slowed down nor sped up. The skin behind her ears was starting to burn with embarrassment and anger. She owed these two nothing; why should she give one more moment's thought to anything they said?

On the other hand, they were nearly at the trees. Close to the place where she had met the lion, Bold, before she had led her back to the baobab . . . before she'd gotten the cubs killed. . . .

Perhaps the others were right. Perhaps she never belonged with the clan at all.

"That's far enough," said Hidetearer, with a nasty snigger in her voice that Tailgrabber didn't like. "I think it's time to finish this."

She turned to look back at her escort, her heart sinking. Skullcracker was already circling her while Hidetearer stood between her and their home, licking her lips.

"Why wait for the inevitable," Skullcracker giggled. "We can let her starve alone, or we can honor Legsnatcher, and the Great Devourer, and make her a meal for two *real* hyenas."

That's right. Of course it comes down to this.

There was no shame in eating another hyena if their death didn't grieve you at all. That was something some other creatures didn't seem to understand. Meat was meat.

But that didn't mean the idea of *being* eaten by these two giggling thugs didn't make Tailgrabber's fur stand on end in horror and disgust.

"Why bother?" she said, trying not to give away her fear. "I'll put up a fight, you'll get tired. Go back now, and you'll never see me again either way. You don't have to do this." Her voice shook on the last few words, and she twitched, trying to follow Skullcracker's path without turning her back on Hide-tearer.

"Oh, I know we don't *have* to," Skullcracker chortled. She stopped in front of Tailgrabber, puffing herself up. "I just *want* to."

She crouched, teeth bared. As her muscles bunched to spring, time seemed to slow. Tailgrabber's instincts threw her down, even as her mind went blank with terror. Skullcracker's leap began—and then, in a flash of fur, she was down on the ground, on her side, with another hyena's jaws in her throat.

Nosebiter!

Her sister pinned Skullcracker, clamping her teeth on her neck.

Skullcracker gave a wheezing yelp of pain.

Nosebiter gave a small shake to show she was serious, then raised her head, showing off her bloodied jaws to Hidetearer, who took a hurried step back.

"One last thing for my sister," Nosebiter said. "The very last."

She turned her gaze on Tailgrabber. Her expression was baleful.

"I love you, and I have one wish for you. *Survive*," she said.

"I will," Tailgrabber tried to say, but her voice came out squeaky and uncertain, like a cub's. She cleared her throat and spoke again, and tried to show her sister how much she meant it. "I *will*."

Nosebiter nodded. Then her face turned hard. "Now, I never want to see you again. After today, I have no sister. Run, Cub. Run far, far away."

Tailgrabber ran.

CHAPTER TWENTY-FIVE

Stride growled, a hoarse and cracked sound that seemed to shiver through the air. The vulture that had tried to land beside him took off, in a flurry of feathers, and went back to circling overhead, patient as a rock.

Stride could be patient too. There was nothing else left for him now.

He lay back down beside Flicker, suppressing a shiver as he felt the coolness of her fur, the stiffening of her joints. Nevertheless, he pressed his face to the fur at the back of her neck and shut his eyes. Her scent still lingered. Soon it would drift away too, overcome by the smell of Death. Soon, there would be too many vultures, and the hyenas would come skulking, and he would have to make a choice. He knew this.

But for now, just for now, he could tell himself she was sleeping. He could press his face to her fur and memorize everything about her, her scent, the beautiful darkness of her spots, the way her flank fit against his.

"Good night," he whispered. "Tomorrow we'll explore the territory more. . . . Tomorrow we'll find the clear river, and the herds of prey animals, and the long grass. It'll be perfect. We'll find it all. Tomorrow. Go to sleep, now. Don't worry about anything. I'm here. I'll protect you."

The silence hurt, like a sharp thorn digging in between his ears. He squeezed his eyes shut and kept on talking to Flicker. He promised her cubs and a territory and a future. He began to repeat himself. He said things he barely heard or understood, because when he stopped, the silence came in and began to strangle him. It was almost a relief when the vultures overhead croaked to each other, or the grasses around them rustled.

Until suddenly he became aware, with a flash of anger, that the rustling was coming closer. Some creature was creeping through the grass toward them.

It was too soon. He wasn't finished here.

They already stole her from me. They already gave her to Death. Can't they give me this moment to pretend?

The scuffling sound came closer, and suddenly fury shot through Stride, propelling him to sit up and turn, snarling at the interloper. He was ready to fight and die for Flicker, whether it was a hyena or a whole pride of lions. They would not touch her.

For a second, he couldn't see the creature who'd been moving through the grass. Then he looked down and saw a small black body, striped with white from nose to tail.

The honey badger sniffed derisively. "Get up, spotty. You're in my way," he said.

For a moment, Stride simply didn't understand. "In your way," he whispered. How could that be something any creature could care about when Flicker was dead? How could *this* be the thing that had torn him from her side?

In the next moment, the anger came back, and he faced the honey badger, nose to nose, and growled. "Go around!"

The honey badger's lips pulled back, and he reared up on his hind legs, displaying two paws full of long, black claws and rows of pointed teeth. "Watch yourself, you . . ."

But then his eyes flicked around Stride, and he seemed to see Flicker's unmoving body for the first time. He didn't drop back to all fours, but his snarl vanished.

"She's dead?" he asked gruffly.

Stride said nothing. He couldn't say it aloud. It was all he could do to stay on his paws, facing off with the strange little creature, and not drop to the ground and wail.

"How did it happen?" asked the honey badger.

His voice was surprisingly gentle.

Stride didn't intend to reply, but something seemed to force the words out of him, as if they'd been waiting behind his teeth for a chance to escape. "It wasn't her time. But she ran too fast, and Death . . . Death caught her."

"Too fast," muttered the honey badger, returning to all four paws at last. "Always knew it was better to walk slow."

Stride bristled. Was this creature mocking him? *"Leave,"* he croaked.

The honey badger nodded. He backed up a little and began to pad a wide circle around Stride and Flicker. Stride sat and watched him go, feeling like he couldn't turn his attention back to Flicker, not until they were alone once more.

The honey badger walked a few steps away and then stopped. Stride pawed uneasily at the ground as he turned back. What did this thing *want*?

"Listen," the honey badger said. "No point sitting next to a dead body. Nothing good comes of it. Unless you're planning to eat it?"

Stride took a shaky, horrified breath. How could he even respond to that?

"No, I didn't think so," said the honey badger. "But it looks like someone else would like to."

Stride spun around just in time to see the vultures landing, much too close to Flicker, stretching their long necks toward her.

"Get off!" he yowled, springing across her body and swiping at one of the vultures. They took flight in a flurry of feathers and squawking, but instead of circling above, this time they just landed farther away, sitting and staring at Flicker with an intensity that made him step protectively over her again.

"Hmm," said the honey badger behind him. Stride turned, trying to keep the small creature and the vultures in sight at the same time.

"What?" he snarled.

"Well . . ." The honey badger tilted his head curiously. "What's your name?"

"It's . . . Stride," Stride muttered.

"Stonehide," said the honey badger. "That's me. Do cheetahs always do this?"

"Do what?" Stride asked. He was almost too distracted to lash out at a vulture that came too close. "What are you saying?"

"Do your kind always guard their dead?" Stonehide asked. "Or is it just weird ones like you?"

"I'm not *weird*," Stride yowled, "I just can't . . . I can't leave her to be eaten. I'm not . . . it's not fair. She didn't deserve to die!"

"Hmm," said Stonehide again, and if Stride could have left Flicker's side, he would have aimed a paw at his head, danger or not. But the honey badger was too far away for that. "Do grass-eaters *deserve* to die? What about that ostrich you chased off last time we met? I assume you ate it."

That's different, Stride thought, but he didn't say it. He knew how it would sound.

"Death happens," said Stonehide. "It's not fair. It just is."

That sounds just as stupid as "That's different"! Stride thought.

"What would you know about it?" he growled at the honey badger.

"A little," said Stonehide, blinking placidly.

"I have nothing else," Stride found himself saying, though he knew he didn't owe this creature any answers. "I had a mate. Plans. A territory. Now I have . . . a body, and nothing. I know she's not here! I know that! But if I move . . . I have nothing left."

"You have your teeth and your paws," said Stonehide. "You have your heart. It's still beating. That's something. If you had nothing, you'd know it. You'd be in the stars with her, wouldn't you?"

When Stride didn't answer him, he looked as if he was finally going to leave, and then thought of yet another thing to say.

"If you want answers about Death, the one to ask is the Great Mother."

Stupid suggestion. She can't help me.

"She can't bring Flicker back," Stride said.

"No. But these are her vultures, yes? Would Flicker want you to lie down and die, or would she want you to go to the Great Mother and find out what she knows about her death?"

Stride couldn't look at Stonehide. He couldn't look at Flicker or the vultures, so he stared into the distance, into the bright sunset.

High above the plain, something twinkled as it shot across the sky, leaving a thin trail of white before it vanished into the setting sun.

A shooting star.

He stared at it, and then at the patch of sky where it had been, in dazed silence. He stared for so long that Stonehide turned and looked too. Even one of the vultures craned its neck to the sky.

A sign? Flicker . . . is that you? Did you send me a sign? Is this strange animal right, do you want me to ask the Great Mother about your death? Is there . . . His heart began to speed up a little, and he felt a strange rush of *aliveness* in his paws. *Is there really something to find out?*

He took a deep breath.

"Where does the Great Mother live?" he muttered.

The honey badger sniffed. "As it happens, I'm off that way myself. But none of this charging about, and we take proper naps. Don't worry. You'll be safe if you're with me."

Stride stared at the creature, less than half his size, and the casual way he turned his back on the vultures and began to walk off. Stonehide didn't look back this time. He clearly thought—*knew*—that Stride was going to follow.

Stride looked down at Flicker's body.

Already, somehow, it looked less like her. She was not sleeping. She was not *here*.

Still, he lowered his muzzle to hers, and whispered in her ear.

"I love you," he said.

Then he followed Stonehide.

Behind him, he heard flapping, and then cawing.

Stride didn't look back.

CHAPTER TWENTY-SIX

Whisper's hooves felt heavy, as if the sucking sand was following her, dragging at her steps. She was exhausted, and grief rode on her back like a massive shadow. The sun rose, and the day grew hot, and she walked on, swaying a little under the weight of it all. Her head bowed, and her vision narrowed down to just the ground in front of her hooves. Any predator could have picked her off, but instead of snarling and the snap of teeth, she suddenly heard her name.

"Whisper?"

She looked up.

It was the herd. She had made it back to the herd. They were blurry and indistinct behind a heat haze that rose from the plain, but she could hear their voices as she lumbered toward them.

"Is that Whisper?"

"What? What do you mean it's Whisper?"

"It is, it's Whisper!"

The ground shook, rattling Whisper's tired bones, as a group of females charged toward her.

"Whisper," gasped Clatter, nuzzling against Whisper's cheek in a gesture that almost knocked her over on her unsteady hooves. "We thought—Quake said you were dead!"

The mention of his name sent a shiver of anger through Whisper, cutting through the shadow of grief like a bolt of lightning on a moonless night.

"Where is he?" she croaked.

"There, with the males," said another buffalo, tossing her head.

Whisper had to squint for a moment, but then she could see them, a group of males, gathered around the unmistakable bulk of Holler.

She began to walk toward them, ignoring the fussing and the questions of the other females. They let her pass and followed in her wake, turning to ask each other the questions she wasn't answering.

"How did she escape?"

"Did he say he saw her die?"

"Where's Murmur?"

The males began to spot Whisper's approach too, and as she reached them they stepped aside, until she suddenly came face-to-face with Quake, standing by his father with his mouth hanging open and his ears flicking back and forth in surprise.

"Hello," Whisper said.

"Whisper," Quake gulped. He cleared his throat. "By the Spirit, I thought you'd died! It's a miracle! I saw the sand swallow you!"

He was doing a good impression of a buffalo who cared if she lived or died, with his wide eyes and his glances back at Holler.

"You tried to kill me," Whisper said flatly. "You led us into that quicksand. Said it was a shortcut, but stayed behind us till we'd both stepped in. Then you left us to sink."

"I didn't!" Quake said, though his voice was mingled with the shocked whispers of the females around them. "I didn't know. I came back with a branch to help you out, but you had gone."

"Whisper."

Whisper looked up to see Thunder standing at Holler's side, her eyes red and watery.

"What about Murmur?" Thunder asked.

She begged, and begged, and there was nothing I could do but stand by and watch her die.

Whisper took a deeper breath and spoke as loud and clear as she could. She wanted every buffalo in the herd to hear.

"Murmur is dead."

Thunder let out a bellowing howl and fell to her knees, shuddering with sobs.

"No! No, Whisper," Quake said, in a soft, sympathetic tone that made Whisper feel sick. "It was an accident. A horrible accident. I wanted to help, but there was nothing I could do!"

The buffalo looked at each other, uncertainty creeping in. Even Thunder was looking between Whisper and Quake, as if she couldn't decide who to believe. It made Whisper feel like screaming.

"I loved Murmur," Quake said. "I promise. It was an accident."

"An accident," Whisper said. "Just like what happened to Echo?"

"Thank the Spirit that Whisper is alive," said Holler loudly. "Quake was inconsolable when he returned alone. You poor calves went through something horrifying. I am so sorry about Murmur."

Heads turned as the buffalo looked to Whisper to see how she would react.

"Quake is a liar," she said, but her dry, tired voice cracked, and she couldn't speak above a whisper.

"A terrifying ordeal," Holler said, shaking his head. "Murmur will be remembered with love, always."

Thunder looked up, and her expression was strange, as if blank confusion, burning anger, and terrible grief were fighting it out behind her eyes.

"But at least in this tragedy, there is a point of light," Holler went on quickly, before Whisper could speak again. "We have word from the Great Mother. Starlight sends us hope for the future. I humbly accept her instruction and will take on responsibility for the migration. We leave at once."

Whisper took a deep breath.

"Liar!" she screamed. The attention of the herd snapped

back to her, and she tried to steady herself, though she was dizzy with exhaustion and this all felt like a horrible dream. "Starlight said we should wait! Quake is lying to you all. She said we need a *real* leader before we could go. . . ."

"That's right," said Quake. "She said we need a strong leader. And now we have one."

"She said only the Great Spirit could decide the leader!" shouted Whisper. "She said to *stay*, and she would look into Echo's death, and . . ."

Quake looked up to Holler, as if for reassurance.

"Quake," Whisper snarled under her breath, not sure what she would say next, but certain it would be violent. Before she could come up with something, though, Holler interrupted again.

"Be assured, Whisper, we will not go against the Great Parent's wishes," he said, soothingly. "And that's why I was so anxious when Quake returned alone with this news—and why it was such a relief when the oxpeckers came to me."

"What?" said Clatter. "When did this happen?"

"At sunrise this morning," said Holler. "I was down by the water, and they came and alighted on my back. I guess the Great Mother must have sent word through her birds that it was time to choose a new leader."

"I was there," said Grind. Two more males spoke up to agree with them.

The mood in the herd shifted. Whisper could feel their support slipping out from under her. Even in her own mind, even *knowing* that Quake had tried to kill her, there was a tiny flicker of uncertainty—Starlight *could* have sent the birds on ahead to tell the oxpeckers to choose. There was no way she could prove that didn't happen.

But the males who had spoken had something in common, apart from being supporters of Holler.

They were all in Echo's escort the day he died.

She looked up at Holler and took a step forward, still a little unsteady on her aching hooves.

"How long have you been planning to steal the leadership of the herd from your brother?" she asked.

Gasps of outrage and furious lowing rose all around her. Several males snorted hot air from their nostrils and smacked the ground with their hooves, as if they might stampede over her in their rage. But Whisper kept her eyes trained on Holler.

"Whisper!" Thunder said. She tried to close her teeth on the hair at Whisper's neck and drag her back. "Calm your tongue!" But Whisper tossed her head and wriggled out of Thunder's grip.

"Ah, but she's right," said a low, sad voice behind them.

The herd's intake of breath was followed by still, tense silence.

Bellow moved through the buffalo like a storm cloud passing across the sky, huge and dark and slow.

"I didn't want to believe it myself," said Bellow. His legs shook, but he kept moving forward, until he was standing over Whisper's shoulder, facing Holler. "But I have seen the darkness that has grown in your heart. For years, I have felt your malice, my brother. Your jealousy. And then, while I was focused on my duty as leader, protecting an innocent, blameless calf from crocodiles, I was wounded by something I didn't see. In fact, nobody saw the crocodile that bit me."

Holler opened his mouth as if he might speak, but then slowly closed it again. Silence hung over the herd as Bellow took a breath and swallowed, clearing his throat.

"There was no crocodile," Bellow said. "My wound was made by a buffalo horn. Your horn. And even then, when I knew you had wounded me—had condemned me to death—I hoped that it had been an accident. I told no one. I wanted to give you a chance to let the Great Spirit guide the herd, to accept another's leadership. But you chose death, and lies, over the good of the herd."

Quake's tail swished, and he glanced between his father and Bellow.

"Brother, I am sorry you believed these lies," Holler said. "They are the fantasies of a grief-stricken calf, and nothing more. But the time *has* come to pass on your wisdom. The Great Spirit chose a leader, and now he is not here. It is time for you to pass on your wisdom, and if you refuse to do that, then it is *you* who betrays the herd, not I."

"I will not pass our secrets to an unworthy leader," said Bellow.

"Then you leave me no choice," Holler said, and fear filled Whisper's heart as he raised his head to cry out over the whole herd. "I, Holler, chosen of the oxpeckers and future leader of this herd, challenge you, Bellow, to a duel!"

Shivers of confusion and surprise ran through the herd. Whisper was still standing close to Thunder, and she felt all the air rush out of the adult buffalo's lungs in a long sigh.

Whisper had seen buffalo fight duels before, once or twice— usually over something to do with mating, or petty grievances that seemed like excuses to have a fight. But Thunder had told her and Murmur once that if the leader was challenged to a duel, he could not refuse, and if he lost, the leadership would go to the winner.

Thunder had said it hadn't happened in many, many years.

"So, it has come to this at last," said Bellow quietly. He raised his head and shouted, "I, Bellow, true leader of this herd, accept your challenge, Holler!"

"But—you can't!" Whisper cried. Both Bellow and Holler looked at her—Bellow with kindness, Holler with scorn. "It's not fair! Bellow's injured, it's not a fair fight!"

"It's all right, little one," said Bellow. "I know that Holler has chosen the coward's path, to fight an opponent who is already mortally wounded." Several voices from the herd cried out in shock or gave quiet jeers. "But I must accept this challenge. And so I put my faith in the Great Spirit, one more time. May it guide me to victory—for the herd, and all of Bravelands."

CHAPTER TWENTY-SEVEN

Tailgrabber was alone.

She had traveled by herself plenty of times, of course, on solo hunting expeditions. But every time, she'd known that she was not *really* alone. She hunted for the clan. She scouted for the clan. The clan was behind her, even when they were sniping at her heels.

But now, there was no one relying on her, and no one to hold her back either.

She had never felt so lonely.

I could go back, she thought. *I could try. . . .*

But as soon as she'd thought it, she knew it was hopeless. What would she do? Hang around the edge of the territory like a male, hoping they would just forget that they'd banished her? Or try to hunt and give prey to the clan? Would she attempt to *talk* to Gutripper? Even if her mother changed her mind, for the first time in her life as far as Tailgrabber could remember, the others would never allow it. Sooner or later, one of them would find her throat. Nosebiter couldn't—no, she *wouldn't*—protect her little sister again. The clan had spoken. They had turned their backs.

Maybe if she destroyed Noblepride, all on her own . . .

But I don't want to.

Tailgrabber stopped in the shade of a thorn tree and shook herself from head to tail.

She didn't want to fight the lions, even when she was part of the clan, and now she didn't have to.

Tailgrabber let out a small giggle. It sounded strange to her, one hyena laughing by itself. But she could laugh if she wanted to. She could do whatever she wanted.

"They will never win against Noblepride," she said out loud, walking on a little way. "They will kill each other first, and that's *stupid*. It was all so stupid!"

They should have gone to the Great Mother in the first place.

Tailgrabber stopped again, struck by a strange thought.

I could go to the Great Mother now.

And not to ask what the clan should do—even if she told them, they wouldn't do it. What if she went to Great Mother . . . Sunbeam, or whatever she was called, and offered her service to the Great Spirit?

Hyenas didn't follow the Great Spirit. She knew that her clan would lose their pelts laughing if they knew of her intention. But Tailgrabber didn't care what they thought. She didn't want to be alone forever, and the Great Mother was the Great Mother for all of Bravelands, right? She wouldn't turn her down, would she?

One of the old females, who'd died before Gutripper took over, had told Tailgrabber a story about hyenas who'd worked with a gazelle Great Parent to defeat a giant snake. It sounded a little far-fetched—why wouldn't the hyenas just eat the gazelle, Great Parent or not?—but maybe it was true. Maybe Ribsnapper was real. If anyone knew, presumably the Great Mother would.

She thought she knew roughly where Sunbeam—no, Starbright—lived. Her ears pricked up and her paws felt a little lighter as she set off in the right direction, hurrying around the edge of the thorn trees and clambering over a jutting ridge of rock and down into a long, shallow dip that had probably once been a river. But it wasn't dried up because the rains were due, like the watering hole near the baobab tree—at the center of the valley, Tailgrabber found herself walking over the dusty surface of a black rock river.

She pawed at the mud, exposing the strange rock. It was creepy stuff: too hard, too flat, too shiny, and too black. Plus, it could be slippery. Normally she would go around until she found a place to cross that was covered in enough mud to feel like solid ground, but she didn't want to waste time. She would still have to find something to eat today, and nobody was going to help her. . . .

"Oh, it's you," said a wheedling voice. Tailgrabber startled and looked around, one paw squeaking unpleasantly on the black rock. A lion emerged from behind a rock on the other side of the river.

She was thinner than when Tailgrabber had last seen her and bore a jagged scar across her nose, but she was still recognizable.

"Bold," said Tailgrabber.

"Breathstealer, isn't it?" Bold said, and Tailgrabber felt a shudder of a laugh run through her. Of course, that was the name she'd chosen for herself. . . . "But maybe a better name would be Cubkiller, since you led me straight back to your den," sneered Bold.

The laugh died in Tailgrabber's throat. The sight of Cub and the others, lying dead outside the den, came back to her in a violent flash, and before she knew what she was doing, she leaped at Bold. The lion let out a surprised yelp and ducked away. Tailgrabber missed, but Bold tripped over her paws and went sprawling on the hard rock.

"What's the matter?" Tailgrabber yelled, stumbling but righting herself and spinning around to face the lion. "Big scary lion, afraid to fight me?"

"Stupid hyena," Bold spat, showing her long fangs. "I'll kill you!"

And at least I'll die doing something, Tailgrabber thought. *I'll have revenge for Cub, and all the others we've lost because of this war.*

Tailgrabber had no home, no family. No name, even, now that they had stripped hers. She was Cub, and she would die Cub. All she had left were memories, and this lion was about to pay for the most painful of them all. Tailgrabber threw herself at the lion again, heedless of the danger from the snapping jaws. Bold reared back and caught her in both paws, driving claws into Tailgrabber's ribs, but Tailgrabber snapped and snarled, lunging forward instead of trying to wriggle away, and she got her teeth into the lion's cheek. With an awful tearing, part of it came away, and Tailgrabber spat out a patch of skin and tawny fur.

Bold screamed and tried to rake her claws through Tailgrabber's heart, but she was dizzied by the pain of the bite, and Tailgrabber managed to wriggle her legs under the lion and kick, hard, dragging her claws out and pushing her away.

They scrambled up and faced each other again, panting. Tailgrabber couldn't breathe in all the way without a spiking pain that made her reel, and Bold's eyes were filming over with pain and dizziness. But still they circled, blood spattering onto the black rock, both leaving sticky pawprints across the smooth surface.

"Come on!" Tailgrabber screamed.

I'm not a hyena anymore, she thought, hysterical with adrenaline and pain. *I'm not bound by the Code. I don't need to survive!*

She ran at the lion, sliding on her bloody paws, and ducked under a swipe to headbutt Bold right in the throat. Bold staggered back, choking. But then she reared up and wrapped her front paws around Tailgrabber and tilted her head to the side, sinking her fangs into Tailgrabber's shoulder.

The pain of the bite seemed to burn, hot and horrible in Tailgrabber's flesh. Her vision pulsated for a moment, blue and purple shadows crossing it as she felt blood begin to run through her fur.

But Bold's neck fur was exposed, and Tailgrabber's neck was longer than hers. She twisted as far as she could reach and closed her jaws around the lion's throat.

Bold's body convulsed. Her claws tore out of Tailgrabber's back, her teeth loosening their grip on her shoulder, as she tried to get free. But Tailgrabber held fast. She tasted blood pouring over her tongue and dripping from the sides of her mouth, felt Bold's throat tighten and spasm as she tried to take a breath, but could not. Or maybe the lioness was trying to talk, to say all this was a mistake, a play-fight, and that it was time to stop. Tailgrabber did not stop. She squeezed harder.

The plains of Bravelands seemed to fall silent, apart from the sound of Bold's strangled gasps, the scrabble of claws on black rock, and then . . . nothing.

Bold went limp. Tailgrabber still hung on for a moment, then opened her jaws and let the dead lion thump to the ground.

She stood above it, panting, shivers of pain still passing through her whenever she filled her lungs, her fur clumping and her paws sticking to the rock with blood, Bold's and her own mingling together.

But she was alive, and Bold was dead.

She felt a moment of terrible, exhilarating clarity as she stood there, victorious, a lion-killer after all.

"I did survive," she whispered, her voice a harsh rasp. "I *am* a hyena! I was a cub again, and now I have earned my name. And my name . . . *is Breathstealer.*"

Nobody heard her pronouncement, but that didn't matter. She didn't need the others. She felt the flush of pride and the shudder of excitement she had always thought she would feel when she finally took her name, feelings that were absent from her first naming.

She sat down beside Bold's corpse, licking her wounds. They hurt a lot, but they wouldn't stop her for long. Her shoulder ached when she moved it, but she could move it, and she was slowly able to breathe deeper as she calmed and the deep claw-marks in her ribs stopped bleeding.

Breathstealer looked down at the lion, tilting her head.

She had killed it. She could eat it. She was hungry, and meat was meat. But part of her said, *No.* It said, *Leave it here for the others.* If they found it, covered in Breathstealer's scent, her blood, then they would know. . . .

That was, if there was anything left by then. Even now, Breathstealer looked up as she heard the harsh cry of vultures overhead.

At first, she couldn't see the birds, though she knew they were there. Then she did see something circling, catching the light. It wasn't a vulture, though. It was pure white.

But it flew like a vulture and dived like one, and when it landed on the lion's corpse, barely out of swiping distance, she saw with a shock that it *was* a vulture.

A flash of recognition and memory passed through Breathstealer's mind. A memory of being in the cub den with Nosebiter, when they were both Cub, and Breathstealer was very small. Of hearing the stories that some hyenas would tell.

The Great Devourer has its own messengers, they said. *It comes in the form of insects and mold, and sometimes it sends a pure white vulture from the realm of death. No creature can pass through the Great Devourer's presence without losing the color from their fur or feathers. . . .*

The vulture didn't hesitate, but dipped its head into the bloody wound at Bold's neck, tore a strip of flesh, and swallowed it. Its white feathers seemed to glow against the red that stained its beak and its chest as it raised its head and let out a cry.

"*Follow*," said a voice.

Breathstealer startled. The voice was very deep—deep in her chest, or deep in the earth, she wasn't sure, but it boomed silently within her, and she found herself getting to her paws, without thinking.

The vulture turned to fix its gaze on her, a dark eye glittering behind a mask of lion's blood.

"*Follow*," the voice said, again, and then the vulture was flying away. It landed a short distance from her, on the other side of the black rock river.

There was not a flicker of doubt in her mind about what she must do. As quickly as she could, with the ache in her shoulder and her ribs, Breathstealer hurried after it. The vulture flew again as she drew closer, leading her out onto the plains, through the grass, across the side of a kopje, and on.

Where it was going, and why she must follow, Breathstealer had no idea at all. But to refuse the summons was unthinkable.

After all, she thought, *I am Breathstealer the hyena, and I survive.*

CHAPTER TWENTY-EIGHT

"Well, this Jinks sounds unbearable," said Stonehide.

"He *is*," Stride said. It jarred a little, to be describing the faults in Jinks's character, when his actions were so bad—he had sent One-Ear to kill Fleet and had almost killed Stride himself. But at the same time, it felt good to spill *all* of it to his strange companion, from the very first time he joined the coalition to—hopefully—the last time he saw Jinks, limping away with impotent fury in his eyes. "He's *awful*. Just the worst leader you could imagine."

Stonehide paused to scratch his chin against the rough trunk of a tree. He'd said they were close to where the Great Mother was supposed to be, now that they'd reached the edge of a deep-seeming forest. Dry leaves crunched under their paws, ferns curled tight, and bushes were turning brown, but even so the trees stood tall and spread their hardy branches wide, so the contrast between the moon-drenched plain and the shadowy forest was stark.

Stride wasn't so sure that Stonehide was right about this—elephants usually lived on the open plains, didn't they?—but he followed the honey badger into the trees anyway. He put his trust in Flicker's star. He would see where it led him. It was all he had left.

And it was good to talk. Stonehide, for all his gruff bluster, was a good listener. He often butted in, but it was always to make sharp comments, like the one about Jinks, that reinforced what Stride was trying to say. When Stride had mentioned Jinks's strange, possessive conviction that Flicker was supposed to be his mate, Stonehide had snorted and simply said "Dung-heap!" under his breath.

"I will miss Pace, though," Stride said, sniffing around the forest floor. There were trees, so there had to be water somewhere, and he was very thirsty. But if there was water, he couldn't scent it through the mingling smells of plants and other creatures and the faint, hot overlay of baking earth. "He was my best friend. I wonder if I'll ever see him again. . . ."

"Friends are overrated," said Stonehide.

"Really?" Stride said, wondering whether to bring up that someone who would lead you halfway across Bravelands and listen to you talk about your feelings all the way might be described as a friend.

Stonehide wrinkled his long nose. "Don't need 'em. The open plain under my claws, silence when I want it silent, room for my thoughts. That's the life for me."

But then . . . why? Why tell me to come with you?

Stride didn't say that. He'd learned on this journey that Stronghide didn't answer direct questions if he could help it. For such a blunt creature, he was oddly evasive too sometimes. So instead, Stride sighed and said, "I would definitely get lonely."

"Some creatures aren't built for the single life, I suppose," Stonehide said. He sniffed the air. "This way, definitely. Can't you smell them?"

He could, Stride realized. The scent seemed to have arrived suddenly—but he understood that a little better when they passed through a small gap between two trees. Stonehide strolled through, and Stride had to squeeze, but on the other side they found themselves in a tall green tunnel, faintly lit by the moonlight and the grayish-blue light of the approaching dawn. Branches had snapped and bushes had been trampled to form a long passage through the forest that smelled very definitely of elephant.

Of course. No elephants out there in the undergrowth, Stride thought.

"Oh!" cried a loud, deep voice right by Stride's ear. Stride spun around, saw a wall of gray flesh coming toward him, yowled, and startled all the way up the closest tree trunk and onto a branch. He ended up at about tusk-height, his tail lashing.

"Hey!" shouted Stonehide. He turned, stood his ground, and snarled up at the massive creature. The elephant stomped the ground and flapped her ears as she came to a sudden stop. "*You* watch where you're treading!"

The elephant blinked at the small creature, apparently nonplussed.

"My apologies," she said slowly.

Stonehide sniffed. "Should think so too. Now, we're here to see the Great Mother. I assume you can show us to her?"

"No need," said the elephant, a slow smile curling under her tusks. "You have found her. I am Great Mother Starlight."

Stride looked at the elephant in awe. She had seemed like an ordinary elephant—if there was anything truly *ordinary* about such a massive, powerful creature—but this was the Great Parent for all of Bravelands, the one elephant who had a deep connection to the Great Spirit. A grass-eater who could speak skytongue and sandtongue, and maybe much more besides. . . .

Stonehide made a *hmm* noise in the back of his throat. "Really? You?"

"I apologize if I don't live up to your expectations, master honey badger," said Starlight, a gleam in her eye.

"You can call me Stonehide," he replied.

"Well, Stonehide. Why don't you come to my clearing and tell me what you need from me?"

"It's him," Stonehide said, tossing his head at Stride in the branch above. "Stride the cheetah. He wants to talk to you."

Starlight's great head swung around to face Stride, fixing him with a long look from her great dark eyes.

"Greetings, Stride," she said. "Follow me."

The Great Mother's clearing was a strange place, not the natural kind of clearing that Stride had seen before, but a place where animals had intentionally changed the shape of the forest. Great Mother Starlight sat down with her back to a large jutting rock about as tall as she was and invited Stride and Stonehide to join her and tell her their questions.

Stride tried to keep his voice steady and calm as he told her all about Flicker, Jinks, and their exile from the coalition's territory, and the death of Fleet, and the lions, and finally Flicker's encounter with Death.

"It's just . . . not *fair*," he said at last, the words coming out strangled. "Why does Death hunt us like this? She was taken by something . . . unnatural, invisible. There must be some way to get her back."

Even as he said it, he saw the sadness in Great Mother Starlight's eyes, and he knew there was no hope. He turned his head and laid his chin on his paws. Part of him wanted to get up and run, be far away from this place before she could speak. But a larger, deeper part of him wanted to know what she would say.

"I am so sorry for your loss," Starlight said slowly. "Flicker sounds like she was a wonderful cheetah. But I knew of this death before you arrived."

"You did? The vultures told you . . . ?" Stride's ears pricked up. If the vultures had told Great Mother about Flicker, maybe Stonehide was right, maybe there *was* truly something . . .

But Starlight's soft, sad expression didn't change.

"It was a good death, Stride," she said.

"*Good?*" Stride yowled.

"I apologize, that's not what I mean. It did not break the Code," Starlight said.

"But . . . the Code is *only kill to survive*, isn't it? No creature killed Flicker *to survive*. Death doesn't *need* her. . . ."

"Stride, Death takes creatures through accident, or foolishness, illness, age, bad luck . . . every single day, hundreds of creatures. There is no point in *blaming* Death for it, even for cheetahs. It is just what Death does. It is the price we pay for living at all."

"Well, what's the point then?" Stride mewled, sounding like a cub even to his own ears. "Is it worth it? To live, knowing Death can come and snatch up the creatures you love at any time?"

"The point?" Starlight echoed, and then fell silent for a long moment, as if she was giving this question serious thought. "I believe that every life has a purpose. Let me ask you, what do you think the point of Flicker's life was?"

Stride sat up and stared at his paws, frowning. What was she getting at?

"Perhaps it was so she could meet you and share the precious short time you did. Perhaps it was to send you to me. Or to teach a lesson to Jinks. Or, perhaps, her purpose was just to run on the plains and eat good prey, and laugh, and feel the wind in her fur. The purpose of life is a mystery that most creatures never solve, but that doesn't mean it is worthless."

Stride let her words wash over him, scratching at the ground with his claws, struggling to hold back a grief-filled yowl. He could see Flicker as she had been, running, laughing, catching prey . . . and the pain of her loss hit him harder than ever.

"She was my purpose," he muttered. "That's what I think. And now she's gone."

"A creature can have more than one," said Starlight. Stride glanced up at her and found her staring thoughtfully into the sky. "I wonder. Has the Great Spirit brought you to me at just the right time?"

"What do you mean?" Stride said, bristling a little. Was she saying that Flicker's death had *helped her* in some way? "Anyway, it was Stonehide who brought me here."

Great Mother Starlight gave a light chuckle, and Stride frowned even more. Was she laughing at him?

"I'm sure it was," she said, turning her gaze on the honey badger. Stonehide met her eyes, unwavering, giving nothing away.

Wasn't there something he wanted too? Stride thought, suddenly puzzled. *If so, why hasn't he said?*

Bravelands is in perilous times," continued Starlight, and Stride's ears pricked up in surprise. "Its future is uncertain, far more so than I think most creatures realize. Our fate balances on the edge of a deep ravine, bound up in the fate of the buffalo herd."

"The buffalo?" Stride asked, surprised. Buffalo were . . . solid, intimidating, reliable. Like independently mobile rock formations. Not the kind of creature he'd ever thought might hold the fate of Bravelands in its horns.

"Indeed. The herd is fractured, the migration threatened.

If the buffalo's problems are left unresolved..." She hesitated, as if there were words on the tip of her tongue that she was not sure she should say aloud. Stride's fur prickled. Anything the Great Mother couldn't bring herself to say must be *very bad indeed.*

"I want to help," he said hesitantly. "But... what can I do?"

"I am not sure yet," said the Great Mother. "But you have come to me for a reason. You and your rude friend."

"Now, hang on," said Stonehide, looking from the elephant to Stride. "I'm just passing through...."

"Aren't we all?" said Starlight. "But that doesn't mean we don't have a destiny."

Stonehide sighed. "Ugh! Not this destiny mumbo jumbo again."

Starlight chuckled and swished her trunk. "You don't believe in fate, honey badger?"

"Sometimes it rains, sometimes it's sunny," said Stonehide. "I take the rough with the smooth."

"Then you won't mind helping me with this problem," said the Great Mother.

Stonehide grumbled incoherently.

Stride looked up, and in that moment, the sun climbed above the horizon behind him, throwing the pattern of the canopy onto the rock behind Great Mother—it turned a glowing, beautiful pale yellow color dotted with dark, dark shadows.

It reminded him of Flicker's pelt, so strongly that he caught his breath.

She's here, somehow. She wants me to be here . . . to help Great Mother.

Suddenly he felt as if he could hear Pace's voice in his head, telling the story of the cheetah who outran Death to steal back the sun. How the sun rose every day in that cheetah's honor, even though Death eventually caught him.

"What say you, Stride?" asked Starlight.

Perhaps one cheetah could be the difference between night and day. Stride didn't understand how exactly he could help with the buffalo problem, but it couldn't hurt to stick around and find out.

He took a deep breath.

"We accept," he said.

CHAPTER TWENTY-NINE

The plain hummed with the singing of insects, the chattering of the oxpeckers, and the hushed voices of the buffalo. A tense wave of sound that was somehow worse than silence vibrated around the massive circle that they had formed, with an empty space at the center. The sun beat down on them, pitiless and terrible.

Whisper knew that the males fought. They fought for big things and little things, and just to see who was tougher. Sometimes they got hurt. She'd even seen a fight once, between two males who wanted to mate with one female—they were both hurt by the end, but nobody died, and she saw the two males laughing together only a few days later.

This was different.

"What do we do?" muttered a female, Tremor, behind Whisper.

"'Do'?" replied Thunder. There was a chilling, bleak sound to her voice. "Nothing. He accepted the challenge."

"But it's . . . it's *cruel*," whispered Tremor.

"Don't count Bellow out yet," said another female. "He's survived a lot."

No, Tremor's right, Whisper thought. *And so is Thunder. It's terrible, and there is nothing I can do.*

No buffalo fight had ever had so much depending on the result. And no buffalo fight had ever been so wildly unfair.

On one side, Bellow sat, staring up at the sky, already panting from the effort of even walking to the ring. His legs were wobbly as he stood and made his way slowly to the center of the ring.

On the other, Holler stood proud and tall, and when he went to meet his brother it was on a wave of encouragement and cheers from his cronies.

Breath snorted from both their nostrils as they faced each other.

Great Spirit, please, Whisper prayed, squeezing her eyes, not wanting to see the moment it happened. *Please let Bellow win this somehow. We need him. We need a true leader. . . .*

She heard the mighty crash, the clatter of horns, and the first grunt of effort and pain. Her eyes flashed open, almost against her will. Bellow and Holler were locked against each other, horns almost intertwining, their forehead plates smacking against each other with a hard thud that almost gave Whisper a headache just to hear. Their hooves scrabbled on the dry ground, jostling for purchase.

Obviously, Bellow was struggling. But he was not down yet. His hooves dug up clumps of earth, shaking like tree branches on a windy day, but he didn't fall. Holler roared and gave a great heave of his head, trying to toss his brother onto his back. An *ooooh* rose from the crowd as Bellow shifted his weight, and the great effort Holler had put through his neck and shoulders failed to topple him. In fact, Holler's balance was thrown off, and Bellow pushed his advantage and forced Holler to take a step back.

"Come on, Father!" Quake's voice called out. "Holler! Holler! Holler!"

About half the males, and several females, joined the chant. Holler tossed his head and stepped back, regrouping, readying himself for the next attack. He reared up a little, kicking his hooves out and snorting.

Bellow didn't have the strength for ostentatious moves, but he had gathered himself, waiting for Holler to charge once more. When he did, their bosses met with such an almighty *crunch* that Whisper winced, thinking their heads could split open like nuts. They locked horns again, wrestled again, and Bellow lost his footing and dropped to his knees—but it had been another ploy, and he pushed back to his hooves, sweat pasting his hair to his sides, sending Holler stumbling forward into the dip in the ground that Bellow's hooves had dug. Gasps and cheers broke through the low background rumble of the crowd as they turned to face each other once more.

Could Bellow do this after all?

Hope stabbed into Whisper's heart—and then just as she

had taken a deep breath, it was knocked out of her by the sight of Bellow's injured leg giving way, just as Holler roared and charged again.

Bellow was unbalanced. He tried to meet the charge, but his leg was too weak. He was driven back, his legs folding awkwardly beneath him. He kept his horns locked with Holler, his eyes fixed on his brother's, even as Holler gave an almighty grunt and lifted, raising his brother up to his hooves and then right off the ground by the horns.

Then he tossed his head, there was a *crack* like the sky splitting in two, and Bellow was down on his side, on the ground. Something hit the ground beside him, rolling a little way before coming to rest.

It was his horn. One of Bellow's horns had sheared off completely.

Whisper thought she would never forget the sound of it breaking. It was the sound of the buffalo herd's doom.

Holler's supporters roared, thumping their hooves and bellowing, sending startled oxpeckers flapping around their heads.

Holler loomed over Bellow. He looked strong, authoritative, *glorious* with his two great curling horns, standing over his defeated brother with his one horn and one cracked stump. Whisper's stomach turned, her whole body shuddering at the sight of Holler's unjust, unfair victory.

Everything had gone so wrong.

"It is decided," cried out Holler. "The Great Spirit has spoken! Bellow's horn is broken, his leadership of this herd ended!

You fought bravely, brother," he added a little quieter, but still loud enough that the herd could hear him. "Go in peace, and no more conflict will be needed between us."

It was a threat. Bellow knew it. The whole herd knew it.

Bellow said nothing, but he didn't challenge Holler, or try to get up again as Holler turned and triumphantly strode back to his joyous, roaring supporters.

Bellow was left sitting in the dirt beside his broken horn, his head bowed, his breath coming in uneven gasps.

"Everybody!" Quake cried out. "Pay respects to your new leader! Your rightful leader!" He dropped to his knees in front of his father, and the rest of the cronies followed suit.

Whisper watched in disgust as most of the herd began to circle Holler and bow down to their knees in front of him.

"We must have a leader," muttered Tremor to her as she passed to go to Holler's side. "If we cannot be honorable, we must at least be practical."

Whisper's stomach flipped as she felt movement at her side and saw Thunder begin to walk toward Holler. Her steps were slow and labored, her eyes downcast and strangely blank, but still she knelt in front of the buffalo who'd had her calf killed and bowed her head in his direction.

Whisper could not do it. She would not.

Instead she rushed to Bellow's side. She knew she couldn't help him, but *someone* had to stay with him. This herd was not her herd, not anymore.

"Bellow," she murmured, and Bellow looked up and gave her a slight, weak smile.

"Dear calf," he gasped.

Holler was speaking again. Whisper tried to block it out, touching her nose gently to Bellow's broken horn. But she couldn't completely ignore what he was saying.

"My friends. We have stalled too long already. I may have only my own wisdom and the Great Spirit's guidance to rely on, but I say to you that if we hold together, that will be enough! There is no time to linger. Your loyalty will be rewarded, with green pastures and good health for your calves, and for all of Bravelands! The rains must come! The migration begins *now*!"

The rumble of hundreds of buffalo getting back onto their hooves, talking of migration and other normal things, began to sound across the plain.

Whisper ignored it, looking into Bellow's wide, black eyes. She would not pledge loyalty to Holler, not ever, not even if doing it would save Bravelands. . . .

"Whisper," said a raspy voice. It was Thunder. "We have to go."

"I'm not going," Whisper spat.

Thunder looked over her shoulder. Behind her, the herd was already moving—milling and jostling, waiting for Holler to point the way, but still moving. Before long, they would be gone.

Good. Let them go.

"Whisper," said Thunder again.

"Holler is a cheat and a liar, and he killed Echo!" Whisper said. "He's going to lead the herd to disaster, I know it. Quake killed Murmur at his father's behest, and he tried to kill me too. How can you go with them? How can you kneel to him?"

"Because the herd only lives if we stay together," Thunder said. "Those who are left behind will die. Please, Whisper. I don't want that for you. Not after . . ." She stopped, swallowed, gathered herself. "Don't make me say goodbye to you too, not after we had to say goodbye to your mother."

Mother. The word made Whisper shiver, despite the heat. She remembered that awful day again, the herd drawing away, the knowledge that her mother was alive but that she would soon be dead lying heavy in her heart. . . .

"I can't," she told Thunder. "I'm staying here with Bellow. We can both die together."

"Oh, Whisper," said Bellow, barely audible now. He nodded as if he was falling asleep. "I am grateful for your support. More grateful than you can know. But you must leave. Do not let Holler's treachery cost you any more than it already has."

Whisper shook her head, squeezing her eyes shut, bitterly fighting against her instincts. Everything told her that she *must* go with the herd, except for her heart.

Perhaps she did have to go. Perhaps there was more a living buffalo could do to put things right than a dead one.

But what have I been able to do so far? she thought. *Nothing at all.*

She opened her eyes and looked around. The herd was moving off, several females casting anxious glances back at Thunder and Whisper.

But something else moved, too, on the ground where the herd had been standing. A small flock of oxpeckers had landed on the earth and were fluttering their wings and chirruping together. They weren't going with the herd. They were staying behind.

They're waiting, she thought.

Great Mother Starlight's face flashed before her eyes, and she stood up and faced Thunder, a new certainty filling her heart.

"I'm not coming," she said. "But not just because of Holler. The Great Mother's real message was that we should stay here and wait for her to send word before we chose a new leader. So that's what I'm going to do. I will join the herd, but not until the oxpeckers leave this place. Not until we hear from Starlight."

Bellow took a labored breath, a faint smile crossed his face again, and he nodded. His single horn made his movements lopsided and strange.

Thunder closed her eyes for a moment. Then she gently lowered her head to Whisper's and pressed her nose to the place between Whisper's eyes. "If you stay, so do I."

"You can't," said Whisper. "Your place is with the herd."

"My place is by your side," said Thunder. "I made a promise to your mother, and I will keep it."

Whisper's heart was full with gratitude as she sat back down beside Bellow. She listened to his labored breathing grow slower and calmer, and watched the herd leave her behind. Her mother had seen this same sight once, but she had had no choice. Whisper had chosen her fate—whatever it would be.

The herd gathered speed, until Whisper could feel their

steps vibrating up through the earth, filling her chest with mingled uncertainty and fear. Did they feel it too as they followed their false leader, or were they content simply to be on the move? Dust flew up around them, until the buffalo were completely obscured. Whisper watched until at last the dust faded into the distance, and as if they had been blown away on the hot wind, the herd was gone.

EPILOGUE

The first thing he knew was pain. It shivered up and down his body, like the water that lapped around him, cold and unrelenting. He took a shuddering breath and then coughed and spluttered as the water splashed into his nostrils and his throat.

Where was he? Above his head there was nothing but gray stone. His hair was drifting in the shallow water, and he was lying on something hard. He raised his head and saw a line of light between water and rock. Then he gasped and let his head fall back into the water as pain blossomed behind his eyes.

He didn't know how long he had already lain there, and he wasn't sure how long it was after he'd seen the light that he could bring himself to look again—but the light was different when he did. It was much fainter, a blue-silver glow that was much easier to look at.

He moved his head, trying to sit up, and began to clumsily

push himself along, out of the overhang where he'd woken up. His whole body was sore, from his hooves to his horns, and panic overwhelmed him for a moment as the water deepened and he felt the current begin to tug at him. But he managed to keep close to the edge of the water—it turned out to be a wide river under a bright full moon, with sloping banks interspersed with rock formations like the one he'd struggled out of. After a few moments' desperate attempts to swim, his hooves caught solid ground, and he managed to pull himself up out of the water and collapse to his knees in a reed bed, surrounded by swaying stems.

Aching and exhausted, he passed out there for a little while longer, and when he awoke the moon was gone, but the stars shone bright overhead.

And there was a bird standing on his horn. It chirruped loudly, waking him from his stupor. He startled, until it walked down onto his nose and he managed to see what it was. A little brown bird with a bright, bright orange beak. It walked up and down his nose and over his forehead, singing continuously. It was as if it had something urgent to say.

He struggled to his hooves. It took a couple of tries, but at last he was standing. He tilted his head back, trying to look at the bird, then trying to look around himself. He couldn't see much except for reeds, water, and starlight.

"Where am I?" he whispered. His voice felt raspy and tired, but it came back to him with a few throat-clearing coughs. "How did I get here?"

He tried to cast his mind back, and it came to him in flashes.

The bluff, the hyenas, the sudden feeling of utter abandonment. He had fallen. She had been there, watching—his sister.

"Whisper?" he called.

Nothing returned to him, except for the word coming back from the rocks around him in a faint, uncertain echo.

He couldn't stay here in the reeds. Perhaps if he climbed out of the river valley he would know where he was. Perhaps he would see the herd nearby. They'd be looking for him.

So he climbed on wobbly legs up the slope and over the ridge. It was darker now, and he almost lost his footing several times, but the little bird seemed to fly ahead and perch on rocks and bushes, its vivid orange beak showing him obstacles he might have missed.

At last he crested the hill and looked out into a vast starlit plain. It was dark, and it was empty. Far off, the faint shadows of rocks and plants loomed in the darkness, but there was no sign of other creatures. He listened, and heard the sounds of creatures he couldn't identify.

Terror hit him suddenly, and he hunkered down in the long grass, hoping he was hidden. He was not supposed to be alone. He was in danger. He knew it deep in his stomach, with the first flash of real certainty he'd had since he'd woken up beneath the rock. He was never supposed to be alone.

He hung onto the knowledge, repeating it to himself. It was important, and if he didn't hold on tight, he was afraid it might slip away with everything else.

The herd was out there somewhere. So was his sister. He just had to find them.